Fenway Fiction

Fenway Fiction

Short Stories from Red Sox Nation

Edited By

Adam Emerson Pachter

Adam Emerson Pachter

Rounder Books

Cambridge, Massachusetts

Published by Rounder Books

an imprint of:
Rounder Records
1 Camp Street
Cambridge, MA 02140

This book is a work of fiction. Names, characters, places, and events either are products of the authors' imaginations or are used fictitiously. Any resemblance to actual events, places (well, except for Fenway Park) or persons, living or dead, is entirely coincidental. This book is independent of and neither sponsored nor endorsed by Major League Baseball and/or the Boston Red Sox baseball organization.

ISBN: 1-57940-119-8

Cover design by Steven Jurgensmeyer
Interior design and typesetting by Swordsmith Productions
Front cover photo by Mary Kocol

"The Shadow of Manny Ramirez" first appeared in an October 2003 issue of the *Improper Bostonian*
"The Autograph" first appeared in the 1995, no.49, issue of *Spitball* magazine
"The Long Dark Voyage" first appeared in *Sane Magazine*, http://www.sanemagazine.com
"First Start" first appeared in the *Elysian Field Quarterly* (vol.16, no.4)
"Life, Death, Love, and Baseball" first appeared in *Undertow: Crime Stories by New England Writers* (Level Best Books 2003); and was published in German in an anthology entitled *Tödliche Widder*

9 8 7 6 5 4 3 2 1

This book is dedicated with love to my own bambino, Lucy Emerson Pachter, who was born on July 16, 2004, at a hospital just four miles from Fenway Park, and patiently waited 103 days for the Red Sox to finally win the World Series.

Table of Contents

Foreword

Bill Lee

Bill Nowlin invited me to write a foreword for this book. I've worked with him before; he took the cover photo for *The Little Red (Sox) Book*. He even has a short, short story included in the collection. I perused these stories while aboard planes, trains, and automobiles on my way to someplace else.

A love of baseball is no prerequisite to either coach the game or, as a matter of fact, write about baseball, although it may help. The writers within these pages all suffer from, or relish in, the Red Sox madness. It shapes their prose.

This is a collection in which the diversity of style and genre is striking. Previous fictional stories grabbed at us, stories like *The Natural* and Kinsella's *Thrill of the Grass*. Some of these stories will grab you, too, and some—like Rick Ankiel, the pitcher who couldn't let go of the ball—couldn't hit the paper from six inches, in my opinion. But then reading, like the umpire's strike zone, is subjective.

Take me, for instance. I could throw strikes, but I failed when I tried to pitch my masterwork to a publisher. I knew I couldn't carry Kinsella's jock as a writer, but when I submitted "Caminiti's Incredible Shrinking Jock" story, it was rejected as crass, untimely, and I was accused of kicking a dead horse. But, I said, "It's funny! Vonnegut writes black humor." The editorial umpire threw me out of the game.

The best fiction is really akin to non-fiction, anyway. These stories emerge from real life, reflecting real personal connections to the Red Sox and their generationally handed-down history. You can talk about the tragedy, oh yes, and the curse. What curse? The Yankees didn't win right away. It took until 1923 when 81 Yankees victories by at least 11 ex-Red Sox players propelled them to their first World Series win. But we fixate on Ruth, because he's good copy. He represents tragedy for us and triumph for the Yankees. He is our tragic flaw, our Achilles heel.

Former Red Sox GM Ed Barrow followed by giving the Yankees 14 pennants and six World Series. You can't make up tragedy like that! Like I said, good fiction is born in truth, and thrives in tragedy. We remember Henderson's great swing on a low forkball, but do we remember the true story of Donnie Moore's personal tragedy, shooting his wife five times and then turning the silver-plated gun on himself?

What follows, then, in Adam Emerson Pachter's collection of stories, is a glimpse of real tragedy, of the Fenway faithful's response to the Evil Empire. Red Sox lore is an enticing playground for the imaginations, fantasies, and despairs of these writers. This is emotionally charged ground, like Fenway itself.

Enjoy this book and look for more books to be written as non-fiction by retired players like myself. My next novella will be titled "Free Ted's Head."

The Spaceman
Vermont, May 2005

Introduction

Adam Emerson Pachter

Happy baseball teams are all alike; every unhappy baseball team is unhappy in its own way. Is it any wonder that the Boston Red Sox have inspired so many writers over the years? Tragedy begets great drama. Tolstoy knew that, even if he was fated to die two years before the Red Sox moved into a brand-new Fenway Park and promptly won the World Series. The Red Sox won four of them, in fact, during that fertile period from 1912 until the trading of the Bambino. And so far as I know, they failed to stir a single novelist or rate a mention in any significant literary work during that whole time. Fenway Park, as it turned out, opened just a few days after the sinking of the Titanic. And let's be honest; if you were an aspiring fiction writer looking for a subject at the time, which would you have chosen?

No, a tragic history takes time to develop. And since for a baseball team nothing is more painful than the repeated failure to win championships, over the next few decades the Boston Red Sox began to look very tragic indeed. There was the first real failure in '46, then heartbreak in '49, the Impossible Dream from which New England awoke a game too soon, Fisk's immortal shot in '75 (again, one game too soon), Bucky Bleeping Dent in '78, and the ultimate "coulda been a contender" moment that slipped right through Bill Buckner's hobbled legs. I'm not sure exactly when the Sox made their debut in fiction, but the team's mix of recurring tragedy and regional identity eventually proved irresistible for both writers and Hollywood. The Sox haunted the background of several Stephen King novels, eventually emerging front-and-center in *The Girl Who Loved Tom Gordon*, and the Olde Towne Team made a key appearance in W.P. Kinsella's most famous work of baseball fiction, the short story that became the movie *Field of Dreams*. Robert B. Parker's chief P.I. Spenser was a Sox fan, and celebrated *Cheers* character Sam Malone used to pitch for Beantown. Red Sox fandom has provided grist for memorable sketches on *Saturday Night Live*. The Sox (and Fisk's shot) were an integral part of Matt Damon and Ben Affleck's movie *Good Will Hunting*. And other recent literary efforts have included Troy Soos' *Murder at Fenway Park*, David Ferrell's *Screwball*, and C.W. Tooke's *Ballpark Blues*.

One thing that drew all these writers together was their love for baseball and the Sox; in fact, I don't think it's possible to craft memorable fiction about a team that some part of you doesn't love. It's hard for me to remember the moment when I began to love the Red Sox, any more than I or anyone else can actually recall the first time we took in the magic crispness of a perfect autumn afternoon. Others, often parents, can tell you when they think it was, but that's not the same. I do know that I was born just a few miles from Fenway Park, and also that my parents whisked me down to Washington, D.C., while I was still quite young. So my first attraction was to baseball in general, rather than the Red Sox in particular. I still have some trading cards from the mid to late '70s, many featuring my father's hometown team, the Los Angeles Dodgers; and a few fading scorecards indicating my obsession with Strat-o-Matic baseball.

But the real magic began on July 13, 1978, in Baltimore's old Memorial Stadium. I was turning eight, and to celebrate that momentous event, my parents decided to take me and a bunch of friends to watch the Orioles host the Minnesota Twins. We had good seats, right behind the visitor's dugout, and at some point during the game (no one now can remember exactly when), something happened that was really quite miraculous. A member of the Twins came out of the dugout, and we gasped when we saw that the back of his shirt read : "Adams 8." Which I was. And after that, me and baseball were pretty much hitched. I've attended some kind of baseball game to commemorate my birthday every year since, most recently on July 11, 2004, when I saw the Red Sox play the Texas Rangers. In recent years the All-Star break has often precluded me attending a major league game on my precise birthday, but the magic of that first July outing still remains some 27 years later.

So I loved baseball, but not yet the Sox. That came later, during lazy August afternoons spent at my grandparents' house on Cape Cod, listening to games on the radio. August is the perfect baseball month, all savor and little stress, particularly for a team like the Red Sox, who usually save their collapses for September or October. After a few summers, I was hooked.

But I still lived in D.C., which meant that the triumphs and heartaches would, for the most part, have to be lived vicariously. I can remember Dave Henderson's majestic homer against the Angels in the 1986 ALCS, screaming and racing around my father's house, wishing there were some other Sox fans to share the moment with. I have no recollection of Game Six of that year's World Series, even though I know I watched it—some moments are just too painful for our memory banks. The years went on, and the images accumulated—trying to scalp Yankees-Sox tickets my freshman year at college, living in Chicago during the playoff run of 1995 and cursing the fact that only a few of Red Sox games were nationally televised, watching Pedro strike out hordes of enemy batters during his debut Red Sox season. And then came the momentous summer of 1999.

I met Debbie Miller on a bus heading down to the Cape that July. Debbie had grown up in southern Wisconsin as a diehard Cubs fan, so she was genetically predisposed to look favorably upon the Red Sox and their following when she moved to Boston in 1996. We sat next to each other on that bus, hit it off immediately, then started dating. And a few months later, Debbie performed the most selfless act of baseball love for me that I have ever known: she played hooky from work one cold and wet October day, standing in line for hours before managing to secure us seats to Game Five of the 1999 ALCS against the Yankees. I played a little hooky myself from the

D.C. law firm where I was working, flying up for the game and then back the next morning. We shivered together through that tough loss, using hot chocolate and nachos as hand warmers during what turned out to be the last game played at Fenway Park in the 1900s.

But even though the Yankees prevailed, my love for both the Sox and Debbie was confirmed (my friend Andrew put it best when he said, "A woman could do a lot of things wrong, and that would make up for all of them"). I experienced many dramatic baseball moments after I moved back to Boston in 2001 to be with her: Manny's homer in his first appearance as a member of the Red Sox; the debut of the Green Monster seats (Debbie again stood in line to get me those tickets, bless her heart); flying out to California to see Game One of the 2003 ALDS against the A's. But perhaps the most telling anecdote comes from a late August game against the Yankees in 2002, just a few days before Debbie and I got married and also close to the date set for a possible player's strike. Beneath the Fenway bleachers, I ran into my friend Sam Polyak, a contributor to this book whose wife Christina was one of Debbie's bridesmaids. "Are you nervous?" Sam asked, and the first thing that I thought and said was, "No, I don't think they're gonna strike." They didn't strike, our wedding went off without a hitch, and from that point on, we made our baseball journeys together as husband and wife, including cursing Grady Little in that fateful playoff rematch against the Yankees.

By the time the bitterly cold off-season of 2003 began, I had endured enough love and loss at the Red Sox's hands to begin writing about them; I had experienced all the tormented highs-and-lows that mark the committed Bosox fan as surely as a wedding ring. But I still might never have been inspired to assemble this anthology if it weren't for my friend and fellow novelist Rachel Solar. In the spring of 2003, I first heard Rachel read the story that now leads off this collection. I loved it, encouraged her to submit to a local magazine's literary competition, and was not at all surprised when "The Shadow of Manny Ramirez" won. Now flash forward to early 2004, and I was working on a short story collection where each piece is inspired by a different location around the world. When it came time to write something about Boston, I naturally gravitated towards Fenway Park, and my story "Green Monster" was born. I was sitting at my computer one day, thinking about her story and my story and how the Red Sox had served as a muse for both, when it occurred to me that there might be enough Sox-inspired tales out there to fill a book.

I did some research and was amazed to find that despite the dozens (hundreds?) of books about the Sox that had been published over the years, no one had ever put together an anthology of Sox-inspired fiction. All the compilations and collections of Sox writing were non-fiction, with only an occasional poem or fictional story thrown in for balance. True, there were novels with a Sox theme to them, but no gathering of short fiction. So I began to put a call out for Sox stories, first in local literary circles and then in a wider and wider net that included contacts at NESN, the *Boston Globe*, and various Sox-themed blogs. The response was immediate and enthusiastic; writers sent submissions from as far away as California, and although not every story idea panned out (I would have loved to see the tale about the hunt for Babe Ruth's piano come to fruition), over the next several months I assembled an impressive collection.

In selecting the 18 stories that made the final cut, I have tried to mix genres, tones, and periods of Red Sox history. Humor jostles with heartache, lost love brushes up against murder mystery, the Babe takes a seat at the proverbial bar next to Manny Ramirez. I chose many stories based principally on their literary qualities, and I think several (Rachel's story, Jennifer Rapaport's Kafkaesque "Prospect," and Elizabeth Pariseau's bittersweet "Heirloom" spring immediately to mind) would fit readily in non-baseball compilations. Others, like Cecilia Tan's "Bambino Road," though peopled by imaginary characters, do as good a job evoking Fenway as any non-fiction I've read. And, being a fan of both Shakespeare and political satire, I found Jon Winickoff's "Saint Red Sock's Day" and the Polyaks' "Prophecy" impossible to resist. I had originally thought to limit the book to short stories, but *Fenway Fiction* would be incomplete without a selection from David Kruh and Steven Bergman's superb musical "The Curse of the Bambino," and Kruh's one-act "Ice Age" provides a fitting coda to that part of the Ted Williams saga that began only after his death.

In assembling this book, I have chosen to focus on original fiction; only a handful of these stories have been previously published, and none of them had very wide distribution. I decided against including excerpts from well-known Sox-themed novels as well; I love Stephen King, but he has enough chances to see his work in print. Most of the contributors here are published authors, but no one is yet famous for their fiction. Which leads me to emphasize another point: all the stories here are fiction, and even where they incorporate real-life Sox players, the players are used fictitiously. Put another way, Manny never came over for dinner, Schilling is not a litterbug, that's not how Johnny got his beard, and Kevin Millar didn't rally the troops for Game Seven by quoting Shakespeare (although with enough Jack Daniels, who knows?). Much of Red Sox history is accurately referenced, but even when the stories take place at Fenway, a lot of the on-field action is invented. Take my own story, for example. While I have dropped in several real-life incidents from the summer of 2002 (Guapo's glove toss, Grady's comments, Shea's inability to lay off pitches), the actual game I describe never happened; it's a fictional backdrop to the more important events taking place off the field.

I never could have put this book together without the help of many people, and my first roar of appreciation goes out to the contributors: Rachel, Jen, Bob, David and Steven, Beth, Jon, Andy, Matt, Tom, Jeff, Tracy, Cecilia, Mitch, Sam and Christina, Skye, Bill, and Mary, who took the front cover photo. Without their stories I would have nothing, and I'm grateful for the patience with which they saw this process through. Special thanks to Bill Nowlin of Rounder Books, who spearheaded publication of the book; to Jeff Copetas, who put me in touch with him and has been using the ominous phrase "agent's cut" ever since; and to Bill Lee, who wrote, and Jim Prime, who helped with, the Foreword. I'm grateful to my parents Marc and Lisa, my sister Gillian, and my wife Debbie for their encouragement and support. I'm also in debt to my baby daughter Lucy for being such a good napper, since much of this book was completed while she slept. I'd also like to thank Andrew Howell, who knows you should never bet against the Red Sox; Amy Miller, for the signed Big Papi T-Shirt; my baseball friends at Covington: in particular Jeanne Turner, who shared my admiration for baseball's finest gentleman, Cal Ripken, Jr.; Pam McGhee, who cheered on the 2004 victory; and Neil Roman, who never missed a chance to bring up the Curse of the Bambino. Thanks also to everyone who attended a birthday baseball game with me, especially Bronson, Sef, Michelle, Heather, Mal, Clara, Barb, and Bill. A tip of the cap to Theo, Tito, and various parts of the 2004 Sox, especially: Pedro and Manny's hair, Big Papi's shoulders, Johnny's beard, Trot's helmet, Millar's goatee, Arroyo's dreadlocks, 'Tek's fists, Pokey's leap, Bellhorn's shadow, Schilling's ankle, and Dave Roberts' legs. You did it guys; you made us all believe.

So there you have it; the story behind the first all-fiction anthology devoted to any sports team; and I can't think of a better subject for such a book than the Boston Red Sox. I hope that *Fenway Fiction* will serve as a sort of literary capstone for the 86-year drought that ended on October 27, 2004, and I should emphasize that every one of these stories was composed before the Red Sox won the World Series. As I write this, snow covers Beantown and spring training is still a month away. It seems fitting that this anthology will be published in September 2005, while the Sox are still World Champions and the Hub is preparing for what I hope will be another thrilling playoff season. But one natural question remains—what if we keep winning? What if by some cruel twist of fate the Red Sox should continue in this surreal run, taking home the trophy year after year until they become as arrogant and uninspiring as the team two hundred miles to the south? What will be left to quicken the pulse of the playwright or novelist?

I can't predict the future, but I do have a back-up plan. There is one team that has suffered even longer than the Red Sox, a team whose tragic history continues to unfold. And I'm sure I can find someone willing to share their stories. After all, I'm married to a Cubs fan.

Adam Emerson Pachter
January 2005
Arlington, MA

The Shadow of Manny Ramirez

By Rachel Solar

When I invite Manny Ramirez to dinner, Jack is skeptical. I tell him after I've already mailed the letter to Manny, in care of his agent. "Dear Manny," it says. "Everyone is so excited that you're coming to Boston. Don't worry, you'll do fine. And if you ever get homesick, my husband and I live in Brookline, right near the ballpark. Call us. You can come over for some home cooking!" I include our phone number.

"They probably put you on the list," Jack says.

"What list?"

"The list of suspicious fans. Psychos. People to watch."

"They did not," I say.

"There's probably a van outside our house right now. And FBI bugs."

"It is not a federal offense for one nice person to invite another nice person for dinner."

"What makes you think he's a nice person?"

"Hello! Did you not read the papers all week? His best friend was a clubhouse attendant. He has pictures in his locker of minor league players!"

"And this makes him a nice guy?"

"Yes. Quiet. Salt of the earth. Understated. Humble."

Jack shakes his head and walks out to the backyard with a cigar.

I don't seriously expect Manny to call. Except for that little part of me that does. Sure, he might be suspicious of me and my intentions. But it's equally as easy (and feels much better) to believe that he just might look at my letter, my careful, looped script, and somehow see me, my earnestness. How much I need him.

Sometimes, days go by and I'm so consumed with daily life—or nonlife—that I lose Manny completely, stop reading three sports sections, stop letting his words—"Boston fans are nice. They're cool. They're pumped up"—come in and live in my mind, stop thinking of him as a sweet friend. But then I check voicemail and hear a male voice and feel a jolt, my heart skipping and unsteady. Hope like a dish I didn't order, a favorite meal from a long time ago.

At first, when Manny does call, I don't believe it. Actually, it isn't Manny per se. "This is a message for Ms. Levine," says the low, unfamiliar voice. "It's Gene Mato. I work with Jeff Moorad, Manny Ramirez's agent. Manny received from you an invitation to some sort of cookout, apparently? And he's asked me to get in touch with you to affirm that he will be in attendance. It is my understanding that there is no charitable component to this engagement. It's just an informal gathering, is that correct? Date and time TBD. Manny would like to schedule that for his upcoming off day, July 23rd, which is a week from Monday. If you could, please fax directions to the location and any other information he needs to my office. I'm sure you must be very excited, Ms. Levine. Manny is looking forward to it as well."

I try to put the phone back on the receiver, but my hands shake, and it falls to the floor. I can't sit, can't stand, so I just slide down the wall like water and pool there. I wonder how I ever breathed before when breathing is so, so hard. How do babies do it? And old people in nursing homes? I listen to the message over and over. Especially the part that says "Manny is looking forward to it as well." A few times, I try to get up, but something catches in my chest, a bubble springs up, sharp, and I just can't get a good breath. So I stay there for hours, just listening to the grandfather clock tick and the phone ring periodically and the mailman push *Town and Country* and *Fortune* and *Baseball Digest* through the mail slot below.

I say, out loud, just to hear it: "Manny Ramirez is coming to dinner." Manny Ramirez is coming in ten days. Manny Ramirez will walk through our door. His fingertip (soft, yet somehow in itself athletic, the color of untoasted wheat bread, I imagine) will touch our doorbell! Normally, if someone important were coming, I'd panic about the menu and convince Mary to cook something complicated from the Olives Table cookbook. And then I'd end up ordering some little dress I don't need from Scoop in New York because Sophie, the salesgirl, who went to Spence or Dalton and has a white tattoo, says Kevin Bacon bought one for his wife Kyra and I imagine it will change my life.

But this is Manny Ramirez! Manny would see through all that. It would scare him. He'd probably say, in a quiet voice, devoid of even a shade of impoliteness, "What's with you, man?" After all, what he was drawn to in the first place was the exact opposite of any air—the glimmer of the real me I let him see. For once I didn't listen to those outside voices that say what's wrong, what's inappropriate, what's not allowed. I was real. And I offered Manny the possibility of home—real home—after a long road trip, and in the midst of his first season away from softer, homier Cleveland. What I have to do is distill down to that essence of me. Clip back all the weeds, relocate that girl inside, that person Manny might want for his friend.

"What's up?" Jack's always short when I call before the market closes.

"You're not going to believe this."

"Whoa. Slow down. You sound really strange."

"Manny—" But that's all I can say.

"Manny what, honey? I don't want to rush you, but I'm pretty crunched right now."

I drag in some air; it makes a rough, scraping sound inside my ears. "Manny—"

"What is it? Manny's number one in homers. Manny went three for four last night. Manny's going back to Cleveland."

"NO!"

"Whoa. Okay, okay. Calm down."

"Manny is coming to dinner."

"Ha, ha. Very funny. That's cute, sweetie, but I really need to go. The market—"

"I'm serious. Manny is coming to dinner."

"Okay, it's ceasing to be funny, because I really need to make a call now. And I'm worried about you, sweetie, and the extent of this whole—fantasy world you've invented. I mean, I know that you're a creative person, but at some point there's a danger to—"

"I am NOT being creative! Manny Ramirez is coming to dinner. A week from Monday."

"Shhhhh. Shhhhh. Honey, you need to breathe."

"Don't shush me. Just call voicemail. Listen for yourself."

I hang up, walk into my study, and boot up the computer. Since I quit my job, I rarely use it. When I told Jack I was on the Internet researching at-home business ideas, I was just getting a break from him and reading about the Sox on ESPN.com. Now I go to MapQuest and punch in our address as the destination and "4 Yawkey Way" as the origin. Just typing "Yawkey Way" gives me a shiver. Maybe Jack's right. I need to breathe. I'm going to have to calm down before Manny comes to dinner.

As I print out the map, the phone rings.

"Oh my God," says Jack.

"You owe me a big apology."

"And you don't think it's someone playing a prank?"

"Do you?"

"Oh my God."

"You said that already."

"Jesus H. Christ."

"Wait a minute. You sound not happy."

"Well, honey, how do you want me to sound? It's the middle of the work day, and you drop this bombshell—"

"Bombshell? You act like having Manny Ramirez to dinner, a turn of events beyond my wildest dreams, is some kind of negative thing. "

"It's just . . . What do we have in common with Manny Ramirez? What could we possibly have to talk about?"

"You are such a snob. I'm getting off the phone."

"Hold on a second. I'm not a snob. And if I were, the subject of this alleged snobbery would not be a baseball player with a 252 million dollar contract."

"You're thinking of A-Rod. Manny's contract is only for $160 million. "

"You're right. You got me. This is why I look down on him."

"No, it's because he's not old New England money like you and he didn't go to St. Paul's and he doesn't summer in Chatham."

"That's ridiculous. Okay, you tell me. You're the one who's orchestrated this whole—shindig. What do you plan to talk about with a professional athlete? And how's his English, by the way?"

"You asshole! His English is perfect. He translates for Arrojo!"

"This is working out well," Jack says.

"I have to go." And he lets me.

Manny is coming just in time. I feel more energized than I have in months. I fax the directions and a note ("This is so thrilling!") to Gene Mato. I write a list of simple, homey comfort foods that a pretensionless, salt of the earth type of person might want away from home: chicken, burgers, potato salad, Toll House cookies, lemonade, beer. When I read the list out loud to Mary, she laughs.

"What's so funny?"

"Just that you usually have me make all this fancy stuff. And now Manny Ramirez is coming to dinner and you want me to make—this?"

"No, I don't want you to make it. I'm going to make it. I just wanted your opinion."

"You're going to make all that stuff? Potato salad? Toll House cookies?"

"Mary, don't you have any confidence in me? I was a vice president at Andersen and I can't make a cookie? Even Hillary Clinton can make a cookie."

"No, no of course I have confidence in you. I'm sure you can do anything you put your mind to. It's just—"

"Just what?"

"Well, I don't know. You're just not the cooking type. And the way you've been moping around here—"

"I know. I've been a little down. But I'm putting together a game plan."

"A game plan about what? Manny Ramirez and cookies?"

"Mary, can't you just be happy for me?"

"Of course I can," says Mary. "And instant oats."

"What?"

"Instant oats are the magic ingredient."

"Is something on fire?" asks Jack, walking through the door and sniffing.

"What?" But I hear him. I'm on my third batch of test run cookies. I don't know how Mary does this. I've already ruined a pan, set off the smoke alarm (when I couldn't get it to stop, I smashed it with a grooved wooden mallet I found in a kitchen drawer), and created something so salty it more closely resembled risotto than a batch of cookies. You need an MIT degree in advanced chemistry to bake Toll House cookies from scratch. How will I ever master this in time? I have egg yolk on my H belt and flour hand prints on my best black T.

"Never mind." Jack starts up the stairs, and I know without needing to look that he 's walking to his dressing room, emptying his pockets, separating the change by denomination. I turn the kitchen radio to WEEI for the pregame interviews. Lowe blew a save last night and Joe Castiglione purports to ask Jimy about it, soft pedaling as usual. "So, last night's outcome was unfortunate, Jimy. Lowe seemed to have a tough time. The sinker wasn't exactly sinking. Do you just pick up and move on?"

"Pretty much, Joe. Sometimes you need a little luck in baseball and maybe luck just wasn't on our side."

Slowly, I clean the kitchen from side to side, listening to the game, until only a small container full of my test-run potato salad, a half glass of test-run lemonade, and three cookies from the best batch (the rest were burnt beyond repair) remain on the counter top. I stand at the kitchen doorway for a moment. Down the hall, the blue light from the television flickers as the ticker tape moves. I go back to the kitchen and sit down to the little meal I've made. The lemonade is good—cool and tart. I stay there until after midnight, just listening to the sounds of the game, and then Ted Sarandis's call-in show, the voices rising and falling, keeping me company in the dark.

The next day I don't sleep late. I've been sleeping late since the day I quit. Actually, that was the first thing I did when I got home. I quit in the morning, was home by 11, went upstairs, took off my shoes and stockings, pulled the drapes shut, and climbed under the thick, down duvet, the air conditioning prickling my shinbones. Every day since, I've heard all the normal Jack sounds each morning—the chime of change, the long, heavy breaths as he knots his tie in front of the mirror, the click of his briefcase—but only peripherally, a backdrop to my dreams of endless, endless falling. But today the wink of light that pushes under the edge of the drape seems warm white instead of intrusive. I open my eyes. The Manny call has not evaporated the way some highs do, like some night in college when you thought you were finally alive that grows hazier and hazier, sliding even further out of your grasp every time you try to call it up again. No, this memory stays true, and the feelings come back even stronger when I play the message again or think of the weight of him, of Manny Ramirez standing on our doorstep, the promising shadow he will cast across our threshold.

"You're awake?" asks Jack, straightening his tie in front of the mirror.

We haven't spoken since the night before. Lately, we've been doing that, putting aside the old adage about going to bed angry. Sleeping back to back.

"I'm awake," I say.

"We never talked last night."

"I know." It hangs in the air for a moment.

"Did the Sox win?"

"Yeah."

"Tell me how Manny did."

I sit up in bed, prop the pillows behind my back, smile. "He went three for four with a homer and four RBIs."

"So how does he do it?"

"They say natural talent, but that underestimates how hard he works. First to the park, extra BP, hundreds of balls thrown at him a day, learning every carom. But it's also something else, I think. A love of what you do. Faith. Fate. Maybe magic."

Sometimes I make these little deals with myself. Sometimes I whisper these shocking little things in my head. If he makes fun of me now, I think, I'll just leave him. I'll move into a Holiday Inn, cash in my 401K, road trip across the country.

"Magic, huh?"

I hold my breath.

"I guess I'll have to ask him about that at dinner," my husband says. He walks to the window and peeks out onto the park. "Wow, the sun is out already."

I get up out of bed to see for myself.

Prospect

JENNIFER RAPAPORT

I am slightly shocked when my husband gets picked to pitch for the Red Sox, counting as I had been on a life in academia, summers to ourselves. He is well-built, it's true, and athletic, but when I scan my brain for a memory of his ball-playing, I come up empty. Never mind, though, because he must be good; he didn't even try out.

I watch him pace the room, contract in hand. He has shed his shirt and tie for a well-worn undershirt whose sleeves have just begun to fray. The whole get-up is standard for the small college that employs us, and I wonder how we will be dressing in the fall. Big money, baseball, but big risk, too. These teaching jobs are not easy to come by.

Ear to shoulder with telephone in between, he tells his dad the good news. His voice runs amok, calm and monotonous for the most part, but edgy and shrill in between. Dad played once, too, and there was a story there—its climax Dad's demise. They say that for the one season he played in the big leagues, he was well liked, respected, and by all accounts a moderate drinker. By fall, though, his rotator cuff had deteriorated so badly that he couldn't raise his arm to shake hands. He was eventually rehabbed to the point of functionality, but his manners were gone for good. Retired now from a second career and lazy ever since, he still lives in the house my husband grew up in: same yard, same trees, same backboard. He will no doubt take credit, if only from a distance. He hasn't left Worcester in fifteen years.

"Read him the game schedule," I say. I get up from the couch to elevate my voice, but my husband waves his hand in the air, then presses his ear closed with a finger.

I slink into the kitchen for a beer, peel the schedule magnet off the refrigerator like it's an afterthought: here, away, away, here, etc. Not to mention spring training. Though I mean the shock to be for his dad, I myself am struck again by the erratic nature of this lifestyle— but truth is, I'll get over it. In fact, I like the idea of spending spring someplace warm. It would be good to get away.

"Fort Myers, you know," my husband says. He wears a crooked smile, as if he picked the location just for me, but he is still thinking of Dad. He flips his phone shut with rare flair and stands there looking at it in his hand. When he finally slaps it down on the kitchen counter, it slides faster than expected across the tile, stopping only at the far edge. He picks up a pen and twirls it anxiously between his fingers.

"I know," I say. "Team leaves second week in February."

"February?" he says. The last time my husband and I left New England, his father had a heart attack. At least that's what they told us the first time they called, though I can't say I didn't have my suspicions. By the time we'd packed up and gotten back to the airport, they called again: Angina. My husband's eyes travel to where the phone sits on the opposite side of the counter. "That's spring?"

"That's spring training," I say.

In Florida, on the first day of March, a few of the boys—my husband, Pedro, and Curt—throw the ball around in a park at the edge of the beach. The women watch from a blanket on the sand. Pedro throws to Curt, Curt throws to my husband, my husband throws to Pedro. My husband's back is to the water, whose emerald green exaggerates his new tan, making him look like he belongs. If I had to guess, I'd say he is playing better than was expected. The faces of the other women register similar thoughts and our blanket grows quiet. One of the wives aims a speed gun at my husband. It looks like a cross between an automatic weapon and a hair dryer. "Ninety-two," she says, and I think that we are here to stay.

I excuse myself and make my way to an area of beach with concessions. Near the canteen, a lifeguard sits on a tall white chair under a slack green flag. While my husband throws curve balls half a mile to the north, I am teaching myself to boogie-board—with, I might add, much success. I had hoped to be able to use my hips to swish myself away from the shore on the outgoing remnants of waves, but never to support my weight on the open water. Still, I find myself actually riding the waves. It is a coup of unusual proportions for me, but when I get back to our picnic, I keep it to myself. I am a wife here, not a colleague, a stipulation that stumps me again and again. I take a seat on the blanket and watch some more.

The boys are standing around our oversized thermos, drinking lemonade from Dixie cups. Curt throws one back, crumples the cup, tosses it into our makeshift garbage, takes a new one. He's holding his fifth cup when Pedro jerks the garbage bag—the crumply beige supermarket kind—off its place in the sand. Crushed Dixie cups fly, and sand, too. I can't tell if he's angry or merely used to moving quickly.

"Why can't you just use the same cup?" he asks Curt. My husband looks out at the water, nods at passing trawlers as if counting them. His fingers twirl a phantom pen.

"What same cup?" Curt says. He had a rhythm going there.

"Why can't you drink from the same cup each time?" Pedro says.

"Does it matter?" Curt says. He looks around for his wife. When he finds her, he waves from the wrist.

"Ever see a landfill?" Pedro says. He picks up all of the cups that went flying and puts them in the trash. He holds the bag open for Curt who drops in his final cup without saying anything. My husband hasn't said a word either, but he follows them back to the park when they go.

They are practicing fielding when it happens. Same order as before. My husband to Pedro. Pedro to Curt. Curt to my husband.

The pitches are still fast. Record-breaking, in fact, though the wives say that's how it always is during training. You have to slow it down for control.

My husband has his back to the water again, and the tide is coming in. The surf has picked up considerably since I was in, and it is getting windy. The lifeguard works the clips on his flag, changes it from green to red. I read the placard at his feet: green, low hazard; yellow, medium; blue, man-o-war; red, no swimming.

Pedro's grounder is no different than any other, except that it goes toward my husband in left field, instead of Curt in right. They have changed directions, but my husband missed the switch. He recovers, though, and moves quickly toward the ball in that sideways-forward motion that makes things happen in baseball faster than you'd think they could. His arms are stronger now than they were when we first arrived, and his movements more fluid. He plants his front foot solidly and lays down his glove. He looks up at Curt to place his next throw and looks back down to the silent shifting sand between his legs. And then the ball is wet, under the sea and popping up again and again, twenty feet farther out each time. It still has momentum, pulling against a sea of green.

The Autograph

Robert Weintraub

It was only by chance that I was walking down that street in Herkimer, New York—its name escapes me—and looked into the window of a store that gave the appearance of being a cross between a pawn shop and the unlikely resting place for an assortment of items I would have expected to find in a flea market. The name of the shop, painted on the glass in faded gold lettering, was "The Treasure Chest."

Several electric guitars, some brass instruments, and an assortment of men's suits and women's dresses hung from two parallel wires that looked to be pieces of an old, orange-colored extension cord. In front, there were a number of china cup and saucer sets, a collection of foreign coins, and glassware of all types, some of it the opaque green variety that was given away to movie house patrons during the Depression. Further back, several beat-up dolls joined a display of tin containers that once held tea or soap or crackers, and odd-shaped bottles that once were filled with unpasteurized milk, medicinal cure-alls, and Moxie. But what captured my attention was the baseball, sitting on a small square of red carpeting, near enough to the front of the window that I could read the signature, a name that for several moments I almost couldn't believe I was seeing again: Denton Heywood.

My daughter and I had left our home outside of Boston early that morning on a mission to visit five colleges in upstate New York over a period of three days. The first was already out of the way.

"I don't know. Don't ask me for all kinds of details," Tracy said, irritated by my persistent questioning after she had rated it "about a 6" on a scale of 1 to 10. We had joined a group of other parents and high school seniors on a student-led tour of the campus, watched a film extolling the virtues of every academic department in the college, and sat through a welcoming presentation with one of the assistant deans of admission. He was prepared to take questions at that point, but despite the nervous glances that we mothers and fathers gave to the prospective members of the Class of '87, they indicated by their detached silence that they were not there to take risks but only to be entertained.

On the thruway heading toward Syracuse, our first stop the next morning, we saw signs for the General Herkimer Inn. The name seemed to amuse Tracy, and she suggested we stay there. I had no reason to disagree. Tracy wanted to rest after we checked in, so I changed into some comfortable clothes, put on my factory-discount New Balance sneakers and began exploring downtown Herkimer.

I turned twelve years old on October 2, 1945. It was a Sunday, and the last day of the major league baseball season. Baseball had entered my life for the first time that summer when I became friendly with some boys with whom I spent the better part of each day at the huge field in our neighborhood.

My father, who worked a grocery store owner's typical fifteen-hour day, had responded to my plea for a baseball glove—"I need my own mitt"—by purchasing what looked more like an extra large leather mitten. It had very little padding, and there was no webbing at all between the thumb and fourth finger. I never associated the words "mitt" and "mitten" until years later when my father said he thought he bought me exactly what I wanted; that he understood a "mitt" to be a training glove that one used before being ready to play with a regular one. But the glove served me well that summer as I learned how to play the game.

Sunday was my father's only day of rest, and he normally slept until noon. But on that particular morning he had washed and dressed and was at the breakfast table before ten o'clock. My mother made apple pancakes for my two sisters and me because she knew what would please me the most. It was my birthday.

"We haven't had a chance to buy you anything," my father said, pausing for some theatrical effect, "but maybe you'd like to see the Red Sox with me today."

I was thrilled. "Yes," I said, almost shouting my response. My father could see the huge smile breaking out on my face. My mother told me years later that it was the happiest moment she'd ever seen me have.

"Can we come too?" my sisters asked, almost in unison.

"Not this time," my father told them. "Another time we'll all go together, but today it's just for the men." He waited a few seconds before turning back to me and winking.

Our trip to Fenway Park that afternoon was probably one of the rare occasions on which a father and son experienced together—for the first time in *both* their lives—the thrill of emerging from the dark entrance ramp into the sunshine of the field and being momentarily spellbound by the lush green carpet of grass filling the ballpark. I was overwhelmed by the noise of the crowd, the shouting of the vendors who moved up and down the aisles with their peanuts, soft drinks, and hot dogs, and the smack of baseballs hitting leather as players from both teams loosened up in the area between the dugouts and the foul lines. I wanted to get as close to the field as I could, but the ushers in their red blazers and blue pants allowed only ticket holders into the box seat sections. As game time approached and the lineups were announced, we moved away from the action and out to our seats in the right field bleachers.

The competitive season had ended for the Red Sox weeks earlier when they were eliminated from the pennant race, but they were playing their last series of the year against the Yankees, their hated rivals. I spent much of that cool, sunny afternoon teaching my father the rules of the game and sharing with him the accomplishments of the Boston hitters as they came to bat. He wondered why the players left their gloves out on the field when they returned to the dugout each inning, and seemed disappointed that no one on either team had made his prediction come true by stumbling over one while running to make a catch.

There was drama in the game we saw, right to the very end. The Red Sox were down by one in the ninth inning and had runners on second and third base with two outs. The public address announcer informed the cheering crowd that Denton Heywood was being sent up to pinch-hit for the pitcher. Heywood, a left-handed batter, would face the Yankees' right-handed pitcher. "They'll walk him," I told my father, anticipating my being able to explain the strategy to him as soon as the intentional pass began. The Yankees' manager ran out to talk to his pitcher at the mound.

Most of the major league baseball players who had gone off to war in the early forties did not return to their teams in 1945, after the Japanese surrender in August. They were content to go home to their families and take a long rest before getting their bodies ready for spring training the following year and a new season of baseball. The teams competing for the championship that year were stocked with minor league players who wouldn't have been there if the real "big leaguers" hadn't had to interrupt their careers.

Denton Heywood was born and grew up in Dorchester, about nine miles from Fenway Park and a dozen blocks from where I lived. I discovered years later, while looking through a biography of wartime ballplayers, that he had just passed his twenty-second birthday when he batted in the first game I ever saw. The Red Sox had promoted Heywood to their Triple A farm team in Louisville that summer when injuries forced them to bring several players from that club to Boston. Then, as soon as Louisville was eliminated from its playoffs in September, he was called up for the last few weeks of the season so that everyone in management could get a look at him.

Heywood had asthmatic problems that kept him out of the military, and the Boston sportswriters, skilled at impugning any rookie's ability on his arrival in town, were almost unanimous in telling their readers that he lacked the talent to play the game at the highest level. He had made their stories about him in the city's four major newspapers appear accurate to that point by failing to reach base in the dozen pinch-hitting appearances he'd had since coming to Fenway Park.

To the surprise of the crowd, and to my embarrassment, the Yankees manager decided to go after Heywood instead of loading the bases for the leadoff hitter. "I knew it," my father said, when he saw what was happening. The count went to 1 and 2, and then Heywood barely managed to stay alive at the plate by foul-tipping the next three pitches. He looked completely overmatched. "Hit one out," I begged, in desperation, and was rewarded an instant later with a fly ball that rose on a glorious arc and carried over the visitors' bullpen into the right-field bleachers, a game-winning home run. Rising to my feet along with everyone else, I watched the flight of the ball, certain for most of its ten-second journey that it was heading directly at me. And then, in the most jealous moment of my life, I saw it come down into the glove of Billy Killian, a boy who was two grades ahead of me in the same junior high school in Dorchester.

On the following day, I got the chance to hold the baseball at school and listen to Billy exaggerate the difficulty of his catch. I heard him tell everyone around him during the morning recess how he waited at the players' gate for Denton Heywood to leave Fenway Park and asked him to autograph the ball. On the side opposite his name, Heywood had, for some reason, also inscribed the date, "10/2/45."

The store where I discovered the baseball was located on Herkimer's main street, several blocks of rather seedy looking establishments. Next to it on one side was a movie theater, long since abandoned, I suspected, when I saw the poster for a Steve McQueen/Ali MacGraw picture still encased in plastic on a wall just beyond the iron grillwork that closed off the entrance. The two sides of the triangular marquee that pushed out high above the sidewalk carried a complete message between them in foot-high black letters, "CLO" on the left and "SED" on the right. A jewelry store, with a display of Timex watches that moved around in the front window on an oval-shaped conveyor belt, was situated on the other side.

When I entered the Treasure Chest, the proprietor came out of the back room to help me. He was a man about my own age whose heavy black mustache struck me almost as a stage prop that was there to try and distract attention from what otherwise was the most outstanding feature of his head, a crew cut that wouldn't have been any shorter had he just finished his first day of Marine Corps training. He nodded at me, offered that it was a nice day and asked if there was something he could help me with.

"Believe it or not," I said, pointing at the baseball in the window, "I remember the guy who signed that. He played for the Red Sox when I was a kid."

"Is that right?" the owner answered, and hesitated a few moments. "Well, I'm not much of a fan myself, beyond Pete Rose or Joe DiMaggio or a few others. You know, the great ones. But no one who's been in here ever heard of this fellow. What's his name again?"

"Denton Heywood," I told him. "He had one hit in his whole major league career. But it was a home run on the last day of the season. He won the ballgame with it."

He watched me looking down at the ball and probably sensed that I would be the only person coming into his store who'd have an interest in buying it for whatever added value it received from the autograph. He encouraged me to pick up the ball and hold it. "Have a feel of it," he said.

I did. The signature was written so clearly, as if Heywood had wanted to be certain that everyone would be able to read it. I flipped the ball in the air, not more than a foot above my hand, and when I caught it I saw the writing on the other side for the first time. Just numbers. "10/2/45." A shiver moved through my whole body.

Denton Heywood reported to the Red Sox camp in Sarasota, Florida, for spring training in 1946. By that time, Bobby Doerr was back playing second base, and Heywood realized that his only chance of staying with the team was as a utility infielder. He played in about fifteen exhibition games, splitting his time in the field between second, third, and shortstop, but didn't impress Sox manager Joe Cronin. About a week before the team headed north for the start of the season, Heywood was assigned to Louisville.

On the Saturday after Thanksgiving in 1945, Heywood had married Patty Ann Shea, his high school sweetheart. She didn't accompany him to Florida when he left in February, not wanting to distract him in any way from the goal he hoped to achieve; but she packed up their few belongings and joined him in Louisville a few days after he rented an apartment within walking distance of the ballpark.

The club installed Heywood at third base, grooming him to play that position in a year or two in Boston, and he responded by having an excellent season both at bat and in the field. He was ticketed for a return trip to the Red Sox in September, as soon as the team was allowed to expand its roster for the final month of the season. With Ted Williams leading the way, the ball club had overpowered everyone that year and was able to coast to the pennant. Heywood's only concern was that his wife, Patty Ann, was pregnant and would probably give birth in the latter part of September.

On August 29th, while the Louisville team was playing a three game series in Utica, Patty Ann got into an automobile accident just a few blocks from their apartment. She was rushed to Memorial Hospital by ambulance and spent the next four hours on an operating table. Word reached Heywood in the middle of the game, and the local police drove him to the airport. By the time he arrived at the Louisville hospital, Patty Ann had given birth by Caesarean section to a baby girl. Heywood was told that his wife was dying and that a priest had already prayed with her. He spent the last thirty minutes of Patty Ann's life at her bedside, watching her cradle the daughter she wanted them to name Christina. By the time the funeral took place back in Dorchester several days later, Heywood knew that he would never wear a professional baseball uniform again.

"Where did you get this ball?" I asked the store owner.

"A woman brought it in about two weeks ago," he told me. "Lives a couple of towns over. Said it belonged to her husband and asked me to try and sell it. He's the one that got hit last month out on the thruway, just a little west of here. Said she needed to raise whatever she could." As he spoke, he walked over to the counter where the cash register was located and stepped behind it. "The paper said he was changing a tire in the rain—a nasty night out there—and got killed by some hit-run driver they haven't found yet. You might've read about it."

I told him I was from Massachusetts and just passing through the area. "Do you know her name?" I asked.

"Not offhand," he answered, "but I got it written down in back with her phone number. I'll go get it if you're interested."

I said I was and asked how much he wanted for the ball. He answered right away, telling me he thought thirty dollars was a fair price, especially since I'd known Denton Heywood. He turned a key in the register, took it with him as he headed toward the rear of the store, and returned a few minutes later with a small spiral notebook.

"Her name's Ruth Killian," he informed me, "and she gets half if you buy it."

I told him I would take it, and said that I wanted to leave a note for Mrs. Killian. "Do you have a piece of paper I can use and an envelope?" I took three ten-dollar bills out of my wallet and handed them to him. He tore a page from the back of the notebook and gave it to me.

It took me a couple of minutes to think about what I wanted to say. At home, I would have written the note out on a scrap piece of paper and edited it until I was satisfied that it expressed all my thoughts. But as I leaned over the counter at the Treasure Chest, the words didn't come easily.

By the time the owner returned, I had finished, telling Ruth Killian that I had seen her husband make a spectacular catch of the ball Heywood hit for a home run. The owner had wrapped the ball in tissue paper and put it in a plastic bag. I turned around, folded two twenty-dollar bills inside the note to Killian's wife and put them in the envelope he had handed me. I sealed it and wrote her name on the front. "Be sure she gets this," I told him. "It's very personal."

The next two days passed quickly as Tracy and I visited the other four colleges. The baseball I'd purchased seemed to have me thinking about my own diamond heroes a lot of the time. Heading back, I contemplated a third night on the road and a visit to the Hall of Fame in Cooperstown the next day, but my daughter wouldn't hear of it. Still, I resolved to try and find out what had happened to Denton Heywood. Perhaps he still lived in Dorchester. Maybe the Red Sox would know. I might even have the chance to show him the ball, I thought.

We got off the highway in Albany and stopped for dinner at a Chinese restaurant. We talked about the schools we had seen, Tracy's feelings about possible career choices, and her strong desire to backpack by herself around Europe during the upcoming summer. The fortune cookies we opened relieved some of the tension and were good for a laugh because the messages inside would have been perfectly appropriate if only she had picked mine and I'd gotten hers. I had already found my true love and Tracy wasn't in any position to receive a big promotion. Then I told her about the baseball and Billy Killian. "That's weird, Dad, it's really weird," she said.

Shortly after we crossed back into Massachusetts, Tracy rested her head on a pillow against the passenger door and closed her eyes. A few minutes later I turned on the radio, looking for some soft music, and picked up a New York station that was doing the news on the hour. Before I could turn the dial, the announcer began reporting that a Massachusetts man had come forward in the hit-and-run death of William Killian on the New York Thruway twenty-six days earlier. He said that the individual was a regional distributor for Eastman Kodak in Boston who had driven home from the company's Rochester plant the night of the accident and couldn't account for a dent in the right fender of his automobile when he discovered it the following day. But on his next trip to Rochester, he read a story about the ongoing search for the hit-run driver and suddenly recalled the thump he felt against his car that night during a heavy rainstorm near the Herkimer exit. Police inspected the man's Buick LeSabre and determined that it was the car that struck Killian. The driver, against whom no charges had yet been filed, was identified as a fifty-nine year old one-time professional baseball player for the Boston Red Sox named Denton Heywood.

Unbelieving, I looked over at Tracy, but she was already asleep. I spent the rest of the night wondering about the ways that fate had of entangling the lives of total strangers. Surely, I told myself, Ruth Killian had to be thinking about the same thing if she read my note. Somehow, I felt better knowing that she would never have to see that baseball again. And I was suddenly glad that it wasn't me who had caught Denton Heywood's home run.

Excerpt from THE CURSE OF THE BAMBINO

A MUSICAL

WITH

BOOK AND LYRICS BY DAVID KRUH

MUSIC AND LYRICS BY STEVEN BERGMAN

PROLOGUE

(The stage is quiet and dark, except for an eerie blue glow emanating from a TV set that sits downstage center. The screen of the TV faces upstage towards a couch.)

ANNOUNCER

Well, if you're a Red Sox fan you've got to be asking yourself: is this the moment I've been waiting 68 years for? It's the middle of the tenth inning of the sixth game of the 1986 World Series, and the Boston Red Sox are leading the New York Mets by a score of five to three.

(A middle-aged man dressed in a bathrobe enters, carrying an infant. He settles on the couch, his face illuminated by the glow from the TV.)

ANNOUNCER

Which means the Sox are just three outs away from what has eluded them, in often frustrating fashion since 1918: a World Series championship.

(The lights rise on the father. The sound from the television fades.)

FATHER

(Speaking to his daughter)

I know you're too young to realize what's happening, but someday you'll be able to tell your children that you saw the Red Sox finally win a World Series. You know you come from a long line of Red Sox fans. Did I ever tell you that your grandfather worked for the Red Sox? Maybe that's where we got this family tradition of having our hearts ripped beating from our chests every year.

ANNOUNCER

You know, back in 1920 Red Sox owner Harry Frazee sold Babe Ruth to the New York Yankees and the Red Sox, who had won five of the first 15 World Series ever, haven't won another one since. Now some folks up in Boston call that the Curse of the Bambino, but with a two-run lead over the New York Mets here in the bottom of the tenth, even the most hardened Sox fan has got to admit that the old Curse may finally be broken.

FATHER

My dad—God rest his soul—he was one of the most conscientious men I ever knew. Started working when he was only 14 and never took a day off of work, no matter how sick he was. Except for two days each year—Good Friday . . . and the Red Sox home opener. Said both God and the Sox counted on him being there, but that the Sox needed him more. He used to say they couldn't start the season unless old Joe Waterman was sitting in his usual seat along the first base line.

ANNOUNCER

Wally Backman lofts a fly ball to left where it is grabbed easily by Jim Rice, and now the Red Sox are now just two outs away from a World Championship. Up next is first baseman Keith Hernandez . . . .

FATHER

When I was old enough he started taking me, too. He'd buy me a hot dog and a soda and get a beer for himself . . . He'd look around the field, watching the rookies and the veterans. Then he'd smile at me and say "this is the year. We finally got the pitching we need" or "we finally got a slugger to drive in the big run . . ."

ANNOUNCER

There's a ball, high and away . . .

FATHER

They'd start off great, some of those teams, but most years they were 14 games out by August. By then my old man is screaming at the morning paper "they're nothin' but overpaid bums" and he was swearing off the sport entirely. Wouldn't even watch the World Series. But he always came back the following April. Too bad he isn't here to see this . . .

(The lights slowly rise near the back of the stage, silhouetting four men.)

ANNOUNCER

And there's another fly ball, this one easily caught by Henderson in center, and now the Mets are down to their last out. Here in New York's Shea Stadium, you can almost hear a pin drop . . .

FATHER

One out.

(Looks briefly up to heaven)

You hear that dad? Gramps?

(To his daughter)

You hear that sweetheart? Just one more out.

(The upstage lights rise to full, revealing four solemn men.)

ANNOUNCER

Gary Carter, the catcher, the Mets' last chance to keep this game alive, steps up to the plate.

(pause)

The first pitch is a fastball high and inside for strike one.

FATHER

Two strikes honey. Just two more strikes.

ANNOUNCER

Schiraldi winds, delivers, and it's another fastball. But this one is high and inside. A ball.

FATHER

That's all right, honey. They can't all be strikes.

(The music gets louder.)

ANNOUNCER

Schiraldi steps onto the mound, there's the windup, and—

(Total surprise)

a hit! A hit to left field and Carter is safe at first. The Mets now have one aboard with two outs, and this New York crowd begins to come alive . . .

(We hear the sounds of cheering as the music gets louder, more ominous. The four men move forward just downstage of the father, who rocks gently with his baby.)

ANNOUNCER

Stepping up to the plate is the Mets' *next* last great hope—Kevin Mitchell.

ANNOUNCER

Schiraldi delivers a fastball, high and inside. Ball one.

(Father clutches his baby tighter. The Rooters look on sympathetically.)

ROOTER #1

Behold, a fellow Rooter.

ROOTER #2

A noble Red Sox fan,

ROOTER #3

His team up by two

ROOTER #4

They need but a single out

ROOTERS (all)

To win the prize of World's Champions!

ANNOUNCER

If Schiraldi gets in any more trouble, the Red Sox have several men in the bullpen to help out.

FATHER

Jesus, God, no please.

BETTY

Among them the man they call the Steamer, Bob Stanley . . .

(Frightened, the father crosses himself.)

ROOTER #1

Look at him. Though he knows only the past.

ROOTER #2

He can see the future.

ROOTER #3

As can every Red Sox fan.

ROOTER #4

Poor bastard.

ANNOUNCER

Schiraldi delivers . . . Mitchell swings . . .

(Excited)

. . . and rips it into center field! Henderson grabs it on the first bounce but has no chance for a throw. Carter takes third and Mitchell takes first. So, how about this? The Mets are still alive with two outs in the bottom of the tenth.

SONG:
SO MANY YEARS AGO

ROOTERS (all)

SO MANY YEARS AGO IT WASN'T QUITE LIKE THIS,
YOU WOULDN'T RECOGNIZE THE OLDE TOWNE TEAM.
WE HAD PRIDE. WE HAD CONFIDENCE.
WE HAD CHAMPIONS ON THE FIELD,
AND FIVE WORLD SERIES VICTORIES IN 15 YEARS . . .

ROOTER #1

FANS WHO WENT TO FENWAY SAW GREAT BASEBALL,
THE RED SOX ALWAYS MADE THEM GLAD THEY CAME,

ROOTER #3

BUT SINCE THAT AWFUL DAY THE SOX SOLD BABE RUTH,
THE FORTUNES OF OUR TEAM ARE NOT THE SAME.

ROOTER #2

IT'S ONE THING WHEN THE UMP FORGETS HIS GLASSES,
OR ANOTHER WHEN YOU CANNOT SCORE A RUN,

ROOTER #4

BUT HOW DO YOU EXPLAIN YOUR GOLD GLOVE FIELDER,
JUST LOST A CRUCIAL GROUNDER IN THE SUN?

ROOTERS (all)

WHEN A MAN NAMED HARRY FRAZEE
MADE THE BABE A NEW YORK YANKEE
HE HAD NO IDEA THE IMPACT IT WOULD HAVE.
FOR NOT SINCE WORLD WAR ONE,
HAVE THE RED SOX WON
LEAVING US TO WONDER, ARE WE CURSED?

ROOTER #1

WE SAW PESKY HOLD THE BALL,

ROOTER #2

WE SAW GALEHOUSE GET THE CALL,

ROOTER #3

IN '49 THE RED SOX BLEW A ONE GAME LEAD,

ROOTER #4

'72 CAN'T ROUND THIRD BASE,

ROOTER #1

TWO YEARS LATER—LOST FIRST PLACE,

ALL

THEN WE WATCHED AS CARLTON YELLED OUT GO GO GO

ROOTER #2

BUCKY DENT HITS A FLY BALL,

ROOTER #3

THAT SAILS OVER THE WALL.

ROOTER #4

IF THE WIND WAS IN THE SHORTSHOP WOULD HAVE CAUGHT IT!

All

AND NOW WE HAVE ANOTHER CHANCE TO END THE CURSE,
WE'RE IN THE LEAD AND WE NEED ONE MORE OUT
COULD THIS BE THE MOMENT WE HAVE
WAITED FOR ALL THESE YEARS

FATHER

OR WILL THIS TWO-RUN GAME TURN INTO ONE . . . MORE . . . ROUT?

(END.)

(The Rooters and the father turn towards the television with great anxiety. The lights slowly fade.)

ANNOUNCER

Calvin Schiraldi will stay in the game to pitch to the next Mets batter, Ray Knight. So, just think about it. The Red Sox are just one out away from ridding themselves of the Curse of the Bambino after 68 years.

FATHER

68 years? Wow. Imagine that. 68 years . . . 68 years . . .

ACT 1
Scene 1

(It is late November, 1919, in a bar, in which a sign reads: WELCOME TO THE THIRD BASE. "Nuff Ced" McGreevey is behind the bar. A large sign reads BEER: 10 cents, SHOT: 10 cents. BOILERMAKERS: 20 cents. NO CREDIT. Patrons Carelli and Wiznowski sit at the bar listening to MacMullen, who sits with Myron, a recent Russian immigrant, at a small table, looking at a book.)

MACMULLEN

And it was right here in Boston that a bunch of patriot fellows—dressed as Indians they was—dumped the King's tea into the harbor.

MYRON

Why they do this? What did the King to do them?

MACMULLEN

What did the king do? He did what an Englishman always does.

(Loud)

Tried to rob us of our freedom! And that, my fine lad, is why we had the American Revolution, so we could be free to do what we wanted, when we wanted.

MCGREEVEY

(Bitterly)

Except take a drink.

CARELLI

You mean legally.

(The others laugh)

MYRON

Ah, yes, you speak of this . . . how you say, Pro-bi-hi-tion.

MACMULLEN
(Correcting him)
Pro-hi-bi-tion.

MYRON
Prohibition.

WIZNOWSKI
You know, I hear that on the Beacon Hill they have a supply of the good stuff that will last for many years.

MACMULLEN
Ain't that the way? One set of rules for them and one for us.

WIZNOWSKI
Listen to you.
(Indicating Myron)
You sound like that Red.

MACMULLEN
Now, now. Myron here is no Red. A little pink, maybe, but he works just as hard at the factory as any of you loafers and I'll not have you besmirching the lad's name just 'cause he's got a few crazy ideas about the, what is it you call us, the Pro-te-la-riat?

MYRON
Pro-le-ta-ri-at.

MACMULLEN
Proletariat, yes.

(Satisfied, MacMullen picks up a newspaper, which Myron studies from his chair.)

MYRON
Mister MacMullen, explain please.

MACMULLEN

What is it, lad?

MYRON

(Pointing to the paper)

It says there that "There is much . . ." what is word, please?

MACMULLEN

(MacMullen turns the paper around.)

Eh? Ah, speculation.

MYRON

(Taking the paper back)

Speculation, yes, "speculation these past days and weeks over the fate of Babe Ruth, who batted cleanup and was our greatest hero on the diamond." Tell me, MacMullen, why is baby named Ruth forced to clean up diamonds?

MACMULLEN

Babe Ruth isn't a baby, lad. He's a grown man. But the fans call him the Babe.

MYRON

And how does a grown man get to be named for a baby?

MACMULLEN

(Looks to the others for help. They are amused.)

Well . . . I guess because he's so large.

MYRON

(Momentary confusion)

Because he is so large. What about this diamond?

MACMULLEN

A diamond is a field made of grass.

MYRON

A diamond made of grass?

MACMULLEN

Yes.

MYRON

I see. And it is this grass that this Babe must clean up?

MACMULLEN

No, the Babe doesn't clean up. He bats cleanup.

MYRON

So he cleans the diamond with the bat.

MACMULLEN

No, he does not clean anything.

MYRON

But you just said—

MACMULLEN

He bats cleanup and if he hits a home run, he *clears* the bags.

MYRON

He clears the bags but he doesn't clean them.

MACMULLEN

Right.

MYRON

And where did these bags come from?

MACMULLEN

The bags are on the diamond.

MYRON

Ah, now I see. So it is these bags that the Babe uses when he cleans the diamond.

MACMULLEN

No, the Babe bats cleanup and clears the bags if he gets a home run.

MYRON

A home run? What is this home run?

MACMULLEN

It's a hit that clears the bases.

MYRON

(Horrified)

You mean top of everything else they hit this Babe?

MACMULLEN

No, the Babe hits the baseball.

MYRON

I am so confused.

MACMULLEN

It is really a simple game, Myron. Children play it every day.

MYRON

(Points to the paper)

But what child gets thousands of dollars to play a game? This is just what they tell me in Russia, how in America the bourgeois exploits the workers for the profit.

MCGREEVEY

That's it! I'll have none of that Red talk in me bar! Nuff said!

(McGreevey starts to roll up his sleeves, but Carelli and Wiznowski restrain him.)

MACMULLEN

Take it easy, McGreevey, it's not his fault. The lad got off the boat only a month ago.

MCGREEVEY

You know how I feel about that stuff, MacMullen.

MACMULLEN

Don't get your knickers in a twist, McGreevey. He just doesn't understand the game, that's all.

(To Myron)

Don't you worry, lad, I'll teach you all you need to know.

(Steve enters the bar.)

MCGREEVEY

Ahhh, how are you going to get that Red to understand anything?

STEVE

Hello, big brother.

WIZNOWSKI

Eh? Who is that speaking to me?

STEVE

Philip, it's me. Your brother, Steve?

WIZNOWSKI

My brother? If I had a brother his name would be Wiznowski, not . . . not . . . what is that you call yourself? Ah, yes, Waterman.

(To the others, who are listening in)

My brother, he have the brains, so the family send him here to America to learn so he not have to work factory, get his hands dirty.

STEVE

Philip . . .

WIZNOWSKI

So he learn and he get job. Becomes the business manager of the Boston Red Sox.

STEVE

I wish you wouldn't do this every time—

WIZNOWSKI

Then he sends for family. But when we arrive with mother and father, what do we find? Not a Wiznowski. But a Waterman.

CARELLI

I have cousin. Is no longer a Carelli. Is now a Smith. I guess that makes them Americans, eh?

WIZNOWSKI

It is such . . . disrespect, you know. For the family.

STEVE

I noticed no one in the family minded the money I sent back home.

WIZNOWSKI

(To Carelli)

My brother. The big shot American. Listen how he speaks like American. Goes to college. Wears a tie and works for great baseball team.

STEVE

Are you through?

WIZNOWSKI

(Smiling)

Yes, I am through. You may now buy me a beer.

STEVE

Why do I come in here? Why do I spend time with you?

WIZNOWSKI

Because you can change your name but you cannot change who you are. My brother. My *Polish* brother whose name is Wiznowski.

STEVE

And it has nothing to do with the fact that I get you into Red Sox games for nothing?

WIZNOWSKI

Brother. I am hurt.

(There is laughter from everyone.)

CARELLI

So, Steve, you are at the Fenway Park every day.

WIZNOWSKI

Of course he is. Works side by side with the owner, too.

CARELLI

So tell us then, are we are going to do better than the sixth place we did this season?

STEVE

I think we have a good chance, Thomas.

MACMULLEN

With Babe Ruth on the team, they always have a chance.

CARELLI

That is why Babe Ruth is the greatest Italian since Columbus!

MACMULLEN

Italian? Where do you get that stuff?

CARELLI

Why do you think they call him the Bambino?

MACMULLEN

No no no, the Babe is from Baltimore, right Steve?

STEVE

Yes. From a place called . . . Camden Yards, I think.

MACMULLEN

Which is the Irish section where he grew up as O'Ruth!

WIZNOWSKI

Where do you get that stuff? It was the Polish section and his name was Ruthinski. Right, brother?

MACMULLEN

Don't let your big brother bully you. You tell him the truth, that the Babe is Irish!

CARELLI

The Bambino is Italian!

WIZNOWSKI

Polish!

MYRON

No, the Bambino must be Russian!

ALL

What?

MYRON

Why else would he wear the Red Sox?

(There is a roar of disapproval, some of it good natured, against Myron, as the bar explodes in simultaneous yelling by the patrons.)

MCGREEVEY

(Shouting to be heard over the noise)

Lads, lads . . . listen to me!

(They finally quiet down)

What does it matter, as long as he's on the Red Sox?

(McGreevey bangs his fist on the bar)

Nuff 'ced, right?

ROOTERS (all)

Nuff 'ced, McGreevey!

SONG: EVERYBODY'S GOT THEIR HEROES

MCGREEVEY

GENERAL PERSHING LED OUR NATION'S TROOPS
TO WORLD WAR VICTORY,
BUT BABE RUTH PITCHED SIX SHUTOUT GAMES,
AND BATTED THREE HUNDRED FIFTY-THREE,
TEDDY ROOSEVELT LED THE RIDERS, AND
BEAT THE SPANISH NATION,
BUT RUTH ONCE HIT A BALL SO HARD
IT LANDED ON SOUTH STATION.

ROOTERS (all)

EVERYBODY'S GOT THEIR HEROES,
MINE'S THE GREAT BABE RUTH.
HE CAN PITCH, HE CAN HIT, HE'S THE BEST
AND THAT'S THE TRUTH.
NEVER MIND YOUR SOLDIERS
AND THEIR TALES OF BATTLES WON,
WHO EVER PAID A DIME TO SEE A SOLDIER FIRE A GUN?

CARELLI

BACK HOME THEY TOLD ME THAT THIS WAS
THE LAND OF OPPORTUNITY.
AND EVEN THOUGH THE WORK IS HARD
I'M GLAD I'M NOT IN ITALY.

MACMULLEN

CAUSE HERE'S THE PLACE WHERE ANY LAD CAN
MAKE ALL KINDS OF RICHES.
WITH HOME RUNS, HITS AND RBI'S
IF HE CAN HIT FAST PITCHES.

ROOTERS (all)
EVERYBODY'S GOT THEIR HEROES,
MINE'S THE GREAT BABE RUTH.
HE CAN PITCH, HE CAN HIT,
HE'S THE BEST AND THAT'S THE TRUTH.

WIZNOWSKI
THE FACTORY WORKER'S LIFE IS HARD
BUT WE GET OUR REWARD,
WHEN WE READ HOW MANY RUNS
OUR HERO BABE HAS SCORED!

STEVE
Woodrow Wilson says we need a League of Nations to end all wars. But here's how I'd do it . . .
I'D TAKE THE KINGS AND THE PRESIDENTS
WHO RULE THE MANY LANDS,
BRING 'EM DOWN TO FENWAY
EAT A HOT DOG IN THE STANDS,
WATCH 'EM CHEER AND HUG EACH OTHER
WHEN BABE STEPS TO THE PLATE,

ROOTERS (all)
AN AMERICAN LEAGUE OF NATIONS,
WHO WILL CURE THE WORLD OF HATE!

ALL
EVERYBODY'S GOT THEIR HEROES,
AND MINE'S THE GREAT BABE RUTH.
HE CAN PITCH, HE CAN HIT,
HE'S THE BEST AND THAT'S THE TRUTH.
GO ON KEEP YOUR SOLDIERS AND EXPLORERS WITHOUT FEAR,

MCGREEVEY
WITH BABE RUTH ON THE SOX
WE'LL WIN THE
SERIES EVERY YEAR.

ALL

EVERYBODY'S GOT THEIR HEROES,
AND MINE'S THE GREAT BABE RUTH!

(END.)

(Another cheer arises from the patrons, who sit down at the bar as McGreevey pours them all a beer. Betty enters and all their heads turn to watch her warily.

Steve crosses and sits down at her table. The other patrons shake their heads and slowly return to their drinks during the following.)

STEVE

(To Betty)

Excuse me, miss. Is everything all right?

BETTY

Yes, I'm fine, thank you.

STEVE

Are you sure? It's just that we don't get too many strangers in this place—

MCGREEVEY

—Especially unescorted women.

BETTY

I just needed a place to get warm. It's awfully cold tonight.

STEVE

How about a drink? Might warm you up.

BETTY

(Hesitates)

Well . . . all right.

STEVE

(Motions to McGreevey, who goes to the bar to get the drink.)
I'm Steve Waterman.

BETTY

Betty Danvers.

STEVE

So, are you from the neighborhood?

BETTY

No, my husband is . . . was. He was killed in France a month before the Armistice. My sister-in-law took me in until I could get settled. She has three kids and I've been helping out, you know, as a way of paying her back. I just wish there was more I could do . . .

(Steve eyes her sympathetically. McGreevey arrives with the drink and breaks the moment.)

STEVE

Betty, meet "Nuff 'ced" McGreevey. He owns the Third Base.

BETTY

The Third Base?

MCGREEVEY

It's the last place you stop before you go home.

MACMULLEN

Hey McGreevey, I want to settle up. I've got to be getting home to the wife.

CARELLI

Me, too, Nuff 'Ced.

MCGREEVEY

(To Betty)

What did I tell ya?

(McGreevey returns to the bar.)

STEVE

So what more could you do?

BETTY

(Downcast)

With all the men back from the war there isn't much work out there for a woman. I was the bookkeeper at my husband's filling station.

(Sees Steve looking at her with a big smile)

Is that funny?

STEVE

Betty . . . do you like baseball?

BETTY

I guess so. I don't get out much.

Steve

Well I'm the business manager of the Red Sox. I work for the owner, Harry Frazee, and we've been looking for a bookkeeper.

BETTY

A job?

STEVE

A job.

BETTY

I don't know what to say.

STEVE

Say you'll come to Fenway Park tomorrow and meet your new boss.

(The lights fade to black as Betty smiles gratefully.)

CURSE #1

(The soft blue glow of the television begins to fill the stage, as we hear the announcer speak. During the following speech the lights will slowly rise on the four Rooters, who appear back in their raccoon coats. Now the pennants they carry read 1946.)

ANNOUNCER

Welcome back to our coverage of the 1986 World Series. You know, before the last commercial break we started talking about the fact that the Red Sox haven't won a World Series since Babe Ruth was sold to the New York Yankees back in 1920, what some call the Curse of the Bambino. Could there really be a curse on the Red Sox? Well, if you think about all the times it looked like they would win the World Series or get into the World Series only to have things go terribly terribly wrong, it just might be. Like in 1946 . . . .

SONG:
1946—RED SOX BOOGIE

ROOTERS (all)

WHEN THE SOX CAME BACK
FROM THE SECOND WORLD WAR
FROM THE ARMY AND THE NAVY
AND THE MARINE CORPS.
THEY HAD JOHNNY PESKY AND DOM DIMAGGIO, PLEASE,
AND WITH THE MIGHTY TED WILLIAMS,
WON THE SEASON WITH EASE.
SO FOR THE FIRST TIME SINCE THE BABE WAS IN TOWN,
THE SOX WERE IN THE SERIES
WITH A CHANCE FOR THE CROWN.

IT'S THE RED SOX BOOGIE!
SINGIN' BOUT THE TEAM THAT NO ONE COULD BEAT.
IT'S THE RED SOX BOOGIE!
SENDING EVERY OTHER TEAM DOWN TO DEFEAT.

THE WORLD SERIES WENT TO A SEVENTH GAME,
'CAUSE THE RED SOX BATS HAD PULLED UP LAME.
SOME SOX FANS ALMOST LOST THE FAITH
WHEN THE ST LOUIS CARDS
HAD A LEAD IN THE EIGHTH.

THEN THE SOX FOUGHT BACK,
THEY WOULDN'T GET BEAT.
THEY TIED THE GAME, THEY TURNED ON THE HEAT.

IT'S THE RED SOX BOOGIE!
SINGIN' BOUT THE TEAM THAT NO ONE COULD BEAT.
IT'S THE RED SOX BOOGIE!
SENDING EVERY OTHER TEAM DOWN TO DEFEAT.

SOX COULDN'T SCORE—THEY REALLY TRIED.
BOTTOM OF THE NINTH AND THE GAME'S STILL TIED.
WHEN A CARD NAMED SLAUGHTER GETS ON FIRST
—oh no!
IF HE SCORES THAT'S ALL FOLKS, THAT'S THE END OF THE SHOW.
THAT'S WHEN A GUY CALLED HARRY "THE HAT,"
REALLY DID SOME DAMAGE WITH HIS NEXT AT-BAT.

HARRY HITS THE BALL INTO CENTER FIELD
WITH SLAUGHTER ON FIRST, MAN! HE REALLY PEELED.
JOHNNY PESKY GETS THE RELAY THROW
BUT HE STOPPED . . . FOR A MOMENT OR SO.

FANS STILL ASK, "JOHNNY WHY WAS IT DONE
THAT YOU STOOD THERE WITH THE BALL
WHILE SLAUGHTER SCORED THE RUN?"

IT'S THE RED SOX BOOGIE!
SINGIN' BOUT THE TEAM ST. LOUIS COULD BEAT.
IT'S THE RED SOX BOOGIE!

SUFFERING THEIR VERY FIRST SERIES DEFEAT,
SUFFERING THEIR VERY FIRST SERIES DEFEAT.
CAUSE IF YOU'RE GONNA HOLD THE BALL THEN YOU'RE GONNA
GET BEAT!
OH NO!

(END.)

Heirloom

Elizabeth Pariseau

We take the train in from the suburbs. As the cars rumble and squawk their way toward the city's core, passengers crowd their way onto the cars until it's nothing but a sea of navy blue and red. By the time we reach Park Street, those not wearing the sacred "B" are in the distinct minority.

We leave the Red Line and stumble up the greasy stairs toward the Green Line platform. As we toe the yellow warning line next to the tracks, one train, then two, groan into the station with people stuffed inside. The cars stop and the doors open out of habit, while the people on the stairs glare over their shoulders toward the platform.

No one moves.

The doors close again, and the cars lumber off.

We wait. The air is thick with diesel fumes.

I'm clutching Amanda's hand, maybe a bit too tightly. Amanda, for her part, is goggling into the bewildering sea of knees around her.

"Yook, Mama," she keeps saying, pointing at things I can't follow in the chaos. "Yookit."

"What you lookin' at, 'Manda?" I bend to ask her, but she's already pulling away from me, her fingers twisting in my palm.

"Amanda!" I yank her back, my heart slamming into my breastbone.

"Stay with Mumma, okay?"

She's too busy looking to be upset. "Yookit," she chirps. And points. "Yookit, Mama."

My father lays a hand on my arm. "Sandy. Want me to take her?"

"No." Just a little too harsh. "I'll be fine. Let's just get on the train."

The fact that he doesn't reproach me for my snottiness just makes me feel worse.

I was born in 1970, three years after the Impossible Dream team almost won it all.

My due date was August 30, Ted Williams's birthday. My father's entire existence was vindicated by that coincidence. While I was still sprouting the buds that would grow into limbs—while I still had a tail but no fingers—my father was pooling his poker winnings to buy a color portrait of the Splendid Splinter.

By the time I'd found my own thumb in the amniotic fluid, Teddy Ballgame was hanging in a place of honor on the wall above my crib, in the tiny pantry that was waiting to become my room. He would stay over every bed I had, as sacred a figure as the crucifixes hung over the heads of my Catholic friends.

In the picture, No. 9 was frozen in the moment just after a big hit—you assumed it was a towering home run—his gangly legs corkscrewed around one another, the bat about to drop into the dust behind him, his squinting eyes buried in shadow as he followed the ball off into the blazing sun of a summer day.

Frankly, I preferred Ted to the gloomy Jesus, dangling from the Cross like a limp fish. My father, raised Catholic and recovering ever since, did too.

In addition to a room and a crib and a picture of my patron saint, I also had a name waiting for me. Theodore.

If it was a disappointment that I was born on September 1, and a girl to boot, he never let me know. For a name, he finally settled on Sandra, Sandy for short, after the great Sandy Koufax, the only player outside Boston my father ever thought was "wuth a dahn."

And Ted stayed.

Finally a car comes groaning up the tracks that looks like it might have just enough space for a smiling old man in a battered Red Sox cap, an increasingly impatient little girl, and a thirtysomething single mother on the verge of tears. If we can beat the milling crowd of college students, homeless people, Rastafarians, and the usual smattering of bewildered suburban families to it, that is.

It's close for a moment. Two girls—probably teenagers, but it looks like each weighs little more than my daughter—almost manage to squeeze themselves past us into the car. But I have hips now, thanks to motherhood, and I sling Amanda onto one of them and use the other to barge our way onto the train, while my father, following in my wake, says, "excuse us, excuse us."

I was five years old in the summer of 1975 and an avowed tomboy. This was my father's fault. He taught me to play catch, to ride a bike, about ground rule doubles and the infield fly rule. He shaped me into what I was, molding my knobby arms and my sturdy legs until I was the only girl in our neighborhood who could throw a ball overhand for more than a few feet or beat all comers in a bicycle race.

I was a strange and exotic creature, a fiercely happy little monster in pigtails tied with elastics in clashing colors, a filthy t-shirt with the faded likeness of Carlton Fisk on the front, and, quite often, a black eye or cut chin. I was wholly my father's creation.

That same year, as the summer wilted into fall, the Red Sox played the Cincinnati Reds in the World Series. My father let me stay up for the games, but when my fashionably late entrances at school reached three in a row, my mother intervened. As punishment, she declared, I was not, under any circumstances, to watch any more baseball.

My father nodded as she lectured us, rubbing one thick hand over the Navy tattoos on his right forearm. When my mother began slamming dishes around the kitchen, as she did whenever she was fed up, he leaned down toward me and winked.

The night of Game Six, though, my father, sternly observed by my mother from the hallway, tucked me into bed as the first pitch was thrown.

He pulled the blankets up to my chin and lightly pinched my cheek. He kissed my forehead, and said, with unusual formality, "Good night." He turned out the light and moments later his creaking footsteps followed my mother's down the hall.

She'd given half a mind to not going to her bridge club, she said, but decided in the end that this baseball foolishness wouldn't keep her from the precious little time she had to enjoy herself.

But if my father thought he could just wake me up as soon as she was gone, she said, he could count on packing his things when she got home, and that was a promise.

The door slammed.

I held my breath. I squeezed my knees together till the tips of my bones were rubbed raw. My fingernails dug ruts into my palms.

My father didn't come.

Instead, he sighed. He went into the living room. He lit a cigarette. I clamped my eyelids shut until infrared stars shot through my brain. Nothing.

Then, carefully, he turned the television up a little louder.

I arranged myself at the very edge of the bed, sure he would come to get me at any moment.

By the third inning, it became clear he wouldn't. It was the definition of unfair.

After several minutes of thrashing around the bed in impotent frustration, I resolved that the most I could do was obey the letter, but not the spirit, of the law. If I was being denied my inalienable right to watch the game, I would stay awake in bed and listen.

But my eyelids thought differently. Waves of gray soon began rolling across my field of vision. Absurd fragments of dreams began winding themselves into the sounds of the game.

The last thing I heard before sleep overwhelmed me was Luis

Tiant, he of the famous corkscrew delivery, freezing Johnny Bench with a called third strike in the fourth.

And then I was dreaming of fly balls and third outs and the Red Sox winning. Some time later, as I was riding a black racehorse over a field of perfect, empty baseball diamonds, I felt hands lifting me up, strong arms carrying me effortlessly over the ground, and I stirred at my father's ashtray-and-Old-Spice smell.

We were in the living room by the time I could force my eyes open. The television blazed the neon green of the Fenway outfield into the dark. My eyes adjusted painfully, and I gasped as I saw a tie score, INNING 12, and Carlton Fisk at bat.

My father balanced me carefully on his lap as he eased himself into his ratty armchair. I looked up into his beer-blurred face. "Watch," he whispered hoarsely.

I turned back to the television.

Pudge stepped to the plate. He windmilled the bat. He took ball one.

I climbed out of my father's lap, completely awake, and stood next to the chair, one hand clutching my father's forearm in quiet desperation. My eyes were wide open, my pupils fixed and dilated, but it still seemed like I couldn't see well enough, couldn't absorb what was happening.

A low fastball, an improbable swing, and *crack*. There goes a long drive to deep left field, if it stays fair . . .

They showed the ball in the air and it was sailing toward the foul pole.

"Get over!" my dad hollered. "*Get over.*"

He heaved himself out of the chair, hunkering down right into the face of the television.

"GET. OVAH. YOU. BITCH."

And *plunk*, the ball rebounded off the yellow spire in front of the great green wall.

My father swept me up into his arms, spinning us around, wheezing and coughing his smoke-stained laughter. The TV screen, ignored, flashed a replay I wouldn't see till years later—Pudge Fisk hollering at the ball just like my father: "Get over!"

My father was spinning me around and all that joy was pooling in my head, making me dizzy, and I threw back my shoulders and let the laughter out, and my father followed, and at that exact pinnacle of celebration, that precise apex of the purest happiness I ever felt in my bittersweet little life, my mother appeared, ashen faced, in the doorway.

No chance of us missing the stop at Kenmore—no sooner does the train ease into the station than people begin to push toward the doors like the thing's on fire. Now I have to haul Amanda back up onto my hip again. Most of the time, her sturdiness is comforting to me, a sign of her health, a sign she cannot be easily broken.

But it sure makes her heavy to carry through a teeming crowd in a subway station.

Once we stumble off the train, I have no choice but to set her down. Her Velcro sneakers are kicking back and forth, trying to take off running before they even touch the ground.

"Mandy," I warn her, trying my best to sound In Charge, "Don't. Run away. Oof."

And I let her go.

She stamps her feet and tugs on my hand, but remains at my side. Thank God for small favors.

We have to get moving—we're still rocks, now, in a whitewater of people. I make sure Dad is following, and the three of us turn into the current.

At first, there was no placating my mother. She slammed upstairs, and my father followed her, and for weeks a tiny buzz of anxiety hung over the apartment.

Gradually, the mysterious machinations of adults came into play. Behind closed doors, they reconciled, and I was never privy to the process. I only knew that, by Christmas, things were stable enough for my father to tuck an I.O.U. for tickets to my first real game at Fenway into my stocking.

I wore my Carlton Fisk t-shirt to the game. It was old, stained and just the slightest bit too small, but freshly washed for the occasion. I wanted Pudge to sign it and brought along a fabric marker stolen from my mother's sewing kit for that purpose.

Fenway Park is famously small. In an era of domed, Astroturfed Taj Majals, it's become the stereotype of outdated and quaint. But when it loomed before my child's body, it was a monolith of brick with all the power I had imagined.

The first thing my father did once we'd wandered through the green garage doors at the gate was buy me an official program. The kid selling them stopped his barking—"Proo-grams, hair!!"—long enough to hand down the glossy book and a short yellow pencil with no eraser. I took it with the reverence of a priest allowed to handle the Dead Sea Scrolls.

My father had taught me how to keep score, but I'd always had to draw my own boxes with a ruler on a piece of scrap paper, or use mimeographed copies from magazines. The score sheets inside the official program were, by contrast, works of art, framed with color photos of players, stamped with the logo, and printed in brilliant red ink. They were far too beautiful to mark. I closed the program and clutched it to my chest, the pencil clicking against the fabric marker in my palm as we made long trudge up the ramp to our seats.

I had pictured us sitting right by the infield, preferably near the on-deck circle, the better to buttonhole Pudge on his way out of the dugout for that autograph. This rich fantasy, of course, hinged on the fact that, being six years old, I wasn't clear on what the word "grandstand" meant. When we finally got to our actual seats, I was speechless for a moment, and not with joy.

Pudge, Dewey, and Yaz looked about the size of ladybugs off in a green distance. We were consigned to the shadows of a rickety roof on the first-base side. And someone had had the audacity to place a pole directly between me and any view of the pitcher's mound. I tried switching seats with my dad, only to discover that, between the two of us, the pole—more like a pillar—meant we had a choice between seeing the pitcher's mound or seeing first, second, shortstop, and the shallow outfield.

"But, Dad," I whined, pointing to the box seats next to the dugouts, "I thought we were going to sit over *there*."

"Heh!" he half-laughed, half grunted.

"Well, can we go over there?" I cajoled. "There's nobody even *in* those seats. Maybe they don't want them."

He cleared his throat, swiped his thumb under his nose, and sniffed loudly. Cleared his throat again, and barked out a strange little chuckle.

"Dad? What are you laughing at?"

No answer.

It was hot that day, and the darkness under the roof managed to be shady and an inferno at the same time. My legs stuck to the seat. Soon, I began to wilt, my chin in my hand, absently looking over at the ads behind the bleachers, watching the CITGO sign blink beyond the left-field wall, coughing and waving my hand in front of my face when the men behind us lit up cigars.

To make up for the disappointing seats, and the fact that the Sox were losing from the second inning on, my father bought me snacks: pizza, pretzels, hot dogs, cotton candy, popcorn, more hot dogs, and lots of orange soda.

Hot, thirsty despite the soda sloshing in my belly, tired, and disappointed, I began riding a bucking bull of nausea into the late innings.

Finally, an out into the ninth with the Sox still down five runs, my dad turned to me and said, "Well, better get goin'. Beat the traffic."

I turned to say, "okay," and vomited directly into his lap.

The Moosehead is now the Cask 'n Flagon. Coming into the neighborhood of the ballpark, you're now greeted with a full-fledged street fair of awnings, souvenir kiosks, memorabilia stands, and concession carts. They shut down the street before game time so that people are free to roam about with their Italian sausages, perusing the ubiquitous souvenirs.

Where there used to be just a net, people now teeter on top of the Green Monster. Coca-Cola bottles cling to the light poles. The word "Budweiser" glows in red cursive over the right-field roof. They've added seats there, too.

Of all the things I remember about Fenway, only the bums are still the same.

The awe of the subway station has given way to a disgust my little girl doesn't know what to do with. We're running the gauntlet of beggars and ticket scalpers that, since time immemorial, have gravitated along with rats to the feast that is game day in Boston, and she's clutching my hand now, bumping my thigh with her shoulder, shrinking away from the run-down men waving hand-lettered cardboard signs, the fast-talking greaseballs hissing, "Sellinticketssellintickets-sellintickets?" the muttering insane reaching for her with filthy hands.

She was born in 1999, on the very same August night that Pedro Martinez struck out 17 batters in a game against the dreaded Yankees. My father showed up at the hospital bearing a gift—a tiny Red Sox outfit.

It is a testament to my inability to bring myself to disappoint him that Amanda not only wore the little blue T-shirt with MARTINEZ 45 home from the hospital, but that she is now wearing GARCIAPARRA 5 and that "B" smack on top of her head to her first Red Sox game at the tender age of four.

I'm off in my reverie about Red Sox sportswear when one of the bums, stinking of urine, reaches out and brushes Amanda's hair with his yellowed fingers.

He rasps out something then, in a tone of putrid, predatory lust that will never leave the darkest reaches of my mind: "Lukkida li'l sweet-haaat."

It's indescribable, the way I respond to my child from the deepest part of my gut—as instinctively as I moved beneath the hands of the man who fathered her (during the first, last, and only one-night stand of my life, and of course I got pregnant). Now I sweep her off the ground, squeezing her so hard that she begins to squirm and whimper.

No conceivable kind of fear in her life is acceptable—even those of which she is blissfully unaware, as she is now, trundling down the street on her chubby little legs in her Velcro sneakers, at eye level with the varicose veins on the back of her grandfather's knees.

She doesn't have a father to protect her. She doesn't have a father to even give her a last name (I never knew it, stupid slut that I am). But I'll be goddamned if she doesn't have me.

Over and over, like an echo, I hear the bum's whisper, see the gleam in his eyes as he looks her over, watch a purple tongue snake out of his mouth and lick over the lipless slit of his toothless maw, and feel as though I've been punched in the chest.

I'm ready to leave now.

1978 was the year of Bucky Dent. I was eight, with as many trips to the ballpark under my belt, and I considered myself a sage of the game. When Bucky Dent defied all the laws of the universe, I adopted a Zen calm worthy of the Buddha.

You know, just a fluke. A crimp in the very concept of logic, but an anomaly nonetheless. Not prone to repeating itself.

I might have challenged you to a fistfight, might have duped you into a game of marbles (anyone who knew better wouldn't play me by that age) and taken your best piece, might have called you "nutso" if you had suggested to me in 1978 that I would have to live another eight years—another entire lifetime—to see the Red Sox win the pennant.

By that time I had taken to giving myself black eyes with powder from a compact rather than through a fistfight. I had taken to snapping tight bubbles of gum and wearing frosted pink lipstick. My hair was permed to the point of diminishing returns.

Pudge Fisk's t-shirt had long since gone to Goodwill. Though Ted still hung steadfastly on the wall, posters of Nikki Sixx were slowly creeping into his territory.

I still loved the Red Sox, but worked slavishly to keep it a secret. Liking sports in a flagrant and public manner was grounds for immediate dismissal from the sullen crowd of yuppie children I was desperate to "hang" with. And a close relationship with my father—who had become about as "cool" as Quasimodo almost the moment I turned fourteen—was out of the question. Therefore, baseball, our favorite shared activity, was to be enjoyed strictly *sub rosa*.

My father didn't understand. But he displayed his usual—and, somehow, infuriating—resignation to the fact that someone had replaced his perfectly acceptable tomboy with a Juicy-Fruit-popping lunatic.

In fact, all the times I would steal into the living room and slump down on the couch when the Red Sox just happened to be in extra innings, my father would act like he didn't notice, would stay as still as a hunter watching a twelve-point buck sniff the wind.

Not once did he ever ask me what I was thinking about, a fact that angered me simply because I desperately wanted the satisfaction of refusing to tell him.

As the summer ripened, and the heat deepened, and our smoke-filled living room traversed the spectrum from stuffy to unbearable, game time still often found me chewing a fingernail or the ever-present stick of gum on that couch, matching my stone-faced expression perfectly with my father's.

All this despite the fact that my bedroom was one of the two rooms in the apartment cooled by a wheezing, window-mounted air conditioner.

Looking back, it just doesn't get much more obvious than that.

Still, in that year of our Lord 1986, my father said nothing. Occasionally, when something either very bad or very good happened, he'd let out a grunt. Other than that, and the flick of his lighter as he lit a cigarette, or the soft crackle of dry tobacco as he took a drag—nothing.

Our monastic silence wasn't the only appeal to these evenings, however. It still pains me to admit it, but around that time a baseball player became my first real crush.

Something about the way Roger Clemens squared his shoulders made a lump rest in my throat. Something about the way he drew his glove slowly from eye level to his belt made me have to look away. Something about his taut hatchet face, the way his blue eyes tore holes through the television screen, something about the way a tiny hollow formed between his collarbones when he shook off a catcher's signal, something about the smattering of stubble that sometimes roughened his cheek—something about the way he blazed with power even in the midst of a world exclusively populated with spitting, barking, chewing, scratching, broad-shouldered men . . .

The first time I watched him pitch in a Red Sox uniform, I went from desperate to terrified. Though I might have been reassured that my hormones were, in fact, in working order, my only real feeling was an inarticulate sense of loss.

Men, boys, had been my friends and my peers. The way I felt about Roger put something alien between me and my old buddies from the neighborhood. And also between me and my father, who raised his eyebrows slightly at the newspaper photos of Roger that began beating back Nikki Sixx from Ted's territory, but still refrained from comment.

The fact was that I was becoming a woman, and that meant I couldn't be a little boy anymore.

Already at a fever pitch of confusion, I sat down on October 25, 1986, to watch Game Six of the World Series between the Boston Red Sox and the New York Mets.

What loyalty I had to that baseball team—what little-girl attachment remained to my father—flowed out of me with the tears after a game that felt like watching someone being slowly stoned to death. There was still another game to be played, but I knew it was over.

Call me sheltered. Call me shallow. But that night, in the darkness that followed Game Six, I first confronted loss in its rawest form. Confronted the fact that no amount of love, no amount of belief, no amount of passion—not even the fact that my entire relationship with the first man in my life hinged upon it—could earn that third strike to win the game.

Confronted the fact that life itself was not just cruel but needlessly and senselessly so.

Childhood was officially over. After 1986, it was over in so many ways.

Months later, in the spring of 1987, my father offered me tickets to a game at Fenway Park. I just looked at him and shook my head.

He slipped them back in the envelope and said nothing.

And both our hearts were broken, just like that.

Now here I am with my child amid the clamor and violence of the city, where at any moment some sick bastard might decide not just to look and lick his lips. And where, if my father has anything to do with it, that horrible soul sickness that is faith in the Red Sox will kidnap her instead.

It seems silly, but it's serious to me—allowing my daughter to experience what I experienced—the disillusionment, the bitterness, the very real grief. I might as well hand her over to the disgusting old creature on the bridge.

But my father has been determined. Everything he had failed to teach me, he will teach her. Everything he'd wishes he'd said to me while Roger Clemens wound up, kicked, and released, he will find a way to make my daughter hear.

He'll start early.

So why do I give in? Why board the train, take that long trip in from the safety of the suburbs? Why let my daughter wear a number on her back instead of a Mickey Mouse t-shirt?

Call it a peace offering.

And of course, her first Red Sox game is on the kind of late spring day that brings tears to the eyes of those old enough to harbor regrets. Of course, it's going to be played out in biting, vivid colors just a few yards away from our box seats right next to the dugout on the first-base line. Of course, it will take place, even in this the fourth year of the twenty-first century, the way it always does—designed to seduce, with the heartbreak hidden behind its back.

The Yankees are the opponents, and by the fourth inning, they are winning.

Two men on, one out, and Derek Jeter steps to the plate, the modern ballplayer incarnate, no longer a paunchy, mustachioed poor-boy-made-good but a sleek athletic machine, wind-milling the bat and blinking those frozen blue eyes.

My father, meanwhile, seems to have forgotten that Jeter is one of the few perfect strangers he will go to his grave despising. He's too busy pointing to the field and chattering excitedly into my daughter's ear.

"Ya see that," he stage-whispers. "Pitcha just shook off a fastball. Gonna try a curve now."

Amanda nods solemnly as though she understands.

"Look out!" my father chuckles, leaning back and slapping his knees. "Look out, boy-o, that one's outta the pahk a-ready."

My father hasn't been watching this game for sixty years for nothing. Maybe this year of our Lord two thousand and three really *is* "The Year", and maybe the Red Sox will overthrow the Yankees at the end of this season—but not today.

The pitcher—some kid named Lowe—delivers a curve that hangs for days.

Before it has gone halfway to the plate, you know. It spins on its lazy arc—just a little too low, just a little too outside—as pure and sweet and destined for doom as the afternoon sunlight glinting off Jeter's helmet.

It hangs there in a roaring, timeless silence, white and spotless and innocent. It floats and tempts in midair, as sumptuous a feast for the predator in the batter's box as my daughter's innocent heart.

The *crack* as the ball rockets off over the outfield, rising steadily, clutched in the blind hands of fate, makes me jump. Before I can recover, I have lost my child.

She points at the ball as it disappears into the blazing sky, following it with one tiny finger long after it's lost over the left-field wall.

"Whee!" she shouts and claps her hands with all her strength. "Mommy!"

She turns to grin at me in a way that makes me want to grab her and run up the beer-soaked steps, crunching over the dropped peanut shells till we're safely out of the ballpark.

"Whee!" she shrieks again.

And then she stands and applauds, Nomar cap be damned, for

Derek Jeter as he trots the third-base path toward home.

My father looks pale. For a moment I am sure he will lean down to reprimand her for cheering on the man whose first name he replaced with a curse word years ago.

He cups one hand on the crown of her head. His eyes are glassy. He's swallowing hard.

I hold my breath.

He looks at her, and ever so softly, he whispers, "Whee."

Saint Red Sock's Day: October 20, 2004

being a selection from Act IV, Scene III of William Soxspeare's newe playe "John Henry, the Fifth"

JONATHAN P. WINICKOFF

KEVIN MILLAR: What's he that wishes for more pitching?
My cousin Manny? No, my fair cousin. If we are mark'd to fail, we are enough
To do our Nation loss; and if to win,
The fewer men, the greater share of honour.
God's will! I pray thee, wish not one man more. By Tito, I am not covetous for Steinbrenner's gold,
Nor care I who doth cheered that California club;
It yearns me not what men those pinstripes wear;
Such outward things dwell not in my desires;

But if it be a sin to covet the World Series,
I am the most offending soul alive.

No, faith, my coz, wish not an extra set-up man.
God's peace! I would not lose so great an honour
As one man more, methinks, would share from me
For the best hope I have. O, do not wish one more!
Rather proclaim it, Manny, through the clubhouse,
That he which hath no stomach to this fight,
Let him depart. His passport shall be made to exit Red Sox Nation,
And crowns for Amtrak put into his purse.
We would not play ball in that man's company
That fears his fellowship to play ball with us.

This day is call'd the feast of the Red Sock.
He that outlives this day, and comes safe home,
Will stand a tip-toe when this day is named,
And rouse him at the name of Red Sock.
He that shall live this day, and see old age,
Will yearly on the vigil feast his neighbours,
And say, "To-morrow is Saint Red Sock."
Then will Schilling with bloody stocking donned again
Up roll his trouser and show his scars to all,
And say, "These wounds I had on Red Sock's day."

Old men forget; yet all shall be forgot,
But he'll remember with advantages
What feats he did that day. Then shall our names,
Familiar in the Nation's mouth as household words,

Ortiz the King, Cabrera and Bellhorn,
Lowe and Damon, Martinez and Varitek,
Be in their flowing cups freshly rememb'red.
This story shall the good fan teach his son;
And Red Sox's Red Sock shall ne'er go by,
From this day to the ending of the Curse,
And on to posterity,
But we in it shall be remembered,
We few, we happy few, we band of idiots.
For he to-day that sheds his ankle blood with me
Shall be my fellow idiot; be he ne'er such a Yankees fan,
This day shall gentle his condition;
And gentlemen in Boston now a-bed
Shall think themselves accurs'd they were not here,
And hold their Sox caps cheap whiles any speaks
That fought with us upon Saint Red Sock's day.

My Night at Fenway

ANDY SAKS

There's a lesson that life teaches: you never know. And if you think you know, you're wrong. And if you don't believe me, read on, and learn how a guy who didn't think he'd catch a game at Fenway all season found himself just twenty-four hours later standing next to a naked Manny Ramirez in the Red Sox locker room.

On a Thursday evening in May, I took a walk with my friend Julie along the bike trail near my Arlington home. As she told me about her trip to a Sox game the previous week, I started considering my own prospects. The odds didn't look good. Most tickets were long gone, and the remaining few were expensive and mostly behind large posts. I had no special contacts to call, no strings to pull. It looked like I'd be catching all my games on TV.

But it was spring, the air was fresh and warm, and I was in the mood for baseball. Well, I thought, if I can't get *in* the park, at least I can watch the game nearby. So the next night, I set out for that oasis of Sox fandom, the Cask 'n Flagon, to watch the Sox-Royals game with the other ticketless folk.

I should have recognized a budding lucky streak when I grabbed a free parking space in Kenmore Square just half an hour before game time. What were the odds? Still, I tried not to read too much into such mystical occurrences, lest I upset the space-time continuum. So I grabbed my Sox cap from the backseat and joined the masses marching over the Pike to Fenway.

Approaching the bar, my ears caught the catcalls of vendors pitching peanuts, programs, and pennants. The ticket scalpers added harmony, whispering their plaintive mantra—"Need tickets? Need tickets?"—just loudly enough to reach potential customers, and just quietly enough to evade the police. Together, they created a familiar chorus that stirred my appetite for the game.

The Cask 'n Flagon was crowded, but I managed to wedge myself into a seat at the bar between an older guy sporting a Sox road jersey with "Garciaparra 5" gracing the back and a large bald man wearing a "Yankees Suck" t-shirt. I ordered a Sam Adams draft and joined in the pre-game conversation. Would Wakefield's knuckleball keep the Royals off-balance? When would Nomar and Nixon rejoin the team? Would Manny and David Ortiz bring their red-hot bats tonight? And, of course, were the Yankees losing yet?

The conversation downshifted to a murmur as the game began, and our collective gaze turned to the TV screen dangling from the ceiling. The Royals wasted no time drawing blood. In the top of the first, Angel Berroa singled, moved to second on a ground ball, stole third, and scored on another ground ball. The Sox didn't answer.

END OF THE FIRST: 1-0 Royals.

I ordered another Sam Adams.

The second inning passed quietly, but the third didn't. Two singles and a throwing error produced another Royals run. The Sox seemed off-balance, and my comrades in the bar began reciting their familiar lamentations, blaming everyone from the manager to the A-Rod trade fiasco of the previous winter.

MIDDLE OF THE THIRD: 2-0 Royals.

The Sox bats finally came alive in the bottom of the third. Johnny Damon launched his third homer of the year, scoring Pokey Reese and tying the game. The bar patrons raised their glasses in praise, each insisting they'd never lost faith.

END OF THE THIRD: 2-2 tie.

With two beers under my belt, I stepped outside for some air. Lansdowne Street was empty except for some stragglers hovering behind the Green Monster, waiting patiently for a wall-clearing homer. I took a few deep breaths, stared at the sky, and pondered the pleasure of a Friday night at Fenway—even on the outside.

My reverie was interrupted by angry voices. I turned to see a man and a woman standing near the entrance gate, arguing loudly. The words "know-it-all" and "bull-headed" punctured the air. Suddenly, the man removed a large rectangular card hanging around his neck, offered a few choice profanities, and flung it to the ground. He stormed off down the street, pausing only to yell "Worst decision you'll ever make!" over his shoulder. The woman lingered on the sidewalk for a moment, body shaking. Then she turned and retreated in the other direction.

The abandoned card lay on the sidewalk. My curiosity aroused, I crossed the street and picked it up. As I examined it, I began to have trouble breathing.

The card was green with a red border and featured the Sox logo at the top. Below that was printed: "Guest, Fenway Park. Good for admittance to: Ballpark, Press Box, Clubhouse, Press Dining, and Field." Underneath that someone had scribbled the name Frank Tuttle into an empty white box.

It was an all-access pass to Fenway Park.

Ballpark.
Press Box.
Clubhouse.
Press Dining.
Field.
All access.

What would you do?

The universe works in mysterious ways, that's for sure. But it rarely, if ever, drops an all-access pass to Fenway Park in your lap. I'm not a religious man, but this clearly seemed a case of divine intervention. Like I said, you never know.

My mission was clear, my resolve firm, my pass intact. I was going in.

With a furtive glance in either direction, I hoisted the lanyard over my head and strode to the gate. Of course, my real name was Charlie Blake, not Frank Tuttle, so I hoped they wouldn't ask for any

ID. Steadying myself, I presented the pass to the guard for inspection. He looked it over, smiled, and said "Welcome to Fenway." I smiled back and shouted "Thanks!" over my shoulder as the turnstile clanked behind me.

I was in.

Where to go first?

Clutching the pass, I decided to head for the Monster Seats, the most coveted address at Fenway. I followed the upstairs walkway around the outside of the park on the first-base side. As I reached the elevators behind home plate, I turned a corner and found myself staring at the entrance to the .406 club, a 600-seat private section. Its giant bay window framed an impressive view of the field, but I'd heard it also walled in its inhabitants, denying them any actual sounds from the game. What would sitting there be like? This seemed like a stellar opportunity to find out, but the receptionist at the desk wouldn't let me in. I must have looked crushed, because as a consolation prize, she offered me a look around the nearby Red Sox Hall of Fame Club, something I never even knew existed. My curiosity was piqued, and I said yes.

The Club was well-appointed, featuring a restaurant, a bar, walls adorned with Red Sox photographs and plaques, and a TV monitor in every direction. I walked slowly among the deserted empty dining tables, soaking in the ambiance, and then stopped to read a segment of Ted Williams's Hall of Fame induction speech that was painted in large letters on the far wall.

Yes, the Hall of Fame Club had everything—except, unfortunately, a window to the field. Watching the game on the TV monitor just seemed silly, so after reading Fred Lynn's plaque, I headed for the exit.

In a way, I was fortunate to have missed the action on the field. Five singles (and one error by Sox third baseman Bill Mueller) had brought in four Royal runs, breaking the tie and placing the Sox in a deep hole.

END OF THE FIFTH: 6-2 Royals.

That's OK, I thought; *I'm on my own private adventure.* I sauntered down the hallway behind the left-field stands towards the Monster Seats.

For most of the park's history, the area atop the Green Monster had been dominated by a large net that ate up home run balls before they could reach the street. Last year, management had replaced the net with several rows of seats that had quickly become the park's most coveted real estate. Like many of the Sox faithful, I bristled when the seats were installed, sure that they offended the ghosts of Sox past in some way. And like many fans, after one glimpse of the revelers enjoying the view, I wanted to sit up there myself.

Now my moment had arrived. Fearlessly, I unveiled my pass to the guard. Fearlessly, he explained that I needed a ticket to the Monster Seats to enter the Monster Seats. I was about to protest when a pretty brunette who'd been eyeing this exchange rose from her Monster Seat and walked past the guard to me. "I've got to get home and relieve the babysitter," she whispered, sliding her ticket stub into my hand. "But I wouldn't want you to miss out." The guard looked at us, then sighed and waved me through. Like I said, you never know.

And the Monster Seats sure were all they'd been cracked up to be. There was something mystical about sitting in a spot that'd been empty space for so many decades. And what a view! I gazed down on Manny Ramirez in left, across to the .406 Club and the press boxes, over to the roof deck in the right-field corner, and beyond it to the Prudential Center arching into the sky. The remnants of a spring sunset washed over the horizon, vibrant oranges and reds melting into crystal blues and murky purples.

Oh, and the game wasn't bad from there either. I watched an uneventful sixth inning and mingled casually with the other fans, who called me Frank and marveled at my pass. It was pretty cool.

END OF THE SIXTH: Still 6-2 Royals.

Between innings, I decided it was time to press on. There were still more secret parts of Fenway to explore. My next target: the press box.

I took the elevator and quickly found the entrance to the press area. More confident this time, I charged in through the double doors, flipped my pass at the guard behind the desk, and without breaking stride, marched into the hallway beyond.

The setup was different from what I'd expected. The hallway

contained a series of doors on the right, each leading into small rooms occupied by different media crews. I passed "Visitors Radio," "Visitors TV," and "Red Sox Radio," then stopped at "Red Sox TV."

RemDawg was in there. Once again, I had trouble breathing.

I stood outside and considered how I might penetrate that little room. This wasn't like traipsing into the Monster Seats; these rooms were tiny, with barely enough standing room for half a dozen people. If you didn't belong, they noticed. Without a good excuse, they might assume I was a terrorist, or at least a spy for the Royals. What story could I conjure up to justify my entrance?

As I tried to concoct an explanation, the men's room door opened behind me. A man brushed past, opened the door to the Red Sox TV room, and walked in. On instinct, I grabbed the door before it shut and shuffled in behind him.

I realized pretty quickly that my fantasy of swapping incisive comments with RemDawg while we sipped champagne and inhaled Dunkin Munchkins was just not to be. In fact, I couldn't even see the Sox announcers. That's because the tiny rooms were also split-level. I was on the top floor, and RemDawg was on the bottom. Even the top of his head was obscured by a table full of TV production equipment. I was in the right room, but still miles away.

I stood quietly against the back wall and tried to render myself invisible. People watched me curiously, seeming to sense that I didn't belong. Suddenly, my worst fears were stoked by the man standing next to me, the same one whose return from the bathroom had allowed my clandestine entrance. He turned abruptly in my direction and whispered "Hey, do you . . . " That was all I needed to hear. Panicked, I spun quickly around, opened the door, and jumped into the hallway. Just before the door clicked shut behind me, I heard the man, now a bit dismayed, add " . . . have a pen?"

That misstep cost me a possible RemDawg encounter, but there were other places to explore. I continued down the hallway until it opened up into a big media room. Reporters sat in long rows, pecking at their laptops, chatting, and watching the game through a giant bay window. This was, in fact, the very same bay window view that had looked so tantalizing from the stands for so many years. And it definitely lived up to the hype. I quietly took a seat in the back row and watched some more of the game.

In the bottom of the eighth, Manny Ramirez and Gabe Kapler each singled. Then Doug Mirabelli stepped up to bat. He tapped a high fly ball to left, and Matt Stairs camped out underneath it. At this point, Mother Nature stepped in to help. As the ball sank, a gust of wind erupted, catching the ball and twisting it in manic circles. Stairs couldn't follow it, and the ball hit the ground untouched. Ramirez and Kapler both crossed the plate. Mueller then lined to left and Daubach struck out to end the inning. But the Sox had done some damage.

END OF THE EIGHTH: 6-4 Royals.

With only one inning left, I decided to rejoin the regular fans. Emboldened by my victories, I was determined to capture that holy grail of hard plastic chairs: a seat behind home plate. I'd gone to countless games since the mid-'70s and sat nearly everywhere in the park. But I'd never enjoyed a seat so near the action that the batter's box was closer than the men's room.

I felt it was time.

I went right to the section in question, held up my badge, and asked the guard, "Will this get me in here?" He said yes and showed me to an inexplicably empty seat right behind home plate. I guess the occupant had given up on the Sox and called it a night, but I wasn't going to make that same mistake.

Now there was nothing to obstruct my vision or distract my attention. No tall fans, no peanut vendors, no guards. In this setting, inches from the hallowed Fenway grass, I could almost imagine I was a part of the game, a special ambassador drafted to cheer the home team through a ninth-inning rally.

And rally they did.

First, Johnny Damon drew a walk and moved to second on Santiago's passed ball. Then Mark Bellhorn entered the batter's box and smashed a fly ball to deep right. From my perfect vantage point, I had no doubt about its destiny.

Red Sox 6, Royals 6. Still one out.

David Ortiz was next and went down on strikes. But Ramirez took first base on a walk. In came Royals' reliever Scott Sullivan.

Kevin Millar popped to second. No swirling eddies of wind this time. Two out, Ramirez on first.

I turned around to survey the crowd behind me. Though most of the park was standing and cheering, my section sat quiet and tense. Clearly, as the occupant of the front-row center seat, I had a responsibility here, and I wasn't going to waste this chance. Frantically I moved my arms up and down and yelled "Stand up! Stand up!" imploring my fellow fans to rise to the occasion. They stood, adding their cheers to the cacophony around them.

Jason Varitek came up off the bench to pinch-hit for Kapler. Ramirez represented the tying run on first, but with two outs, any mistake would send the game into extra innings.

But this game wasn't destined for extra innings. Varitek cracked a hard line drive deep into the right-field corner. While Gonzalez struggled to retrieve it, Ramirez chugged around second and turned the corner on third, heading for home. The relay was on its way to meet him, and the play would be close.

Ramirez didn't slide. Instead, the Sox powerhouse stayed vertical, tapping home plate with his arms raised in victory just a split-second before Santiago could swing around to tag him.

7-6 Red Sox. Final score.

Yes, it was only an early-season, non-divisional game against a mediocre team. But for a few moments, the fans of Fenway unleashed a thunderstorm of cheering, jumping, and high-fiving that rattled the whole damn park. While the Sox players stormed out of the dugout and swarmed Manny at the plate, the fans reveled in a comeback win for the ages. And I shared it too, from the front row center seat behind home plate.

Now, you'd think that sneaking into the best seat in the house just in time to watch the Red Sox win the game in the bottom of the ninth would be enough. You'd think that, but you'd be wrong. There was still one undiscovered area to which my pass granted me access: the clubhouse. And by this point, I felt fearless. A visit to the clubhouse now seemed as reasonable as grabbing a hot dog at the concession stand. Except for one thing: I didn't know where the clubhouse *was*. Upstairs? Under the Monster Seats? Down a secret passageway under home plate? I needed help. So as the crowd filtered out of the stands, I asked a passing Fenway staffer for directions. "Follow me," she answered, and walked me through the exit tunnel and over to a small, unmarked, nondescript entrance area next to the men's room.

Then the staffer handed me off to man in a Sox jacket lounging on a folding chair. He checked my pass, nodded, and pointed through the doorway. My heartbeat quickened as I entered a plain dark gray hallway and reached a plain-looking door. I opened it and stepped inside.

And just like that, I was standing in the Red Sox locker room.

Up until that moment, I wasn't sure the clubhouse and the locker room were the same thing. I figured the clubhouse was more likely a side room with tiny cheese sandwiches and waiting reporters and players' wives. Because they wouldn't just let any idiot with a paper pass around his neck walk into the Red Sox locker room, would they?

Yes. Yes, they would.

The locker room was small, just like everything at Fenway. Three walls were lined with lockers, each containing clothes, toiletries, and a freshly-pressed jersey hanging from the top bar. A black leather couch occupied the middle of the room, and a cooler with bottled water hummed quietly against the far wall, next to the showers.

Once again, the sense of history descended on me. This was the room where hundreds—thousands—of Red Sox players, decade after decade, had come together to don their uniforms and prepare for the game. The Babe once had a locker in here. So did Williams. And Pesky. Tony C. Yaz. Clemens. And now, Pedro, Manny, Nomar, Damon, Varitek. All those players who seem so much larger than life to those of us who see them only from a distance. All those million-dollar personalities, all those ghosts, all those memories, concentrated in this tiny room.

My excitement turned to anxiety as I realized that I might be questioned by someone; I had to blend in. I crossed the room and joined a gaggle of reporters interviewing Johnny Damon. Beyond the artificial glare of the TV lights, it looked like a million interviews on that very spot must have looked: a bunch of men gathered around a man in a Red Sox uniform, frantically scribbling his every word on their tiny notepads.

As Damon spoke, I glanced to my left and spotted Manny Ramirez, who had emerged from the showers and stood naked at his locker with his back to me. I was later asked by a female friend to describe Manny's ass, and I can only repeat what I told her. The ass in question was, well, an ass, and it looked pretty much in proportion with his back and his legs. What else do you need to know?

Manny covered his butt with underwear, then added jeans and a sweatshirt. When he was presentable, the reporters migrated to his locker. They asked him why he didn't slide into home plate on that last play, and he responded, "I was just running hard. I was going to run hard, not going to stop." There you have it.

Manny finished up his interview as several other players emerged from the showers and headed to their lockers. Suddenly I felt very conspicuous, fully dressed and without a decent excuse for hanging around. What if someone challenged me, asked to see my press credentials? And what did I know about Frank Tuttle, the man whose identity I'd assumed for this adventure? If questioned, I'd have to invent a whole backstory for him on the spot. Or maybe they'd actually know him and recognize that I had pilfered his pass.

It seemed unlikely that my good luck would last much longer, so I decided to make my exit. As I shuffled toward the door, my hand brushed against a table in the middle of the room. I glanced over and noticed a Red Sox jersey lying there, signed by several players. A black permanent marker sat beside it.

I knew I couldn't walk out with the jersey in front of a dozen Red Sox players, risking arrest and depriving some charity of their prized auction item. Yet I felt compelled to mark this astonishing evening somehow. On a whim, I picked up the marker and scribbled "Blake #27" across the bottom right corner of the shirt. (Carlton Fisk was my brother Evan's favorite player.) Then I scurried from the locker room, stepped out of the park, and joined the masses of fans spreading into the night.

And that is the story of how one man who thought he wouldn't catch a game all season pulled off an impromptu grand tour of one of baseball's most cherished shrines, on a night the Sox staged a comeback for the ages.

They say fifty percent of success is showing up, just being present for the chaos that life serves every day and taking advantages of the opportunities that come along.

Here's how I'd put it: you never know. And if you think you know, you're wrong.

But if you ever see a Red Sox jersey with one out-of-place signature at an auction, go ahead and buy it. It's priceless.

The Long, Dark Voyage

Matthew Hanlon

Sure, he came to spring training with a shaggy beard and a mane of hair thick enough to choke a cat. And he knew for damn sure he was going to get comments. A *lot* of comments. At least it would give the press something to talk about, he thought.

He'd made a list that first morning as he headed out the door: Captain Caveman, Jesus H Christ, Samson, Grizzly Adams, Caveman Pete, Johnny Come-With-A-Lotta-Hair. He figured he'd get 'em all, and more, from the Boston media. And most of them had already been tried out on him.

No matter. None of them knew, none of them *would* know, what really happened that winter.

He told them the stories about migraines after his collision in Oakland. He told them about other stuff; he couldn't quite remember everything he said. If he seemed foggy about things, he could usually get away with a smile and a weary shake of the head. With his longer hair, it made the shake that much more effective. The reporters ate it up. And then they'd move on to Pedro, or Manny, or

Nomar. Curt was always good for a juicy quote. And he'd be able to sit back and relax at his locker. He'd put his head in his hands and let the cool steel mesh make marks on his forehead through a few layers of hair.

In November, he *was* having migraines, truth be told. But that was also when he got The Call.

Some of his buddies from the Oakland days rang up one day, and he could tell they had him on speakerphone almost straight away. He could hear his own voice groggily saying "Hello?" The grogginess really hit home with the echo reverberating in the phone.

"Heya Johnny, how's your head?"

"S'allright. I suppose. How're you guys?"

There was silence on the other end of the phone.

"Hey, guys." He held the phone a little away from his head and tilted it at an angle, as if he could tip the conversation out of the phone like water.

"Uh, yeah. Listen. Wanna come outside, like, now? There's a car out front." There was only one voice on the phone now. Johnny could hear the emptiness of the room that the calling phone was sitting in. He pictured brown walls and those hard linoleum floors of a school cafeteria. He wasn't quite sure why.

He got up out of the chair where he had dozed off earlier and sidled over to the front window. He pulled the blinds back a little bit. Sure enough, there was a car out there. A black four-door sedan, some weird looking gold trim glinting in the streetlights. Not *entirely* unusual for Florida, which has some ugly cars, but odd for his neighborhood. He let the blinds back down gently, so they wouldn't rattle and wake anyone. And that's when the guys burst through the front door, sending a good chunk of the doorjamb flying out into the hallway. Then they grabbed Johnny and half dragged, half carried him to the waiting car.

At first, he couldn't quite tell what was worse, his sea-sickness or the migraines. It turned out they probably weren't migraines at that point; it was probably a different manifestation of the seasickness hitting him. If you get your head shoved in a canvas sack and then are tossed on what appears to be (from the sounds and smells) a large boat, your general well-being isn't so well. He was kept out of the sun, for the most part, but by the end of a couple days Johnny wasn't feeling so hot, and he really wished the rocking of the boat would stop.

On the third day, he woke to the scraping of wood against sand and the sudden vertigo that hits you when you touch land after a long time on the water. He was pulled out of a smaller boat and put ashore, the bag removed from his head, and his arms untied. Then he just sat in some incredibly soft sand, facing out towards the sea, and watched as the two men who had rowed him to shore struggled to get the boat out of some impressive surf. The men dove forward against the boat, trying to push it out of the way of the breakers. The thought crossed his mind that they would look ridiculous doing this on dry land. And just then, they were over, out of the crash zone and bobbing over the waves before the breaking point. By the time the men reached the larger boat he'd apparently arrived on, the sea and sky were a dusky pink. The last thing he saw before night fell was the larger ship angling seawards. The next morning there was nothing on the water.

He found a cave set back from the shore, surrounded by a sort of grassy clearing. Judging from the brightly colored banners he occasionally dug up while looking for grubs, he thought the clearing had been created and then abandoned by a reality television show. He didn't know what he was looking for, exactly, in the grubs, but he kept digging because he seemed to remember something, either from television or some deep-seated primal knowledge, about the easiest-to-catch food often being underground.

The lighter and boxes of matches he found wrapped in plastic at the back of the cave also suggested this might have been used for something else. The lighter ran out of fluid after the third day, but the supply of matches seemed inexhaustible.

As the weeks wore on, he subsisted largely on wild pigs, fish, and fruit. He suspected there were other people on the island, helping him in small ways, because oftentimes the pigs would appear just inside his cave, already cooked and occasionally with an apple in their mouths. Most of the time he heated the pigs back up before eating them, because he wasn't so sure how cold pig would sit in his stomach.

His runs along the beach didn't reveal anything special about his island, though he could occasionally hear the drone of a plane overhead or the rasp of outboard engines coming from somewhere out there on the water. He often scanned the horizon while casting his makeshift line out into the surf, but he never saw any passing ships. Apparently it was just your average, ordinary deserted island, with nice savages around who liked to drop off pre-cooked pigs. And then one day he learned the truth.

"Some bachelor party, eh?" the enormous man said. "Bet you weren't expecting this." His head was stuffed into a black mask, the kind wrestlers often wore when they had nothing else to use as a gimmick. This man had stepped out from behind a copse of trees at the mouth of the cave. He wasn't wearing a shirt, just some faded basketball shorts, a pair of Chuck Taylors, and that mask that made his head look like a baked potato. It had been weeks since Johnny had seen anyone else, and for a moment he worried that this might be his very own painted volleyball.

"I'm not getting married, man." Those being his first words in more than a month, Johnny was disappointed. He had been hoping for something a little more appropriate when being rescued.

"No way. Really?" The guy in the mask stepped back a bit.

"Yeah, no."

"Aw, damn. You're kidding, right?"

"No, man. I'm not. I've already been married. Couple of kids. Sure, I'm seeing someone nice right now, but we're not ready to tie the knot. And I don't think you get a second bachelor party, anyway." Johnny produced what remained of his wallet and pulled out the pictures of his kids.

The big man stepped forward, and his shadow fell over the wallet. "Oh man. But your friends said. . . . " He stepped back again, hand placed where his forehead would be. "Listen, I'm really sorry about all this. I'll give you a lift." The big man pulled a battered-looking motorcycle out of the bushes and hopped on. He motioned for Johnny to climb on behind him. Then the man in the mask spent most of the ride on his cell phone as they drove to a small airfield about a mile, maybe two, from the cave. From there, he let Johnny off down the less grassy end of the landing strip. A plane sat idling there, its steps down and a couple of bored guards leaning on either side of the staircase. They got him on with a minimum of fuss, closed up the door at the top of the staircase and remained there while the plane wiggled off down the runway and back to Orlando.

After that, he had some time. Time to spend with his family, who got used to the hair and beard, and time to work on his excuses for the Boston media. He knew the questions would dog him from the moment he reported to Fort Myers, and a few razor strokes could make them all go away. But Johnny didn't go to the barbershop, not yet. He'd grown a little partial to the beard, anyway.

First Start
Tom Snee

The sun slants across the Fenway Park infield and leaves the pitcher's mound half in shadow as Alex climbs to the rubber and begins his warm-up pitches. This should be a good thing, I explain to my wife, Kathy, sitting next to me in the seats down the right field line. The difference between sun and shadow will make it more difficult for the batter to see the ball and give Alex an advantage in the first inning.

But Kathy only smiles dimly and says nothing, too nervous to speak at the thought of her son's first major league start.

"He'll do great, he'll do just fine," I say as I take her hand. She gives mine a strong, confident squeeze in return, but her clammy palm betrays her nerves.

The stadium announcer is reading the Red Sox starting line-up and I half-listen, paying just enough attention to know when he comes to the last spot, the pitcher's spot. Then I close my eyes and concentrate on the voice, ignoring all my other senses to focus only on the hearing.

"Pitching today for the Red Sox," the voice says, drifting into the corners of the stadium and echoing back off the Green Monster. "Number 38, Alex DeBow."

The name sinks in: Alex DeBow. My son, the pitcher. The major league pitcher. Alex DeBow.

"DeBow," the stadium announcer reminds us, and I smile as my son's name, my name, wraps itself around the 33,000 people who wait anxiously for the game to begin. I'm not kidding myself about the glory of all this—I realize the name Alex DeBow means nothing to the other 32,998 people in the stadium, none of whom have come to see the first start of a rookie pitcher from New Hampshire. But then again, the names Babe Ruth, Sandy Koufax, and Lou Brock once meant nothing, too.

On the mound, Alex is going through his pre-game warm-ups: fastball, fastball, curveball, curveball, change-up, change-up, curveball, fastball. It's the same every game, this ritual: fastball, fastball, curveball, curveball, change-up, change-up, curveball, fastball. The same every game, the same every inning. Alex has very few routines in his life, but this one he has worked on carefully and follows precisely; he arrives at the mound, squeezes the rosin bag, walks once around the mound, squeezes the rosin bag again, kicks the rubber, then stands motionless for four seconds before tossing his warm-up pitches. Then he rearranges the dirt in front of the rubber, walks once more around the mound, squeezes the rosin bag one last time, kicks the rubber again, and he is ready to pitch. His routine didn't appear in this form; it evolved gradually since his days in Little League, the pattern altered, the elements rearranged, some added (the rosin bag, for instance, wasn't included until high school because youth leagues don't have them), others dropped (spitting toward the outfield at the start of every inning, throwing a handful of dirt in the air, genuflecting at the mound, which, as I recall, lasted only two or three games before ridicule prompted him to scrap it). Neither of us knows what the symbolism of any of this means, but ballplayers are too superstitious to let reason alter a routine.

Behind Alex, his defense warms up by throwing easy, high-arching lobs while two Oriole hitters kneel in the on-deck circle, waiting to take their cuts. These last few moments before a game are always a strange time, murky and indecisive. It's relaxed yet tense, the loose feel of the pre-game warm-ups giving way to the focused and serious job of the game these men are paid millions to play. The fielders start to think two pitches ahead, the pitcher and catcher try to find a groove, the hitters study the pitcher for his movements and rhythms, the bored umpire counts to eight. It's like those few minutes of dawn, when it's neither day nor night and the air is heavy as if time has stopped until the sun slides over the horizon and the umpire yells "play ball" and everything moves forward again.

The giant video screen on the scoreboard flashes a digitized picture of Alex and his career statistics: 0-0, .000 ERA, 0 games pitched. I nudge Kathy and point to the screen.

"Look at that," I say, smiling and motioning to our son's disembodied face hovering over tens of thousands of people.

"Oh, my God," she shrieks, shrill enough that several fans sitting around us flinch. "Oh my God, that's terrible. Is that the best picture they have? I have better pictures than that in my wallet . . . "

She's right that it's not a very good picture. He is tight and scowling and seems like he has a very bad stomach cramp, plus the digitizing process has made him look even more alien, moving his eyes closer together and widening his nose. In fact, as I look more intently, I wonder if it's really Alex at all.

"I know I have a better one in here somewhere," she says, pulling a wallet from her purse. "Maybe it's not too late and I can bring it to wherever they do that scoreboard stuff and give it to them . . . "

I put my hand on hers and gently push the wallet back.

"Never mind," I say. "It doesn't make any difference."

"But that picture is awful . . . "

"It doesn't make any difference," I say again, and she puts the wallet back in her purse. Slowly and reluctantly, but she puts it back.

"But what will people think . . . " she says, letting the thought trail off, and we look back to Alex on the field. This is what she is usually concerned about when it comes to Alex: what will people think? Will they like him? Will he be hurt? Will she have to hug him afterwards, console him, assure him that everything will be OK? Kathy tends to remember failure, the blow-ups and explosions and the tears. She doesn't exult in victory as deeply as she is overwhelmed by defeat. For example, she doesn't have much memory of the day he pitched his high school to the state championship, or his American Legion team to their World Series. What she does remember is the day Alex got hammered in his sixth grade Little League championship game, when he gave up six runs in fewer than two innings before the coach finally pulled him. As he walked back to the dugout, Kathy's maternal instincts overcame her and she ran onto the field and wrapped him in a big hug. Alex wriggled away and stormed into the dugout, more embarrassed by her hug than his performance.

Alex has since forgotten that game, an isolated failure overwhelmed by many more successes. But it is still at the heart of Kathy's relationship with Alex's career. Her instinct is to protect her son from failure, not push him to success.

"His name's not in the program," she says, her voice desperate.

"What?"

"Alex's name, it's not here in the program," she says again, louder this time, flipping through it so frantically she's tearing the pages.

"That's because they just called him up from the minors yesterday and haven't had time to add it yet," I explain.

"It doesn't mean they're going to let him go?" she asks, madly scanning the Red Sox roster on the scorecard for his name.

"No."

"It doesn't mean they don't think he's any good?" Her voice is rushed, almost desperate.

"No," I say. She nods, reluctantly admitting that I might be right, and looks back to Alex on the mound.

"He is good, isn't he?" she asks, and I pause for a moment before answering. I'm not sure I should be honest with her, if I should give her a true assessment of his talent, because the truth is, no, he isn't very good. It hurts me to say this, but I can't help but think Alex is not ready for the major leagues. He has good stuff, but not great stuff, and as he rose through the minors, he found it increasingly difficult to get batters out. His fastball was a little too slow, his curveball a little too flat, his change-up a little too obvious. He was a star in college, very good at Single A, merely average at Double A. His three seasons at Triple A have been a struggle, and calling Alex mediocre might be giving him too much credit. I can't help but wonder how his maxed-out skill level will fare in the majors.

I've never told anyone my doubts, but I know others think the same thing. One of the Boston newspapers wrote a profile of Alex during spring training, pointedly saying he had yet to fulfill his early promise and this would be a make-or-break season for him. When

Kathy asked what I thought of the story, I said it was garbage and the writer just needed to say something bad about someone. But in my heart, I knew the story was right.

Even Alex began to doubt himself, especially after he began the Triple A season 0-4 and looked bad in every start.

"Dad, I don't know what I'm doing anymore," he said to me on the phone after a disastrous game in Indianapolis. "I think I'm going to hang it up, maybe go back and finish college."

I didn't know what to say. I was never much of a cheerleader.

"If that's what you want, that's fine with me," I said, a part of me happy that he was doing the practical thing, a part of me destroyed that his dream was melting.

I never pushed Alex to do any of this, I was always far too sensible to think my son could ever be a major league pitcher. He had talent, I knew that, but I always thought he'd pursue something safe and ordinary, like selling insurance or industrial equipment, which is what I did.

But safe and ordinary couldn't overcome the aura that he carried with him after we saw our first Sox game at Fenway when he was 6. That day, his career goal was set.

"I want to be a major league pitcher," he'd say when I asked him what he wanted to do when he grew up. I wished I could have said, "Yes, you can do it, keep practicing," while we played catch in the backyard, encouraging him to believe that he could make his dreams come true if he tried hard enough.

But I'm far too conservative for that sort of thing. Instead, I said, "That's great, and it's a wonderful dream, but don't you think you should have a back-up plan in case baseball doesn't work out?"

"Naw," he would answer, pounding the palm of his glove, putting more confidence in himself than I did. It's true I never really helped his climb to the major leagues, but I never hindered it, either. I didn't tell him he couldn't succeed, I never discouraged him from playing ball, I never ordered him to consider other careers. I created a neutral environment, neither helpful nor hostile, for Alex to develop and choose his own direction.

He managed to turn his season around after that game in Indianapolis—in comparative terms, anyway—going 4-3 with a shutout. They weren't great numbers, but they were good enough to earn a call-up to the majors when one of the Red Sox starters got injured. Perhaps the call-up will show him that others have faith in his ability and give him the confidence to get major league hitters out. I have a nagging feeling it won't.

"Yes, he is good," I say to Kathy, giving her the answer she needs to hear. She takes a camera from her purse and aims it at Alex, the motor whirring as the auto focus lens tries futilely to find something to focus on. I'm glad I lied. It seems to have comforted her.

The batter digs into the box, the catcher crouches behind the plate, and Kathy and I hold hands as Alex begins his major league career. He stands on the mound for a moment, his body still, his head turning slowly from one foul pole to the other, and it looks as if he's trying to soak up Fenway Park, realizing that this is the place Babe Ruth pitched, this is the outfield Ted Williams patrolled, this is the plate that Carlton Fisk blocked. Fenway is nothing new to him, we've been here many times. But he's never seen it like this.

He stands a little too long and I wonder if he hasn't forgotten that he's come to pitch, not play tourist. Finally, he leans over, shakes off the first signal from the catcher, nods to the second, takes the ball from his glove, and starts his wind-up. Kathy keeps her camera aimed at the lonely figure on the mound, ready to capture his first major league pitch, and as the ball slides from his hand, her flash explodes. It's the only flash to pop in the entire stadium.

It's a curveball. My son's first major league pitch is a curveball. I make a mental note in my Book of Alex's Firsts, along with first words ("mama"), first grounding (one week for throwing a rock through a neighbor's window), and first date (Christy Neal, a cute enough girl who I knew was way too sophisticated for him). Never his best pitch to begin with, the curve bites well before it should and lands in the dirt three feet in front of the plate.

"Not a good start," a man sitting in the row behind me snickers as a few of Fenway's other merciless fans giggle and snort. I want to get angry with them, tell them that it's just one pitch and how can you possibly judge a career on that? But I can't really argue because I'm thinking the same thing.

"Nerves," I say to Kathy, patting her on the knee, trying to reassure the both of us. "This next one will be a strike, just watch."

His next pitch is a fastball, his best pitch, the one he goes to when he needs to throw a strike and build up his confidence. He never had a blazing fastball, but he could always place it well, paint the corners, as they say, throw it to the spot where the ump will call it a strike but the batter can't hit it. This fastball, though, is over the heart of the plate, and the batter sends it right back up the middle into center field for a single. Alex has to duck to keep from being hit in the face.

"Oh, no," Kathy gasps, and I take her hand again.

"Don't worry," I say. "He'll throw a curve to the next batter, get a ground ball and they'll turn a double play."

But he throws another fastball, and the next batter laces a single into right field. Another fastball is smoked into the gap in right for a bases-clearing double and it's suddenly 2-0.

"What's wrong?" Kathy asks, as if she is trying to figure out some way she can help. "Is he OK?"

"He's fine," I lie, hoping this need to avoid the truth doesn't become a habit. "He's just a little nervous. He needs to settle down, throw a few pitches and get rid of the butterflies."

His confidence in his fastball gone, Alex now throws four straight curves to the next batter. None of them is any closer than two feet from the strike zone. Ball four is so far outside the catcher has to dive to stop it.

The walk brings out the pitching coach, a short, pug-nosed, fire-plug of a man with a baggy uniform who looks like he should have played the game in the 1920s. The Fenway fans razz Alex even more, calling him a bum, loser, third-rate hack, and each shout stings me like a line drive.

I look at Kathy and her eyes are puffy. She's put the camera away and now holds a tissue instead. I can tell she wants to run out on the field and wrap her son in a big motherly hug.

"Don't worry," I whisper to her. "It's only four batters, he has plenty of time to straighten himself out."

But I can tell by the way Alex is standing that he no longer feels right. He looks lost and he fidgets like his shoes don't fit. When he looks up from the mound, I can see his eyes blank with confusion, his face twisted in frustration.

The pitching coach gestures wildly, almost as if trying to catch Alex's attention, and Alex nods slowly in return. The first baseman and catcher give Alex encouraging pats on the back while the coach slams his right fist into his left palm to drive home a point. Alex just nods.

When the conference is over and the coach trots back to the dugout, I take Kathy's hand; it's still clammy, but now her grip is weak and resigned.

"There, now he's had his pep talk from the coach, he should be OK," I say lamely. I know she is suffering from every mother's nightmare; her son is failing spectacularly and she can do nothing about it. I assume she can see for herself the pitcher warming up in the bullpen.

Alex leans forward to get his signal, and I lean forward with him. He looks like he is standing at the edge of a cliff and peering over to see how far it is to the sea raging below. This is the most important pitch of his life. If he gets out of the inning with no more damage, the Red Sox are still in the game, he can settle down in the next inning, and these first few batters will be dismissed as a bad case of nerves. Give up another hit, though, and he'll be banished to the bullpen as a mop-up reliever until he's sent back to the minors. He will never be called up again, will spend another season or two in the Red Sox system, then he will be released and bounce around from minor league team to minor league team until his arm goes to hell and by the time he's 30, he'll be out of baseball and wondering what to do with the rest of his life. He knows that, too, I can tell by the long glance back to check the runner at second, by the careful way he sets on the mound, how he makes sure he has the right signal from the catcher. I can see him mentally check off the fundamentals of good pitching, making sure his set is right and his pace is right and his body motion is right, making sure he's got the basics down, because this pitch is too important to just rear back and throw. It has to be the best pitch he has ever thrown.

He winds up, and as he steps forward, Alex puts every ounce of strength into the pitch, every piece of heart he can dig out of himself.

The batter swings, and from the moment he hits it, I know it's out of the park. From the crack of the bat, the ball rises quickly and soars over the Monster, past the net hanging from the back of the wall, and crashes down onto Landsdowne Street. The left fielder doesn't even bother to chase it—he just looks up and watches it fly over his head.

The runners slowly circle the bases, adding three more runs. Kathy buries her face in her hands as the catcalls from the fans resume.

"You bum," says a man two or three rows behind me. "Go back to the minors."

"You suck," yells a boy in the row ahead of me, not more than 10 years old. "Loser."

He is not a loser, I want to say to them. He does not suck, he is not a bum. He is a kind person, a good friend, and a wonderful son. He is just not a major league pitcher.

"Give it up," yells another man.

"Start selling insurance."

"I want my money back, this guy stinks."

Kathy can take no more of it and runs from her seat, disappearing in sobs down the concourse. The sun has set further now so the mound is completely surrounded by darkness as the manager leaves the dugout and walks slowly onto the field, trying to give the relief pitcher in the bullpen a few more warm-up tosses. Alex has thrown nine pitches and given up five runs. He has gotten nobody out. His ERA is infinite.

It was not a good first start. I'm not worried, though. I know that for Alex, this game will be like the Little League championship in sixth grade, a temporary disappointment quickly forgotten as he moves through life. Someday, despite the result, this game will be a high point in his life, and he'll tell his kids that he once pitched in the major leagues, not that he once got shelled.

I only hope that Kathy can see it the same way.

The Opposite Field

Jeff Parenti

She hated baseball. She hated the creaky pace, the spitting and scratching, the listless bodies defending the outfield grass, the pointless throws to first. She couldn't stand going to bars and staring at the big screen for 9 innings. She didn't like watching the game if it was on at my house, even if she was doing something else. And she absolutely despised the Red Sox, with their losing and whining, the curses and the screwing up, game after game, year after year.

This was all a little strange considering I that met Lisa in the bleachers at the third home game of the 2003 season. It was an ugly 6-5 win against the Devil Rays in which the bullpen blew a 5-1 lead in the eigth, but Sox legend Shea Hillenbrand drove in the winning run in the ninth to save us. Lisa was miserable for the whole game, a cold Tuesday night in April. The temperature had fallen at least 20 degrees since lunchtime, and she didn't realize Fenway would be so chilly. She was wearing a cardigan, a short skirt, nylons, and sneakers. No jacket.

Lisa came with a big group from work. Her friend had convinced her to tag along at the last minute, then ditched her to sit with a bunch of drunken Suffolk U guys. Somehow Lisa ended up near me, with only an empty green seat between us. She was pouting the whole game.

As a 12-year veteran of the bleachers, I knew to expect bad weather—cold, drizzle, burning summer sun—and I always felt for the newbies. I thought about offering her my windbreaker many times over the first few innings, and when I spotted her rubbing her own arms after Manny ripped one foul into the box seats near Pesky's Pole, I finally said something.

And Lisa responded in the perfect way. She didn't act as if giving her a jacket was my duty, and she didn't refuse and continue to freeze. Instead she asked just once if I was sure and then said thank you very much. Then she smiled, and she was gorgeous in my Red Sox windbreaker. At the end of the game, she gave me the jacket back and said thanks so much for lending it to her, it was so warm, and it would be nice to talk again sometime. Since I was brain dead, I didn't ask for her number; instead I said yes maybe I'll see you at a game again. And she smiled one last time, like she thought I was cute and a bit naive, and disappeared in the crowd.

I got pounded by my three buddies—Bobs, Pete, and Lon—on the way out of the stadium for not getting her digits. But she had planted her business card in one of my jacket pockets. She was an executive assistant—don't call her a secretary—for one of the VPs at Fidelity. On our first date at a Central Square lounge called the Good Life, she explained that taking care of one of the million-dollar execs was a solid, high-paying job that turned out to be surprisingly low-stress. And after a year of hard work and bonding with the boss, she had become indispensable. It was rare to meet a woman who told me about anything in her life that was fully satisfying. Within 20 minutes I knew she was a low-maintenance match for a simple guy like me.

At the time, the Red Sox bullpen mirrored my love life. The team had no true closer; any one of three or four guys could be called upon for the save. When I met Lisa, I was working on a girlfriend-by-committee—all people I had met through an internet dating service.

Even this amount of attention from the ladies was new to me since I had spent nearly all of my life on my first love: computers. I wrote a BASIC program in second grade and quickly hopped on the nerd track, joining the math and science teams in high school and then embracing the MIT Electrical Engineering curriculum. I also looked the part, with my horribly outdated clothes, hideous mission-control eyeglasses, and a blond mop tamed only after semi-annual barbershop trips. Cute girls and I never occupied the same sentence, much less the same room.

But one night about a year and a half ago, I was over at Bobs' house for dinner, and his wife Petra, a visionary of sorts, couldn't stop staring at me. Finally Bobs asked her what she saw. A new Kevin, she replied, and the following Saturday Petra took me to Filene's and her favorite hair salon. With her help, it only took a few hours to go from Ultra Geek to Super Kev.

That night we all went to the Rack, and for the first time in my life women started approaching me. I started dating, and found to my dismay that not only was it entirely unnatural, but also that this new lifestyle clashed with my love of the Red Sox. I had thought that adding a woman to my life would be easy just so long as I picked one that enjoyed baseball. And even though I wrote only to those women on the service who liked the Sox, it didn't turn out the way I hoped. These people had other interests too, and sometimes they wanted me to give up my tickets and rollerblade along the Charles, or stroll the stale hallways of the MFA. Even in the off-season, some stupid conflict always arose with the woman I was dating and that would be it.

After a while—and this is the part that really scares me—I developed my own Red Sox curse. The last five women I had taken to Fenway all dumped me within a week—no matter the final score or how much fun we had. I had to stop bringing my dates to games and explain why without sounding nuts.

Of course, I wasn't sure whether the curse applied if I met the woman at the game. But since Lisa didn't want to go back, the problem was moot.

The first few weeks after we met were great—she only hinted that she wasn't as excited about baseball as I was. It was odd that I enjoyed spending more than ten minutes with a sports-neutral person, but Lisa had a spirit that made me forget about double plays and gap shots when I was with her. Besides, she was so gorgeous that when I looked at her my mind tended to quit working anyway.

We did plenty of non-baseball things together, and it wasn't long before I forgot about the other girls in the bullpen. I didn't learn the level of Lisa's dislike for the game until at least a month and a half later, when it came out during our first fight.

It was a night after we lost to the Yankees, and, even worse, Roger Clemens. It was the rubber game of a home series, and it left us a game behind them in the standings. Nothing put me in a worse mood than losing to the Rocket, but before we walked out Gate C, Bobs told me to leave my frustration behind before going to see Lisa. And Bobs knew what he was talking about; a five-game losing streak in the 2001 season almost got him divorced.

So I managed a smile when I knocked on her door, but before I even had a chance to say hello, Lisa started yelling at me. Apparently her friend had spotted me the night before at a bar in the North End making out with some other woman. It wasn't true, of course, and I had an alibi—I was at Fenway watching the Red Sox score five against Jose Contreras. I even had witnesses and a ticket stub at home. But nothing I said made any difference. She threw in some nasty comments about my stupid baseball games, and the stupid Red Sox, and why do I even bother with them since they never win the stupid World Series anyway. It was both hurtful and ironic, since my presence in their stupid ballpark should have exonerated me. But Lisa chose to believe her friend's account and threw me out of the house.

The next day I showed up at her door with the evidence.

"Why aren't you at the game?" she asked through a scowl so harsh her eyebrows touched.

"I wanted to see you," I said with semi-sincerity. In truth it was a travel day for the Sox, but it didn't hurt that she thought I was skipping a game for her.

I showed Lisa the ticket stub and she slowly processed the truth.

When she turned back to me, the regret was written on her face. "I hope you believe me now," I said, and then some caveman instinct told me to turn and storm out.

The next day was Friday and I ignored all her calls. At the end of the work day I finally answered, and she asked me to come over. I said I couldn't because I had tickets to the game in two hours and it was too late to try and sell them. She was nearly crying by then and pleaded with me to come over. I said we'll see. I wasn't still mad at her but I *loved* that she thought I was.

At the game the Fab Four had some great advice. "Wow. She's intensely jealous," Bobs said. "This is a great sign. I can't think of a better sign than that. She's into you."

"Yeah, but she's psycho," Lon lamented. He and I were the Single Half of the Fab Four. We usually had competing date stories, although his were generally more pathetic. So now he oozed attitude whenever I talked about my relative success, and I secretly believed he was jealous of my little makeover. But I couldn't confirm my hunch because men never discuss this sort of thing, and besides, we didn't use words like "jealous" and "makeover" unless we were talking about ugly chicks.

"How was she standing when she called you a liar?" Pete asked. He rounded out the Married Half of the Fab Four and believed that body language meant much more than words. His girlfriend said no the first time he proposed, but he swore to us that she said yes with her eyebrows. Sure enough, he asked again two days later and got it verbally.

"And you did the perfect thing, walking away after you showed her the ticket stub," Bobs said emphatically while pointing at the ground. Bobs always backed me on my adventures with the ladies, no matter what I did. "All day she's been thinking about how much of a jerk she is. You're in the driver's seat, Bub. She'll do anything for you now."

"Man on first and third, only one out!" Lon said, referring both to the situation on the field and my rapidly improving prospects. The Fab Four collectively chuckled.

There is no way to comprehensively describe how lucky I am to have the Fab Four. We all used to work together in the IT group at State Street Bank. I was the New Guy after leaving a crappy start-up that collapsed in the dot-com crash. We bonded after a week of looking at girls during lunch at Post Office Beach—a little piece of grassy Eden over a parking garage in downtown Boston. Even though I left the company a few years later, the Fab Four stayed together by investing in Sox season tickets. Of the Four, I claimed to be the most loyal fan since I had been to Fenway at least once every year since 1983. But we were all hard core.

That night the Red Sox went on to score six in the first off the Indians, while Derek Lowe worked the whole game allowing just two runs on three hits. The blowout is a relaxing experience for the fan, and we spent the last seven innings talking about Lisa, and women, and crazy fights we have had with women. My three friends, plus the monumental green of Fenway Park, put everything into proper perspective. Every out Derek recorded brought me closer to an easy victory. At the end we stood and applauded the win, and the four of us filed out with the happy crowd onto Ted Williams Way.

About an hour later Lisa and I had sex for the first time. Like many first times, there were some rookie mistakes. But Lisa didn't give up after my chopper-to-short performance. Instead, like a talented roving scout, she saw my potential, because afterwards she flashed a Steinbrenner smile and asked me to go steady. I'd always thought that having a significant other without being married was like being a call-up from Pawtucket—you could get sent back to Triple A at any time no matter how well you hit in the Show. Still, you don't turn down a call to the bigs. So I told Lisa yes, I would go steady with her. And I promised not to see anyone else, real or imaginary, and we had a good laugh. Lisa didn't know I'd quit dating other girls a month before. But she saw it as a huge commitment. More points for me.

The next morning I woke up next to her and something seemed different. Although she had no clothes on, Lisa wore the uniform of my team. It was like looking across a crowded room and seeing a beautiful woman talking to some guy, but knowing she is going home with you. Multiply that feeling by 10 when she's smiling at you in bed the next morning. We talked among the pillows for a couple of hours, and then we got some brunch. After that we stood on the breezy Brookline sidewalk and kissed—the exciting kind you have when time is short—until I could hear the inbound trolley coming down the hill.

As it turns out, I was late to Fenway for the first time in a year, so the boys hooted when they spotted me coming up the grimy bleacher stairs.

"We thought you were dead, First Pitch Man!" Lon hollered. "Jesus, it's the third frame!"

"Bobs called the police and reported you missing," Pete deadpanned.

"Yeah, you might want to check in with one of the ushers," Bobs advised. "The whole park is looking for you."

"Boys . . . " I smiled as I squeezed into my seat, and I must have had The Look.

"Ooooooooh!" The three of them shouted in unison.

"You got it, didn't you!"

"Yes I did."

"You rat bastard!" Lon shouted this whenever one of my stories ended well.

"Well done, my friend. Well done," Pete said.

"My boy got some last night! Hahah aha ha hah ah aha hh!" Bobs heaved his hefty frame upright and shared my glory with section 43. We think he starts drinking Bud Light from plastic cups at home before weekend games. "Whoooooooo!"

"Thank you, Bobs, you can sit down now. What's wrong with Burkett? He's only given up two runs so far."

"Forget that, Kev, the game is in the bag." A moment later Nomar bashed a solo shot. Fenway stood and whooped and waved its arms.

"Number fifteen!" Lon screamed. He counted Nomie's home runs and also called his favorite player Nomie, which annoyed everybody.

Garciaparra touched the plate, got a high five from Manny, and returned to the dugout to receive some love from the rest of the team. Then it was my turn.

"So how was it? How was she?"

"What do you mean how was it? It was sex. Sex is always great."

"So was it just great, or really great?"

"Lon, leave the guy alone. Maybe he doesn't want to talk about it."

And they went on like that, outlining the whole experience without my help. Meanwhile, all I could do was wear a smile like it was taped on my face.

In truth they didn't care how good it was. They were happy for me and proud that I had got this far. I'd been whining to them about going nowhere with women for as long as I'd known them, and three years is a long time.

A diving catch in center finally changed the focus a little and had the Fab Four buzzing about the actual play on the field. I felt like bringing it back to me.

"She asked me to go steady, too."

"Whoa," Lon replied. He was falling way behind in his own love life now.

"So what did you say?"

"I said yes."

"Well, that's what you wanted," Bobs observed and vaporized another half cup of beer. "Welcome to the club."

The Red Sox went on to dismantle the Indians 12-3, and I actually thought about leaving early to see Lisa. An instant later I realized that would be the first sign of insanity. We were always the last to leave our section; we liked to stay and see the old ball yard empty.

On the way out the Fab Four recited their plans for the rest of the day. I announced that I was going right back to Lisa's house, and they almost threw me off the Brookline Street overpass. They warned me to not become too clingy and told me to go home and do what I would normally do after a one o'clock game. When I reminded them that would be sitting around doing absolutely nothing, they assured me, unanimously, that I should do that, or anything else but see Lisa until at the very least a late dinner.

"Once you give all your non-baseball time to her, it's over," Bobs said. "Next she'll take your baseball time, and then you'll have no balls left to play with, if you know what I mean."

I did.

A week later, after a Wednesday night 6-5 loss at New York, I said something wrong over the phone. Maybe I shouldn't have called Lisa during the post-game show. It was something small and stupid and she ended the conversation before I could sort it out.

Saturday the Fab Four met at the Coolidge Corner Clubhouse to watch the Sox in Toronto and to talk me down.

"I went over last night, and she just sat there on the couch reading a magazine. She barely even talked to me. I said I was sorry. What else do I have to do?"

"What did you say that was so offensive?" Pete asked.

"I don't know!"

The Married Half chuckled.

"Maybe she's on the rag," Lon murmured.

"Don't be an ape," Bobs said.

"Hey, at least he's still getting some. Sex from an angry lady is better than none at all."

"No, when I was in the bathroom Lisa went to bed early. Didn't even say good night."

Bobs raised his eyebrows. "Well, maybe she is on the rag."

"Were her hips and shoulders turned completely away from you?" Pete asked in his problem-solving voice. "When Abby does that I know I am in serious trouble."

But I hadn't noticed. The Red Sox went on to lose that day's game, 10-7, and fell into a five-game rut. I didn't see Lisa Saturday night as we planned. Sunday I read the entire *Globe* sports section and Peter Gammons's column on-line, but all I could think about was her. None of the sports writers had any answers for me.

Monday was a travel day and I didn't call Lisa. Tuesday the Red Sox were in Pittsburgh for interleague play, and I was encouraged because the Pirates were a bad team. I tried Lisa, but she didn't call back, and the game was rained out. So I sat in my apartment, watching old *Cheers* reruns on TV. Carla Tortelli has never failed to cheer me up, but this time I got nothing.

First pitch the next night could not have come soon enough. I was desperate for anything to take my mind off Lisa. Fortunately, BK Kim shut down the Bucs and we hit four home runs. Plus Lisa called during the bottom of the eighth inning. The W was already secure, but she knew not to call during the game. The timing was deliberate.

"What are you doing?" she asked.

I had to be careful.

"Nothing," I said.

"Do you want to talk?"

"OK."

In ten minutes, the whole fight was forgotten, and we were giggling at each other like second graders. She asked if she could come over and I said yes, even though it was a school night. When she rang the door buzzer, the game was 11-4 in the bottom of the ninth, and I hung around for an extra pitch or two before going downstairs to let her in.

That night I learned that make-up sex is far better than watching the end of a baseball game in a non-save situation.

A few weeks later I threw Lisa a 29th birthday party at my apartment. I intentionally started the party at 1, the same time as the Sox game at Philly. That way Lisa would know when she saw the invitation that I was giving up watching a game to host her party. It was also the first time the Fab Four met Lisa. They were so interested in finally laying eyes on this woman that they gave up watching the game too. This was very impressive, considering Pedro was pitching.

And they each gave me very favorable reviews:

Bobs: "Gorgeous hair."

Pete: "Exquisite posture."

Lon: "Nice can. You rat bastard."

Party central was in the backyard of my building, and I wasn't too surprised when, at about 1:30, Bobs told me he was going upstairs to "get more beer" and the other two followed. Every few half-innings one of them would come down with a beer and give me a secret score update. When Bobs revealed the 11th inning score (2-2), he caught me looking across the yard.

"What's up, buddy?"

"Lisa's over there talking to some guy."

"So what?"

"He's hitting on her like today is his last day on earth."

"Maybe he told her that. I used to use that line. One time it actually worked."

I shot him a scowl.

"Why don't you go over there and put your arm around her? He'll back off."

"I already went over there. He's some doctor over at Longwood. He's two inches taller than me. And he's a *doctor*."

"Yeah, you said that. Does she have a weakness for doctors?"

Another scowl.

"Dude, don't worry about it. She's not going to do anything stupid at the party you threw for her. That's madness."

Bobs' Nextel beeped. "Sox are leading 3-2 in the bottom of the twelfth. Get up here," Lon's voice squawked from the phone speaker. Lisa looked over at me and smiled.

"Shit." He beeped back. "Be right there."

"Hang on a second," I said. "I might have to pop this guy, and I'm gonna need you around to back me up."

Bobs laughed at me. "Be cool, cowboy. You have nothing to worry about."

"Thome just homered of Shiell with two out," Lon sighed over the Nextel.

"God!" gritted Bobs. "Dammit, Grady! Why didn't he walk Thome? I hate that guy."

People were looking at us. Lisa laughed and put her hand on the doctor's inflated arm.

"Is he a friend of hers?" Bobs asked.

"Just met her today. No idea who invited him."

"Let's watch the end of this. You need a break." Bobs beckoned upstairs.

So I had to choose between witnessing my girlfriend make eyes at some asshole M.D. and watching the Red Sox bullpen cough up the win in extras . . . well, the good beer was upstairs.

I joined the rest of the Fab Four for the top of the thirteenth. We got two off Jose Mesa and the world started to make sense again.

"Go talk to her before it's too late," Bobs told me. "We got it sewn up in here. No way we're giving away three leads in one game."

I agreed, but Bobs lent me his Nextel just in case there was a development.

So I marched downstairs with the Sox up 5-3. "Hello again," I said to Dr. Asshole. "Can I talk to you for a second, Lisa?"

"Sure babe!" she chirped, and waved a playful look at the doc I hadn't seen before. I led her out of earshot by her arm.

I squared to face her and she peered at me with a pleased expression. "What's up?".

"Are you having a good time, Lisa?" I asked with purpose but not anger.

"I am having a GREAT time, babe." Her eyes floated in their sockets and I smelled tequila. "Where have you been? You're not inside watching that dumb game, are you?"

"No . . . I've just been hanging with your friends." A double lie. Who was the jerk now?

"Well, I was just talking to Stephen there, and . . . " she leaned over on me and I steadied her. "Ooops! My chalice is empty! Wench!!"

"Calm down, Lisa; I'll get you another drink." She was hopeless. I had to get her seated.

"I like that Stephen. He's *cute*."

Beep beep. "RBI double to left, 5-4. One out."

"What's that?"

"Nothing. Come over here, OK?" I led Lisa to a bench in the corner of the yard. Truthfully, getting this wasted was not something she did only on special occasions. She liked the hard stuff, her hangovers were severe, and afterwards I always asked her to stop drinking so much. She said she would, but obviously she didn't want to. Lisa once asked me if I would break up with her just because she "liked to have a drink or two." I said I didn't know, but secretly I couldn't bear to be around her in this condition.

On the other hand, drunk Lisa couldn't tell a lie.

"Do you like that guy?"

Beep beep. "Pitching change," Lon radioed. "The immortal Rudy Seanez. I got a bad feeling about this."

"What is that?" Lisa shouted. I had no idea how to shut the speaker off.

"Nothing. I told Bobs I would hold his phone for him."

Lisa buried her head in my chest. It was only five o'clock, but she was done. "Thank you for the party," she said, and reached up and kissed me.

This knocked me down, but I dug in. "Lisa, do you like that guy?"

She giggled. "He asked me if I would dump you for him."

"What did you say?"

She sighed. "I said yes."

Beep beep. "Todd Pratt homered. Walk-off. Fucking Todd Pratt."

OK, so Lisa was kidding. She couldn't hold her liquor, but she always managed to hang on to her caustic humor. That damn loss was tough to take, but a four-game series at Fenway against Detroit was just the thing I needed to recover. We swept, of course, and the Fab Four used its time in the bleachers to analyze the party and Stephen the Doctor. My friends assured me that I could survive a raid by a rich M.D.

Meanwhile Lisa and I had a good week. I nursed her back from the party hangover, and we had giddy telephone conversations. On Friday the Red Sox scored 14 runs in the first inning and beat the pathetic Marlins 25-8. Afterwards Lisa and I had sex a record three times in one night. A few days later the Sox went on a two-week road trip and Lisa and I spent busloads of time together. I even missed watching an inning here or there, and on a Friday night I turned off the TV with us up 4-0 because Lisa walked in the door and wanted to watch a rerun of *Law and Order*. The boys went on to win without me.

It was a defining moment in our relationship, even more than the decision we made an hour later (during the *Law and Order* credits) to run away to Martha's Vineyard after the weekend. We took Monday and Tuesday off and hopped on the ferry, standby, and lucked out, finding an available room. Why Monday and Tuesday?

It was, of course, the All-Star break.

The rest of July went pretty well. We took two of three from the Yankees at home and put together another winning streak. The relationship hit its stride after the Vineyard trip. I would switch off away games if we went ahead by more than 5 and go see Lisa. Then August arrived, and the Sox went on a killer west-coast road trip. With games starting at 10 P.M., it was impossible to watch enough of the action and still see Lisa. One Tuesday night she said she had to see me, and for the first time in at least a year I missed an entire game. This might have been easier if we could have watched the games together, or if I could watch while she did something else. But Lisa hated the very idea of me paying attention to the game rather than to her.

And something else was happening. I found myself not missing games I didn't see, and this led me to start questioning my own faith. Fortunately Pete pulled me back from the edge with some amazing news: he had procured bleacher tickets to two New York games in late September—at Yankee Stadium. Pete made the announcement during an otherwise dull 14-5 victory over Oakland at Fenway, and I was psyched.

But there was a problem. "What about Lisa?"

"No wives," Lon murmured.

"No, I mean she won't want me to go."

"So what?" shrugged Bobs. "I never ask Petra if I can go to stuff like this; I just mention that I have the opportunity, and then leave it up to her to tell me she doesn't want me to. She never does. I mean, I can tell she doesn't like it. But not because she doesn't want me to.

It's more like she's jealous I'm out having an entire weekend of fun without her."

"Pete, have you asked your wife?" asked Lon.

"She's the one who got me the tickets."

"Wow," I said. "She must really love you."

"Yes."

"Rat bastard." Poor Lon.

I decided to take Bobs approach with Lisa.

"The boys are going to New York next weekend."

"For what?"

"We got some tickets to the Yankees game."

She looked at me with a disapproving eye. "In Harlem? You'll get killed."

"Yankee Stadium's in the Bronx. I won't be in Harlem."

"I don't want you to go."

"We'll be fine," I chuckled. "There are four of us going. We'll be looking out for each other. If there's trouble, I'll just hide behind Bobs. Besides, I can handle myself."

"They all have guns down there. You're going to wear your Red Sox jersey and all that, aren't you?"

"Sure."

"You'll get in a fight."

"It's not like that. They don't even sell beer in the bleachers anymore."

"You're going to be sitting in the *bleachers*?" I had forgotten that story I had told her about the brawl at the Yankees game in the Fenway bleachers earlier in the year. One New York guy got pushed over the wall behind section 40. She laughed at the time.

So I left for New York the following Friday with the Fab Four but without a kiss from angry Lisa. Down in the Bronx we found safety in numbers—thousands of other Sox fans were on hand. And the games gave us plenty to cheer. We chased Andy Pettite after 2⅓ in the first one, and tagged the Rocket for seven runs in the second. I had no voice left after shouting "RO-ger" over and over. My affair with the Red Sox was gloriously renewed. And when my buddies dropped me off at Lisa's place, she could see in my face I had gone back to my old lover.

She never asked about that weekend, and I never told her. It was as if I had said I was going out of town to see an old college friend, but she knew it was really an old girlfriend. Lisa couldn't confront me about it because she didn't want to hear the truth.

For the rest of the stretch run, while some people forecast the latest collapse, I just watched the magic number drop. I also gave Lisa as much attention as possible, particularly during road trips. Then, with a week left in the regular season, the Red Sox came back against the O's via a Todd Walker home run with two outs and two on in the bottom of the ninth. Ortiz won it with a dinger in the tenth, and there was so much raucous elation in Fenway I even hugged my homophobic buddy Pete. We left with the magic number at two, and I arrived at Lisa's thinking about baseball and gave her the best orgasm she'd ever had.

The next night John Burkett gave up seven runs while recording only one out. Later, Lisa yelled at me because I forgot our six-month anniversary, and we went to bed mad. The next morning she left me a message on my voice mail saying that she needed to see me immediately after work because she had something very important to ask. Good old Lisa. Didn't she know this was clinch day? I called her back and asked if it could wait until after the game. No, she said. So I notified Bobs, who agreed that she was testing me in a major way, I had little choice, and after six months this was going to be some kind of Big Thing. He also wondered if we were maybe a little too old to be celebrating month anniversaries.

That night the Red Sox won the wild card without me. Meanwhile, Lisa asked if I wanted to move in together. The next morning I felt lightheaded, watching the highlights on SportsCenter at her house with the sound turned way down. Ordinarily I never watched bits of game on tape, but to see this celebration occur in my absence made my gut hurt.

I moved some clothes into Lisa's place as the Sox played out the string over the weekend in Tampa. Then, as we made grilled cheese together early Saturday afternoon, I started talking about the playoffs. I told her they would be very intense for me and the Fab Four, with the Curse and 85 years and stuff. She smiled as though I just revealed my deepest secrets and said she understood. "When is the first game?" she asked. "Who are we playing?"

I was stunned. Not only was she taking interest in my Red Sox, but Lisa was using the familiar "we!" What was happening to her? What was in that cheese?

The playoffs began in Oakland that Wednesday. The Fab took our customary table at the Clubhouse, while Lisa waited at home within cell phone range and "sitting on my lap in spirit." But neither BK Kim nor Embree could hold the lead in the ninth, and their catcher drove in the winning run three innings later with a bunt. I could almost hear Lon's brain writhing with Curse talk, but he was bright enough not to let it get as far as his mouth.

Lisa must have peeked out the window before I even opened the door. "Kevin, how . . . " She looked at my eyes in the foyer, then muttered a simple "please don't take it out on me" before turning and heading to bed. I sat in the kitchen munching on a sugar cookie that tasted more like a paint chip and stared out the window until I was sure she was asleep.

Going into Game Two, I had a bad feeling that I couldn't shake. I tried to smile as I walked into the Clubhouse, but Pete saw my doubt. "We will not go down 0-2," he said with the sort of confidence Roger Clemens displayed against the same A's in the '88 LCS. And we all know how that went.

As it turned out, we got nothing off Barry Zito, and Timmy coughed up five runs in the second. People stopped buying beer in the seventh, as if it were a Clubhouse rule. Some patrons even left. I looked at Pete after we went down 0-2. He was the only one of us that never lost hope, and I could see he was already thinking about how to win Game Three. And we had seats. That was the nicest thing about plunking down the cabbage for season tickets: the playoffs.

Playoff baseball at Fenway Park is like milling around the gates of Heaven. Standing there in the crowd, you start shivering with anxiety. Fans stretch and do breathing exercises that they learned from their therapists. Bobs even claimed he was less nervous the morning of his wedding. And Game Three itself did nothing to calm us down.

The ghosts of the old yard sure had some fun us with that night; one Oakland player failed to touch the plate at a key moment, and another got called for interference. When you are on the brink of elimination, extra frames are harder to endure then multiple paper cuts. But Trot finally sent us home with a tater in the eleventh, and I was so excited I nearly turned inside out.

When I got home, I discovered that Lisa had made chocolate chip cookies. And I had to admit, as thrilling as the bizarre playoff win was, kisses served with warm cookies were a pretty close second.

Sunday it was time for the equalizer. Tim Hudson mowed us down in the first, but he got hurt and couldn't start the second. The A's replaced him with Tigers reject knuckleballer Steve Sparks, but somehow he managed to keep us in check inning after inning. Meanwhile, Jermaine Dye chased Burkett with a homer in the sixth to put us down 4-2. Walker helped the good guys with one of his own in the bottom half and made it a one-run game. I started doing yoga.

The enemy sent out a Dennis Eckersley facsimile named Keith Foulke to start the eighth. Foulke was the iceman. He only needed six outs. We were in a little trouble.

But Nomar bashed a one-out double off him and the crowd was charged. We didn't sit at all after that hit. One out later Manny singled but Nomar stopped at third. Two outs for Mr. David Ortiz.

We love David, but he carried an 0 for 16 collar into the batter's box, and even in the best of times, the big man has the sort of swing that smells like a strikeout. Some fans in Section 43 couldn't watch.

Then POW. It was coming for us, straight out of a dream I had. It didn't get all the way to Williamsburg, but the ball did hit on the short wall. Ortiz stopped on second with a double and a 5-4 lead. Then Scott Williamson polished off the A's in the ninth. Now the two teams had to fly out to California to play the series clincher, and I had to make it through the intervening 20 hours. I slept with my hand on Lisa's hip, but I dreamt playoff baseball.

When Lisa called me at lunch Monday, I told her I might go home sick. I didn't mention the madness in my head, how the Game five script had already been written, but no one would let me read it yet. Maybe the Sox would come back from 0-2 in the ALDS to win in miracle fashion, the Curse would be broken, and we would win the World Series! Or maybe the Red Sox would get to within an out with a big lead, making the fans believe that the Curse was about to be broken, but the bullpen would somehow blow it and crush our spirit once and for all, forever!

The scenarios just kept playing over and over in my head. Talk radio made it worse, so I turned that off. We had our best, Pedro, versus Zito going on short rest. It was on the road, but we had the momentum. The hours could not have passed more slowly.

After work I went straight to the Clubhouse without changing. I didn't eat or drink anything. I read the business section instead of sports. I did nothing that would jinx the game.

I was early and the place was empty. By the time my friends arrived, I was going blind staring at the stock prices. No one said anything about the game, the players, or baseball. If you said, "we're going to win tonight, I feel great," and the Red Sox lost, no one would ever speak to you again.

The room was in a good mood when Manny took a swing in the sixth. He knew it was gone, and so did we. He showed up the A's by walking to first base, and we showed up some ugly Oakland fan in the corner. Then Bobs broke radio silence with some strategy talk.

Everything seemed normal enough again, but in the seventh, Johnny Damon and Damien Jackson wrecked in a horrible head-on-head crash in short center. Johnny was hurt so bad an ambulance drove onto the field. Not a single fluid ounce was tasted at the Clubhouse, or anywhere in New England, while Johnny lay on the turf.

Meanwhile, Pedro lasted seven-plus and then it was up to our bullpen. Embree and Timlin were solid in the eighth. I started to breathe steadily.

So we went to the ninth, ahead 4-3. Despite having the renewed Williamson out there, being three outs away felt like leaving your car in a bad neighborhood. Lon made a noise every time Scott threw a pitch out of the strike zone to Hatteberg, and after the fourth ball I wanted to strangle him. Next he walked Guillen. People were holding their head in their hands. I wanted to throw up.

Grady called on Derek Lowe. This sent the room agog—a former closer, current starter, needing the sinker to get a DP, etc. But Hernendez bunted the runners over. Two in scoring position. We needed two outs from Derek without advancing the runners.

Then a gift from A's skipper Ken Macha: he used backup catcher Adam Melhuse to hit for Jermaine Dye. Grady decided not to walk him to set up the double play, and Derek struck Melhuse out. We were all standing now. Singleton walked, but his run didn't matter. Terrence Long hit for Frank Mene-whoever. There was nowhere to put him, but bases loaded didn't scare D-Lowe.

I got a giant charleyhorse when I jumped because I think I hit the table. Someone spilled beer on me. The whole room was whooping and high-fiving and hugging. Will I ever forget the name Terrance Long, the guy that struck out to send us into the ALCS against the Hated Yankees?

At home I gave Lisa a very long and loving kiss. She had been reading a book all night and was very tired, but she waited up. We went to sleep without a recap, although she did ask me about the blood, which of course was only Heinz 57.

Tuesday was recovery day, and I tried not to think about the Yankees. Instead I took Lisa to dinner at Elephant Walk, her favorite restaurant. It's some sort of French-Cambodian place, and I had no idea where the elephant came into play, but I played along and even ordered a meal with bamboo shoots growing out of it. I didn't like it at all, but that wasn't really the point, and Lisa had a great time. That night we did it three different ways, and I didn't think about baseball once.

On Wednesday the Fab Four decided to change venues and maybe improve our chances against the Yankees. We picked Lon's dusty apartment on Comm Ave in Allston; well, really we picked his 60-inch projection screen plus kick-ass audio system and cushy leather sofa. The new location brought us good luck and a 5-2 win. The 8 P.M. start took its toll, though, and by the time the trolley got me home Lisa was unconscious. She did leave me two brownies in the shape of socks, though.

I don't know what happened in Game Two. We didn't change our positions on the couch, or wear different hats. I even drank the same number of beers (two), and we all stood during the seventh inning stretch, as usual. Despite these efforts, we lost 6-2. No brownies this time.

The scene outside Fenway was surreal before Game Three, but inside it was even stranger. Yankees fans were everywhere, and they must have put something in the water, because between the fights, the beanballs, and the bullpen fracas, I wouldn't have been surprised to see a UFO land and beam up Mayor Menino. In the end we lost 4-3, and after the game the whole crowd looked like it had just been clubbed. As I walked home, the crazy events made an audible buzz in my ears. Or maybe it was some sort of Lisa ESP because I was thinking about her, too. My buzz felt like something was going to happen.

When I came home, she was fast asleep with the TV on, the remote in her hand, and a Red Sox hat on her head. It was the one I bought her, and it was the first time she ever wore it. I realized how far we had come. She used to hate the Sox, and now she was watching a playoff game, rooting for them. I wonder if the loss hurt Lisa like it hurt me. My sources tell me I fell in love with her at that moment.

The next morning, a gloomy-looking Sunday, the radio said rain was due in Boston, and the empty spot in bed told me Lisa was missing. Sometimes she went for a run, but she hated jogging and always returned after about 20 minutes. I called her cell and got no answer.

In the Fens, weather postponed Game Four. I spent a jittery day and anxious night at home alone. Lisa still hadn't shown up. I sat in the front window looking out at the rain and worrying about her, feeling like my mom must have on those nights I missed curfew. It was torture.

At 2 A.M., unable to sleep, I went into the kitchen to make cookies. I had no idea how to make cookies, but Lisa liked to do it. I preheated the oven and spotted the corner of a scrap of paper poking out from under the stove.

"Dear Kevin, I'm going out to Amherst to visit my sister for a few days. Left the phone. TTYL, L."

Kevin. She never called me by my full name. This was trouble. I could see it in the ink.

Timmy edged Mussina in the rescheduled Game Four Monday. The score was 3-2. I participated in Section 43, but it was like going to a rock show with my ears full of wax. The Fab Four could tell something was distracting me, but Bobs was the only one I told what had happened. I didn't mention Lisa leaving to the others because I didn't want it to be a topic, even between innings. Still, I couldn't shake Lisa's mystery issue from my head, and I couldn't get rid of a numbing fear that the Yankees were going to beat us.

In Game Five, David Wells topped Derek Lowe 4-2. The Sox headed back to NY down 3 to 2 in the series, and there was still no sign of Lisa. No phone call, no e-mail, no nothing.

We gathered at the Casa de Lon the very next day—a Wednesday—to witness the sixth game. I don't have to tell you how much bad mojo Game Six has. By this point in the series, I was so tense and sick with superstition I could hardly talk. I don't remember showering that morning. When I wasn't thinking about a potential elimination at the hands of the most vile team in sports, my mind was on why Lisa left me and refused to talk. To distract myself from one problem, I darted to the other. I don't know which was worse, but Old Man Burkett was going for us—in the Bronx—so I think the Sox conundrum had a slight edge.

Like me, the rest of the Fab Four were too nervous to speak. Neither Pete's nor Bobs' wives were talking to them (or vice versa). The game didn't help the mental health of the men in that tiny apartment. Burkett was spotted a 4-0 lead and gave it right back. It was yo-yo time with the bullpens as Pettite was chased too.

But it was our guys that came through in the end. Best of all, we scored the winning runs off choke artist Jose Contreras, a Cuban guy that Steinbrenner signed just to spite the Red Sox. A 9-6 decision opened the door to Game Seven.

I used the long trip home to convince myself to enjoy Game Seven rather than worry about it. I even strung together three trolley stops without thinking about Lisa. I reached for the doorknob on the house while deciding that she would come home when she was ready and we would talk about whatever was bothering her. This lasted as far as the bedroom.

Lisa was awake and reading in bed. "You look like shit," was the first thing she said.

I was too stunned to reply. My face said enough, I guess.

"I just couldn't be around here while—during *this*. It makes you—" She didn't have to finish. A little pain crossed her forehead. "It . . . seems like they lost. I'm so sorry."

"No, they won," I managed. "There's one more game."

One more. Pedro versus Roger. It would be baseball history, no matter the outcome. The Sox would finally beat the Evil Empire or the Bombers would renew their dominance in the lopsided rivalry.

Lisa reached for me when I got into bed. "I haven't seen you in a week," she breathed in my ear. "Feels like forever." She kissed my neck. But my head wasn't in the game.

Thursday the 16th started with Lisa clomping around the kitchen banging cabinet doors. She spotted me a frosty kiss before she left for work. I wasn't yet dressed and lamented out loud that I had no idea what to wear—the team won big games with some of the clothes in that closet, lost with others, and I didn't keep any record of which was which. I am a lazy, superstitious bastard, and Lisa offered no help.

I eventually went with the 45 jersey since Pedro was pitching, and that night I skipped dinner and showed up at Lon's a little early. He had a beer waiting for me.

"Lisa back?" he said. I just stared at him. How do people find out this stuff?

"Yuh." I replied. It was nice of him to care, but I said nothing else until the other half arrived. In fact, we could hardly look at each other. It was too risky. There were too many jinxes out there.

We touched the Rocket for three in the second and were feeling good, but Mike Mussina came out of the bullpen and shut our hitters down. We gave Pedro a standing ovation when he came out of the game after the seventh with a 4-2 lead. He was getting high-fives in the dugout and was clearly done for the night. It was up to the bullpen now, which had solidified at the ideal time of the season. We felt good, but said nothing out loud. We got another run the top of the eighth.

Then after the commercials we noticed a familiar face on the pitching mound.

"What?" Bobs demanded.

"What's Pedro's pitch count?" Lon asked.

"Over a hundred," I said.

"Don't worry, he looks strong," Pete assured us. "Grady will take him out after the first guy gets on."

Generic Yank Nick Johnson popped out. But then Jeter doubled to right field.

"OK, come talk to him," Bobs suggested.

Bernie Williams hit a single. The score was 5-3. This time, Grady did come out. "OK," I muttered, "5-3 lead. This is OK. This is OK. Come on bullpen. We need you now."

Grady turned for the bench. Alone.

"Wh—Take him out," Lon told the TV, as if it was an innocent mistake. The rest of us didn't need to repeat it. A microbe was clearly eating the manager's brain away. Pedro's batting average against skyrocketed after pitch 105, and everybody knew it. Everybody!

Then Godzilla pulled one down the line. Help was ready in the bullpen, but Grady didn't move. I was close to eating my own lips. Stupid catcher Jorge Poor-sada hit a bag of beans to no-man's land in center and the agony came anew.

Tie game. I couldn't swallow.

As the Bob Costases of the world always want, the game smeared into extra innings. Mariano Rivera ran to the mound in the top of the tenth, and Lon went to the kitchen. I heard a beep from there and picked up an unmistakable smell. Popcorn.

"What are you doing?" I demanded, a little too hard. Microwave popcorn was not on the approved list of jinx-free snack foods.

"What? I'm starving."

Why do pitchers like Rivera have to play for New York? Every time he tossed a strike, recorded an out, or made one of our hitters look bad, Lon would crunch a kernel. I wanted to choke him with the damn bag. Tenth, eleventh, twelfth. No runs. My pulse rate was hovering around 150. The home half of each inning was even harder to sit through. Anytime the ball came out of the hand of the pitcher, the game could end with a Sox loss.

Timmy pitched the eleventh and came out for the twelfth. Giddy Schoolboy Aaron Boone hit a knuckleball to left, looked up at it, and raised his arms straight out with his palms up. His body seemed to say, "See? We knew once we tied it that it would end like this."

Lon switched off the TV before Boone made it home. "I feel sick," he said, and went to bed. The rest of us let ourselves out.

The remaining three grunted goodbye and walked separately into the dark. It was possible I wouldn't see those guys until spring training. I couldn't look at anyone on the trolley so I hung my head, sitting backwards on the Green Line.

For the first time in six months, my mind was absolutely empty. No thoughts of baseball or even Lisa. It was a lonely and desperate feeling. I almost missed my stop.

I entered the house gingerly so I wouldn't wake her. The door to the bedroom was open, which was strange. I squinted and saw the bed was empty. That meant more trouble, but I could deal with it in the morning. I needed to sleep right now. I stood and unbuttoned my rumpled 45 jersey, then tossed it in the air toward the closet.

Before it hit the ground, Lisa's arms embraced me from behind. "Hi," she whispered. I could feel her smile pressing into the nape of my neck. "It's just you and me now."

She purred in my ear, and we went to bed. We kissed for what seemed hours, but I could not get aroused. I hated Grady Little.

I awoke at about 6 A.M., got up to pee, and when I came back to bed I noticed Lisa wasn't sleeping either. We were both lying on our backs. I was staring at the ceiling. She was rubbing her eyes. She never rubbed her eyes. The bed, the sheets, and the pillow suddenly felt stiff and cold. I couldn't hear her breathe.

I lay there for maybe 30 minutes with an unlabeled dread. This was trouble I might not be able to escape.

But I could try. “I’m going for a walk,” I said, getting dressed.

She sat up. We looked at each other for the first time. She had been crying. It felt stupid to say “What’s the matter?” so I just stared at her. She cleared her throat a little.

“When should I come back?” I asked. She looked down and shook her head. “What’s going on?”

“Your passion for me is gone,” she croaked.

“What do you mean?”

“We don’t have sex anymore, Kev.”

“Oh, that. That won’t happen again.”

“It doesn’t matter. You just don’t like me anymore. Maybe you never did.”

“That’s not true, Lisa.” If it’s one thing I learned from the Fab Four, it’s that you have to walk away from a fight like this, no matter how bad, and only come back after she’s cried it out.

“Meet me at Ankara at one.”

I left the apartment and went to breakfast at B&D where the bustling crowd and familiar environs helped assure me it was going to be OK. I walked all the way down to the Common feeling confident, then I called Bobs for a pep talk. He echoed my own feeling that she would come around and it would just make us closer. We joked about make-up sex. I bummed around Downtown Crossing and Newbury Street before making my way back to Kenmore. I was sitting outside at one of the three tables they have.

She looked composed but not that happy. I asked her if she was hungry, she said no, so I said let’s walk.

We took a left onto Brookline Street, moving slowly with nothing to say. My bad vibes radar told me that Lisa was at the same place she had been when I left the house. On the Mass Pike bridge, the traffic noise below gave me the nerve to break the ice.

“What’s going on?”

“I don’t think it’s working.”

“Why not?”

“Because you killed my passion for you, Kevin.”

“Listen, I’m sorry we didn’t have sex last night, OK? I was just—really tired, that’s all. You can’t go just on one night.”

“Not one night. This has been going on for a while.” Her speech was calculated, methodical. You could have convinced me she sent cyborg Lisa to deliver this message.

"What has? Is this why you left for a week?"

"Yes."

"Why didn't you tell me you were feeling this way?"

"I did."

"No you didn't!" I was raising my voice now.

"Kevin, I told you several times things weren't right and you didn't listen."

"Well, we certainly haven't had a discussion like this, have we? Why don't you tell me what's bothering you?"

"No. It's too late."

I spouted. I ranted. I vented. I made a speech about how much I cared and how much it meant that she was in my life and how beautiful and unique and caring and warm and sexy and—

Lisa was a statue.

I turned us left down Yawkey Way by habit. We passed the ticket office and approached the shuttered Gate A. It was madness that Lisa was ignoring all these sappy but genuine things I was telling her. Had she left her heart on the sidewalk somewhere? It would explain her Dan Duquette demeanor.

But instinctively I knew I couldn't talk her out of a decision she had already made. I needed to fast forward to the end of this movie.

I stopped and grabbed her arm, turning her to face me. I opened my mouth, and behind her head was a red championship banner hanging from the brick exterior that read "1918."

"Do you still have any feelings for me?" I asked.

"Not romantically, no."

"Then let's go home." I wheeled and walked back towards Brookline Street. When I got to the stairs in front of the ticket office, I felt lightheaded and needed to rest, so I stopped and sat.

She stood above me and watched for a few seconds.

"I'm sorry."

"Please go away."

We said these things at the same time, so her apology wasn't fully received, nor did it really matter. She continued back up Brookline

Street, and I stared the other direction down Yawkey Way. There was a placard sticking out of a trash barrel. It said, "What Curse?"

I called a special meeting of the Fab Four at the Clubhouse to watch Game One of the World Series. None of us had planned on watching any of it. (Who do you root for? The evil squad that beat us or an expansion team that would win for the second time in their short history?) But I needed their help, and the most manly way to convene was in a sports bar.

There was so much pain in the group. We all lost a season in the most gruesome manner. And I had also lost my girlfriend. That's double the trauma, or suffering squared. We were a sad sight in the nearly-deserted tavern. We spotted a NY hat here and there, but even the Yankees fans in Boston were smart enough not to rub our noses in it.

I told them how every trace of her stuff was gone by the time I got back late that night. Her Red Sox hat was deposited neatly on the kitchen table with her key. She didn't leave a note.

They all shook their heads. "She's a wacko, maybe she always was," Lon said.

"You did everything right, my brother," Bobs added, with a hand on my shoulder. "Nothing you should regret."

"How could she just ditch a good thing?" Lon wondered. "Sure, you have flaws, but so what? You're a great guy. I mean, would you ever give up Nomar because he's not A-Rod?"

"She said 'lost your passion for her'?" Bobs contemplated. "Hmmm. I think she means you're no good in bed."

Great. All I needed was to worry that I suck at sex.

"She is a little obsessed," Lon said.

"I agree with that," Bobs added. "You did it three times in a night once, didn't you? I don't know. I mean, I like a girl who's good to go whenever, but that's a little much."

"She's a nympho." Lon slurped his beer.

No doubt, Lisa had a very healthy interest in sex, and it never occurred to me that she liked it any more or less than other women. After all, I had no basis for comparison.

"I think she wanted it way more than you did," chuckled Lon. "It's like she was the guy and you were the chick."

"You had a good time, didn't you, though?" Bobs asked. It was a heartless question because having a good time wasn't the point. I loved her, and I'd been looking forward to an offseason that was all about us. The last part of the year was going to be holidays and meeting relatives and buying gifts and playing in the first snowstorm. Maybe even a vacation in Fort Myers. Then again, maybe not.

On the other hand, relationships just end sometimes. And you have to make the most of it while you're there. That's what guys do. A good time is enough to keep us happy.

"Lucky you found out that she has this little problem now, rather than a year after you're married," Bobs concluded.

Right again.

I drained another Octoberfest. That made an even six for the night. Pretty soon they would be bringing in the Sam Adams Winter kegs. On the TV, Florida beat New York. One of them would be champions, but not the Red Sox. Someday I would find the perfect woman, but it wouldn't be this week.

"I guess it's you and me working the beer line for prospects again," grinned Lon, who was thrilled to have me back in the single-guy camp.

The next one, I promised myself, would be a size two blonde in love with Johnny Damon. And Theo Epstein would go out and get us a closer and gold-glove second baseman, maybe even a guy who could steal a base in the clutch. Next season would be even better. Sitting at creaky bar stools with my buddies, I could almost feel it: 2004 was going to be The Year.

Opening Day

TRACY MILLER GEARY

Diana reads the sports page and then tells her boyfriend, "It says here that James Dean was a Red Sox fan." She looks at Joe from over the top of the paper. He doesn't seem impressed, or maybe he's just distracted. Joe is originally from New Jersey and likes the Yankees, though he's finally stopped wearing his NY cap around Boston. Diana loves both Joe and the Red Sox, so she hopes to bring him over to her side. When she first found out he was a Yankees fan, she told her dad it was like discovering he was a Republican, only worse. Her dad is a Republican, but he still laughed at the joke. Her dad has season Sox tickets but only took Joe one time, to a Yankees-Red Sox game right after Diana and Joe started dating. The Yankees won. Usually Diana's dad isn't a sore loser, but 10 months later, he still hasn't warmed up to Joe. Today is Opening Day at Fenway, and her dad is dragging Diana's mother to the game. In their 43 years of marriage, her mother has only been to one game and she brought a book with her, one of those romance novels she's always reading. Diana wanted to call in sick and join her dad, but he wouldn't go for it.

Joe is the coach of the high school basketball and baseball teams, and tonight is the school's winter sports recognition banquet. The indoor track coach died in a car accident the day before the banquet was originally scheduled, back in early March, and it seemed for a while there wasn't going to be a banquet at all. Outside it's raining. Diana teaches preschool at St. Anthony's, just two blocks away from the high school, and when it rains the kids stay inside during recess. The school doesn't have a real gym, just a cafeteria. She and Joe never meet for lunch even though their breaks coincide. They both like to have some time alone, so Diana usually goes and sits in her car during the school break. After the morning kids leave, she's got a full hour before the afternoon group shows up. Mostly she just reads, but today she's planning on listening to the game.

Joe gets up from the table and carries his cereal bowl to the sink. It's Wednesday, which means they're at his place. They live in the same town, but Joe owns a condo and Diana rents a studio apartment over a fabric shop. Tuesday and Thursday nights are at Joe's; Friday and Saturday at Diana's. The other nights they usually don't see each other, but tonight is the banquet, so they'll be meeting back at Joe's and driving over to the school together at 6:00. Diana isn't sure if she'll be staying at Joe's after the banquet.

Joe picks up the phone and dials a number he's reading off a sheet of paper taped to the refrigerator. In her apartment, Diana has a set of magnets in the shapes of various dogs—a hotdog, a Dalmatian, an old car, and a truly ugly woman—a gift from Joe that she uses to hold those things that deserve fridge space. Diana reads more of the newspaper article (*even Churchill was a Red Sox fan*) but really she's listening to Joe. He asks to speak to Tim, which puzzles Diana, until she hears the rest of the conversation. Joe wants to make sure Tim is going to the banquet tonight, and tells him that he's getting a special award. A special award? Diana knows he can only be talking to Tim Dulac, a kid that Joe despises who was on his basketball team. As far as she knows, Tim never actually made a basket. And he was whiny too, always getting hurt and wanting to be taken out of the game. She waits until Joe is off the phone and then says, "Tim Dulac? What kind of award could you possibly give him? I thought he was the worst kid on the team."

Joe smiles at her. "You'll see."

Diana is distracted at school all day. The archdiocese announced a few months ago that they were going to be closing churches and schools in the Boston area, and the official list of closings will be released tomorrow. Everyone is afraid St. Anthony's will be shut down. Even the older kids seem worried about it, though her students are blissfully unaware. Diana works with Chelsea DiMario, who is five years younger and has a much better way with the children. During recess Chelsea leads the kids in a makeshift game of Red Light, Green Light in the cafeteria while Diana sneaks outside and has a cigarette. She's found the one doorway of the school that is completely hidden from the kids and other teachers. Once she forgot to wedge a stick inside the door and had to walk around the entire building to get back inside.

Ordinarily Diana would feel guilty about leaving Chelsea with the kids for so long, but Diana recently found out by accident that Chelsea makes more money than she does. Diana wonders if it's because Chelsea came this close to being a nun. The school is run by a bombastic woman named Sister Martha, and she eats lunch with Chelsea every day. This is Diana's first year at the school, and although she wouldn't admit this to anyone, she's hoping that it will be closed so she can leave without having to make a decision.

Later, when she's home and should be getting ready to meet Joe for the banquet, Diana instead sits in front of the TV and watches the last three innings of the Red Sox game. It was delayed for over two hours because of the rain, so on her lunch break, Diana listened to talk radio in her car instead. Talk radio always pisses her off because everyone speaks in the absolute language of black and white, as if the world didn't hold any gray. Then the Sox ended up losing by three runs. This puts Diana in even more of a bad mood, which she knows is silly because it's only the first game. Still, it feels like a bad omen, and she has a headache. She wishes she'd thought to buy a new outfit for the banquet because most of her work clothes are boring. Lots of navy and brown, skirts on the long side. She wouldn't want to shake up the kids with wild patterns or colors, especially because they have to wear gray plaid uniforms. Throwing color at them would be a tease.

The phone rings and startles her. She'd been dozing off, but now Joe is on the line telling her he's going to pick her up in 15 minutes.

"It'll be easier than you coming all the way out to my place," he says.

Joe lives less than two miles from Diana, but she doesn't say anything. She knows why he's coming to get her; he's afraid she's running late. Diana tells him she'll be ready and hangs up the phone.

When he shows up, Diana takes another 20 minutes to get dressed. She's chosen her one sexy outfit, a black leather skirt and white silk shirt, but the shirt needed ironing and there was something sticky on the pocket of the skirt. To his credit, Joe sits quietly on the couch while she zips around the room, only once losing his temper when she holds up two pairs of black shoes and asks him to pick.

"It's a sports banquet, for Christ's sake," he says. "You could show up in sneakers and fit right in."

Diana picks the shoes with miniature clock buckles. She always enjoys the comments they elicit from people. "You're stepping in time," that kind of thing. Plus, if she's bored, she can always count the minutes going by.

The food at the banquet is better than Diana had expected. Lasagna and meatballs and spaghetti, with lots of Italian bread and salad. She's sitting with Joe and the other coaches and their spouses at the head table. The indoor track coach's widow is sitting between the gymnastics coach and the volleyball coach. The rumor going around school is that the two coaches are lesbians and having an affair—Joe told her this on the drive over—so Diana watches them closely to see if she can pick up on anything. She is relieved that she doesn't have to sit next to the track coach's widow because she wouldn't know what to say to her. There's bound to be some kind of speech about what a great guy the coach was, and then someone will hand the widow a trophy or plaque. It's too depressing for words. Throughout the banquet Joe keeps reaching under the table to check a box that he's brought in from the car. Diana asked about it, but Joe blew her off, saying only that it was for the banquet. The box is about a foot high. Diana keeps kicking it accidentally with her clock shoes.

The other tables are full of students, each sitting with their teammates. She recognizes the basketball players because she's been to every game. Most of them are good kids, but Diana won't be sorry to see a few move on. She's thinking mostly of the identical red-headed O'Brien twins, known for being total assholes on the court, even to their own teammates. She notices Tim Dulac sitting by himself at one end of the table. She can't even count the nights Joe came home from practice swearing about what a pain in the ass Tim Dulac was. He has allergies or is asthmatic, Diana can't remember which, but she remembers seeing his anxious-looking mother at every game. For some reason, Mrs. Dulac was always holding a towel in one hand and an unopened protein bar in the other. Once Tim tried to sit with her during the half rather than run drills with the team. When Joe found Tim sitting with his mother, Diana thought he was going to kick Tim right off the team. He probably would have, but there were barely enough players as it was.

There is a guest speaker, an ancient-looking guy who once pitched for the Sox. Everyone in the room seems to know who he is, even Joe, but Diana doesn't recognize him. Once the fruit cups have been cleared from the tables, he walks up to the podium with help from his son, who looks quite elderly himself. The son stands by his dad's side and introduces him. The microphone isn't on yet, so Diana can't catch the man's name. The principal comes over and fiddles with the mike, then pushes it in front of the old guy.

"You want to talk about the Curse of the Bambino?" he says. The crowd laughs and a few people clap.

"Well, I knew Babe Ruth," he says. "He was quite a guy. And fat!"

The son takes his father's elbow and leads him back to his seat. Diana realizes the old guy wasn't brought in to actually give a talk, just to lend the event a little excitement. She imagines that some of the richer, more influential towns might actually have current Red Sox players attend their banquets, or at least more coherent retirees.

The presenting of varsity letters moves along quickly enough. Diana has stopped paying attention by the time the indoor track coach is mentioned. The widow smiles bravely when she is asked to come to the podium and speak about her husband. Diana is surprised to see that even the O'Brien twins are quiet. The widow says, "Phillip would have loved to be here tonight," and then begins to weep. The gymnastics coach leaps from her seat and helps guide the widow back to her chair. Diana notices that the gymnastics coach has wrapped her arm around the widow's waist rather tightly.

Joe stands up and claps his hands together. The sound is startling in the reverential quiet of the room. "Time for some special awards," he says. Joe bends down and takes out some kind of trophy from the box under the table. Then he holds it behind his back so no one can see.

"As many of you know," Joe says once he gets to the podium, "the basketball team didn't have a great season. There were some close games, especially with Somerville, but we definitely struggled. So I'd like to honor one player tonight for helping to make the team what it was." He pauses and looks over at Tim. "Tim Dulac, if you'd please stand."

Diana looks at Tim, who has turned red in the face. He stands up and smiles.

"Tim, I'd like to present you with this." Joe pulls the trophy out from behind his back. "The Cry Baby Award. Come on up here and get it. You earned it."

The O'Brien twins begin to cheer loudly, but otherwise the room is silent. Even the widow stops sniffling. Diana watches Tim approach Joe hesitantly, like a wounded animal not sure if the outstretched hand will offer food or a slap. The trophy in Joe's hand must have been custom made, since Diana can't imagine there's much of a demand for images of a fat crying babies on pedestals. She sees Tim studying the trophy. Something in his eyes grows dark and cloudy, and then Principal Emery is by Joe's side, telling him to put that damn thing away, just as Tim darts out of the room.

Later, in the car on the way home, Diana feels like she's drifting. She could be out of a job the next day, all depending on what the archdiocese announces. Tomorrow won't be a good day for Joe either; she's sure of that. Tim's parents and the school board will no doubt raise a stink over what Joe did. It's not very often that Diana feels sorry for someone, but at this moment she does feel badly for Tim.

Joe pulls up alongside Diana's apartment building and parks in front of the fabric shop. He doesn't look sorry for how the night ended, with the two of them being asked to leave, escorted to the door by the wrestling coach like they'd been caught stealing the silverware.

"I could call in sick tomorrow," she says.

He just looks at her. "Why?" The car is still running.

"You know, to be there in case things get ugly at school." Diana knows she should be disgusted by what Joe did. Instead, she is merely puzzled, wondering why he would think embarrassing Tim this way could possibly be a good thing. It's the same feeling she gets when Joe defends his love of the Yankees to her: complete bewilderment.

"You're making way too much out of this," he says. "It was no big deal."

He's wrong, and she knows it. By morning reporters from both Boston newspapers will be waiting for Joe outside his condo. Tim Dulac's parents will hold a press conference at noon with their lawyer, and Joe won't have a job by the end of the week. St. Anthony's will be on the list of schools to be closed, and the news will hit Diana in a way she hadn't anticipated. But it is also the start of the longest winning streak in Sox history, and the way Diana looks at it, that's got to count for something.

Bambino Road, Chapter One

Cecilia Tan

The sun is fighting with the clouds on this windy afternoon, autumn trying to sneak in early now that Labor Day is almost here. Charlie Scarinci stands on the porch of his girlfriend's house with his hands in his jacket pockets. Charlie, 34 years old and a graduate of Middlesex Junior College, shuffles his feet on the welcome mat. The jacket is blue and says Bay State Locksmiths on the back, which is appropriate since that's where he works. He pulls a box out of his pocket and tries to decide which hand to hold it in. Charlie feels like a fool out there on the porch, where every car driving by on North Shore can see him, but Ruth's in there with a customer and he doesn't want to disturb her. The purple neon "Palm Reader Tarot Cards" sign is lit in the living room window, and there's a green minivan in the driveway that isn't hers.

Charlie tries dropping to his right knee and holding up the box with his left hand, but it's awkward. Right hand? A little better. But shouldn't he be holding her hand with his right? He tries the left knee, but it's been balky ever since that collision at the plate in the junior college championship game, more than 10 years ago now. He tries again and decides it's going to be awkward no matter how he does it.

The green van belongs to Consuelo Hernandez, a neighbor who lives two blocks away. Charlie can't figure out if she's too lazy to walk or what, but she's down here once, sometimes twice a week. The wind is chilly and Charlie is tired of standing on the porch, so he gets out his key and eases it into the lock, inching the door open as silently as possible. The chimes hung on the back tinkle for a moment until he gets his hand on them, and then he slips the door closed, letting the chimes free one at a time. Yes, it's definitely Señora Hernandez in the parlor with Ruth; he can hear her sing-songy tone of complaint even if he can't make out the exact words. Señora Hernandez has no shortage of things to ask for advice about. Her husband's ill and can't work, her 15-year-old son just got picked up for the third time on a vagrancy charge, and who knows what else. Charlie's sure he'll hear all about it at the dinner table.

He tiptoes into the kitchen and pours himself a glass of orange juice from the carton in the fridge. There's barely enough room for him to turn around in there, what with the small formica table up against one wall and the small stove, sink, and fridge against the other. The house is really more of a cottage, Charlie thinks, but it's a good location for Ruth's business, right on a busy corner, and it's got parking. The house is blue, just like the formica table and the hand-painted flowers on the clock hung on the wall. Charlie hasn't even had a swallow of his orange juice yet when he sees the time on the clock: it's 4:30 already, and C.J.'s train is due in at five. With the Friday rush hour . . . Charlie's thinking expletives as he goes into the living room. He must have stood out there on the porch a lot longer than he thought.

Charlie looms near the curtain of beads in the doorway to Ruth's parlor. The living room's about like you'd expect, full of hand-me-down furniture from Ruth's mother that's old but not really antique. Charlie likes it; he's never been into ultra-modern stuff. Through the beads he can see she's sitting at the small table draped with scarves, the candles are lit, and she's got the deck of cards in her hand. But Ruth's just fiddling with them, nodding as Señora Hernandez keeps talking. He can smell cigarette smoke through the incense.

Charlie doesn't want to interrupt, but he's sure the señora's been in there for more than her allotted half- or full-hour. Ruth's always letting people go overtime—she's just too soft-hearted to cut them off.

"I mean, what am I going to do?" Señora Hernandez says. "His father's in no shape to discipline him."

Charlie's startled by what comes out of Ruth's mouth. "Ah, give the kid a good kick in the pants," she replies.

Señora Hernandez laughs nervously. "Oh Ruth, he's too big for that, you know."

"Yeah? Let me at him." Ruth slaps the cards down on the table, and Charlie sees Señora Hernandez flinch.

Ruth's been a bit jumpy herself lately, he thinks. But ever since he found out C.J. was coming, Charlie hasn't exactly been the most relaxed person himself. Maybe it's me, he thinks. Anyway, there's no more time to waste. He parts the beads with one hand and says, "I'm sorry ladies, but, Ruth, we're going to be late . . . "

"Holy jeezus," Ruth replies and rushes past him without saying another word to Señora Hernandez. La Señora stares at Charlie, a lipstick-red cigarette scissored between her index and middle fingers. She's wearing a canary yellow suit, and as she takes a deep pull on the cigarette, Charlie sees the flash of her gold fingernail. He doesn't know if it's real gold, and he doesn't really care: it would be tacky either way. She stares at him a moment more before grinding the butt into the ceramic ashtray balanced on the arm of the chair she's in. La Señora purses her lips and then stands up, taking a few deliberate moments to brush and straighten her suit before she saunters out of the room. Charlie douses the candles and then hurries out to start his hatchback before Ruth comes down. C.J. is in Massachusetts now, his train speeding toward the station, and Charlie can barely get the key in the doorlock.

The crowd on the trolley is shoulder to shoulder, part commuters heading home and part Sox fans on their way to the game. Kirby

Wilcox, six-foot-one and 185, can see over most of them as he worms his way toward the door. There's no hearing the train's driver, so he scans passing signposts to try and see if this is Kenmore. But any doubts are erased when the majority of the Sox-cap wearing riders pile out as soon as the doors swing open. Wilcox follows them, pushing his own plain blue wool cap down over his shorn hair. The horde of Sox fans moves noisily up the stairs and out onto the street.

The sidewalk is lined with vendors: a pizza cart, a man with a fistful of pennants on sticks, a guy with a folding table covered with baseball caps. Kirby notices that no New York Yankees caps are visible on the table, but he sees people wearing them in the crowd as they walk towards the ballpark. In front of the ATM lobby, guys are scalping tickets. "Sold out, who needs tickets," one fellow says. Kirby lets the crowd carry him past the man and over the highway where he gets his first glimpse of the park's scoreboard and the back side of the big green wall. He's never approached the park on foot like this before, and Kirby feels the collective excitement in the pack build.

The streets outside the ballyard are filled with people and the shouts of sausage and scorecard hawkers. The gates aren't open yet, so Kirby makes his way around to the back side of the park and a small gate surrounded by police sawhorses. There's a cop leaning against one of the barricades, but he's chatting with the sausage vendor on the corner, so Kirby walks right past him and up to the turnstile in the smallish archway in the brick. Inside he sees an old-fashioned ticket window, a brass circle with slots embedded in its center. Fenway Park is full of these kinds of things—even with all the renovations and upgrades, dinosaur bones still poke through.

Kirby nods to himself in relief. He knows the guy behind the window, his name's Jack, and he's probably as old and rickety as the turnstile. Jack is wearing the requisite bright red polo shirt with an "B" embroidered on it and a matching cap. He squints at Kirby's chest and says "You got a pass here, son?" His voice is muffled by the glass and brass.

Kirby shoves his hands into his pockets. "Just got here," he says, trying to look dumb and innocent. "Just up from Pawtucket."

Jack cranks his neck to the side and looks up into Kirby's face. "Call-ups came in yesterday," he says.

His bluff called, Kirby switches tactics. "Come on Jack, I'm just kidding with ya."

Jack's eyebrow twitches when he hears his name and he goes back to looking Kirby in the chest.

"I was in the neighborhood and thought I'd drop in," Kirby continues. "Big game tonight, huh?"

Jack nods.

"Come on Jack, don't you remember me? Wilcox, Kirby Wilcox."

Jack blows air out the side of his mouth. "Can't say as I do."

Kirby starts to blush, but Jack isn't looking at his face anyway. "Kirby, they used to call me the Kirbstone."

"Kirbstone!" Jack laughs hard like he's remembering something hilarious, probably the same thing Kirby's trying so hard to forget. "What're you doin' here, Kirbstone?"

Kirby shrugs. "My season's over, I thought I'd come say hello to some of the guys."

"Who you with these days?"

"Tacoma."

"So you ain't exactly in the neighborhood . . . " Jack's got one of those voices that drips with suspicion.

"Well, I am now."

Jack frowns.

"I just want to say hi to Willie over in the clubhouse."

Jack looks at Kirby again, like he's trying to see if he's carrying a bomb or something. Kirby's holding his backpack below the window where it can't be seen, but he's got nothing to hide.

Jack's eyes crinkle up as he starts to laugh again. "Heh! Okay, Kirbstone, go on in. But watch your step." Jack doesn't write out a pass but just waves him on.

Kirby nods, heads through the turnstile, and enters the dark concrete confines of Fenway Park.

From up on the Tobin bridge, the sky looks strange, an aluminum shine in the background, ragged clumps of cloud floating in the front. Ruth, 36 years old and in business for herself these seven years, pulls her jacket tighter in the passenger seat. Her hair is red and mostly straight, popping out from under the Sox cap she has tried to tuck it into.

She's worried about Charlie. He's been a bundle of stress recently, and they even had a fight last weekend, but she hasn't had a chance to bring up the subject again. Maybe fight wasn't even the right word for what had happened; it was really more of a misunderstanding, but she still had the feeling things weren't the same afterwards.

It all took place last Friday, after she'd seen a young thing with boy trouble out the door and had decided to call it a night. She had flicked off the neon in the window and started neatening up the parlor, straightening the scarves draped over the furniture, pulling the dead candle stubs out of their holders and tossing them into the wastebasket. She could hear Charlie in the living room, walking back and forth.

"You can come in, hon," she had said. He sometimes acted like he was afraid to come into the reading room.

He had poked his head through the curtain. "Can I ask you a question?"

"Sure, sweetie, anything."

"No, I mean . . . " He had stepped through the beads and left them clinking behind him. "I mean . . . professionally."

She had taken one look at the distress on his face and put her arm around his shoulder. "What's wrong?"

But Charlie had twisted out of her grip and sat in the armchair. "I know you said you won't do readings for family, but this isn't really like that."

She frowned and crossed her arms where she was standing. "Now, Charlie . . . "

"I'm just, I just can't stand it anymore."

He had been wringing his cap in his hands and suddenly she had an inkling where he was headed. "Can't stand what, sweetie?"

"The Sox. Should I just quit watching 'em right now? Are they going to fade in September this year, or do they have a chance?"

Ruth wasn't a psychic, but she had known it would be about the Sox. "Honey, I'm not a fortune teller."

"What do you mean?"

"I mean it's not magic. I can't contact the spirit world and ask for guidance."

"You're making fun of me."

"No, honey, no I'm not."

"So you can't help me."

"I didn't say that." Ruth had sat in her chair. "People come to me because they need advice, but really, they know what's best for them most of the time. If I have to use a little hocus pocus to get them to see that, well . . . "

"So it's all fake." Charlie had winced as he said it, because he knew it sounded wrong.

But Ruth had taken it in stride. "Maybe some people really do have extrasensory gifts. My grandmother used to say she predicted the day I'd be born. But I'm just trying to help people, you know?"

"Then why don't you become a doctor or something?" Charlie had looked at the crystals and candles and shaken his head.

"Don't you think I have a good thing going here?" Ruth had started to get a little irked and didn't want to get off the subject. But then again, she hadn't really been sure what the subject was.

"Oh, I mean, of course . . . " Charlie had sputtered right away—he was touchy, a little bit, about how she owned the house and all he had was a beater of a car, but he hadn't wanted her to think this was about that. Charlie couldn't talk well when his foot was in his mouth, and so he had tried to cover for it by getting her to speak. "So, uh, how do those Tarot cards work anyway?"

"Well I don't just make it up as I go along, if that's what you mean."

"That's not what I meant. Please, hon, I'm really curious."

They both had known then that the wheels had come off in the conversation. But at the time, Ruth had felt they had at least rolled to a stop without crashing too hard. She had figured the way to end it cleanly would be to show him a Tarot reading. She would do one on the Sox and show how she could interpret the heck out of it, make it look like anything she wanted to. That would take care of things. But he'd been silent while she showed him the cards, and it was hard to do a Tarot reading when the person wouldn't talk.

Now a week has passed since their misunderstanding, and to Ruth, Charlie still seems moody. Of course, this may have more to do with his ex-wife's phone call and the imminent arrival of Charlie's only kid, whom he hasn't seen in five years.

"Here you go, hon," Ruth says as she hands him money for the toll. "What time is his train due in?"

"Six minutes," Charlie says, sounding like he's hyperventilating.

"Maybe it's late. Amtrak is late all the time." When he doesn't respond, Ruth puts a hand on his shoulder. "Relax, Charlie, will you? It's going to be okay. He'll be okay. And the game doesn't start until seven."

Charles Mendoza Scarinci, Jr., a 12-year-old student at George Washington Middle School in Queens, is dead asleep when a conductor shakes him on the shoulder. The music in his headphones is so loud he can't actually hear what the guy is saying, and in a moment of panic, he thinks maybe he has missed his stop. But as he whips the phones off his ears he sees the train around him is deserted. "Time to get off," the conductor says, then straightens up and walks away.

C.J. shrugs and shakes himself like a dog. Jacket, backpack, duffel bag, cap. He's got everything. He walks out onto the long concrete platform and can't tell which direction to go. He figures that towards the front of the train is a good guess, though, and he's right. Just beyond the locomotive are the glass doors, beyond which lies a cavernous food court. But a quick scan of the field of scattered green tables and chairs doesn't reveal any familiar faces. C.J. plunks down a few bills from deep in his pocket for a copy of *The Sporting News* and then walks towards Mickey D's. He figures if he's going to stick to his game plan of staying out of the way during this week of exile, having food in his stomach is a good idea. Besides, ever since waking up on the train he's had a headache, and although a quarter pounder may not cure it, C.J.'s sure it won't hurt.

He gets in line behind a bulky man in a flannel shirt who's wearing his Sox cap backwards. C.J. wears his cap backwards too, but he still feels the urge to sneer at the guy. Whatever. It's instantly obvious that this mini-McDonald's is painfully understaffed and that the woman at the register couldn't care less. There's some argument about the contents of a to-go bag happening up there, and C.J. fidgets, hoping he'll get his order in before his ride arrives.

"The *Yankees!*" someone says in a sharp tone right behind him.

C.J. turns around and sees a college-age guy in a polo shirt and jeans. This guy's a foot and a half taller than C.J., who has to tip his chin up to give him a "what are you lookin' at" stare.

"I mean, why the Yankees?" the guy asks.

"I'm from New York," C.J. answers, trying to keep his sneer under control. C.J. weighs maybe a hundred pounds batter-dipped, and this guy is not only twice his age but twice his size.

"Okay, yeah, but, why the Yankees then? What about the Mets?"

Here comes the sneer. "Gimme a break. I hate the Mets."

The guy rolls his eyes. "You don't learn anything by winning all the time. Losing builds character."

"I guess that would make you a Red Sox fan." C.J. has turned back around and is now answering the guy over his shoulder.

"I'm serious," the guy says. "And if a man doesn't have his character, he's got nothing."

The burly man in front starts to chuckle, so C.J. replies, "Yeah, you're a character all right."

The guy snorts in disgust and walks away. Now if only it had been the guy in front, C.J. would be one person closer to his fries.

Kirby Wilcox has been a part of many baseball organizations in his career, and he's found that the minors aren't just a place to bury players you don't have room for on the big club. Lots of old coaches and office guys end up there too. Kirby's spent a lot of time drinking with these guys, just listening when they didn't think he was. And he's discovered that they're not so different from the guys in the majors—at least, that's what Kirby likes to think.

Kirby has to duck his head to get under the doorway of the tiny office near the visitors clubhouse. He raps his knuckles on the concrete as he does so, and the leather-faced man at the desk looks up from the worn glove in his hands.

"You gotta see your own equipment manager if you need something," he says.

"Mr. Killeher? I'm not with the Yankees." Even as he says it, Kirby doesn't realize that his left hand has curled up at his chest.

Marty Killeher has been tending the third base locker room at Fenway for several decades, and his father did it before him. But Kirby knows the look on his face. He's one of those baseball men who see players as well-trained animals, and himself as the zookeeper. When he looks at Kirby, he notices what size double-knits the kid needs to wear and not much else. So Kirby clears his throat. "Mr. Killeher, I'm here because I need your help."

Marty pulls a pair of scissors from the drawer of a tough old wooden desk, then turns the glove over with his free hand. "You need a glove re-strung?"

Kirby tries to chuckle but it sounds fake because it is. "No, that's not it," he says. "What I want to know is . . . did your dad talk to you a lot about the old days?"

Marty huffs once. "Hell, you couldn't stop him from doing it." He starts to snip the laces on the glove.

"They say your dad worked at Fenway back when Ruth was here."

Marty huffs again. He slips the scissors between the glove's fingers and cuts. "That he was."

Kirby is still standing just inside the doorway, but the office is so small that puts him more or less up against the edge of the desk. He's not getting anywhere this way. He ducks back into the hall where a bunch of folding chairs are stacked against the cinder block, grabs one, and takes a seat. Then Kirby leans forward with his elbows on his knees. “I’ve heard about The Four,” he says.

Marty doesn’t look up from the glove in his hand, but he stops unlacing it. “You sure picked a night to bring that up.”

“Something special about tonight?”

Marty jerks his head toward the clubhouse. “Just the Yankees. That’s all.”

Kirby swallows. “Did your dad ever talk about The Four?”

Marty nods. “Not much I can tell you, though.”

“Anything. I’m, uh, I’m . . . ” Kirby has no words to explain why he’s here. “I’m on a quest, sort of.”

Marty looks up. If he remembers Kirby, it doesn’t show. If he’s shocked to hear what Kirby says, that doesn’t show either. “The last time I heard him talk about The Four was back in ‘67. He got so drunk that night, I couldn’t shut him up. He started to think it was 1920 again. Just stark raving drunk, that’s what he was.” The look on Marty’s face says the last thing he wants is another nutcase around.

“I’m just trying to find out more. Did he ever tell you what it was?”

“What what was?” Marty starts pulling out what laces are left in the glove.

“The Four.”

“Depends on what you mean by told. Sometimes he insisted The Four were Ruth and three other players Frazee sold to New York. But other times he talked about it like it was a thing that the guys took with them.”

“What kind of a thing?”

Marty looks at the pile of lace bits on the desk top, opens the drawer again, and pulls out a roll of rawhide. “I don’t know. Pops was too crazy to listen to most of the time. Eventually I had to have him committed.”

“Even if it’s wrong, can you tell me what he said?”

Marty thinks for a moment, his lips squirming around on his tan, wrinkled face. “Some kind of good luck charm. Like a rabbit’s foot or something.”

“Did you believe him?”

Marty shrugs. “I still think he was talking about those guys we lost. Never got the same story twice.”

"Because it was such a secret . . . ?"

A heavyset man in pinstripes leans in the doorway. "Hey, Kelley, Jim needs you for something."

"Be right there." Marty stands up and cracks his back. Kirby stands up too, keeping his neck bent so he won't whack his head on the pipe that runs through the office. He holds out his hand to shake Marty's, and Marty says, "You want to find out more, you gotta go to New York. Pops used to trade stories with a clubhouse man down there. That guy swore that Ruth and some of the guys would play cards before games. If you believe him, depending on the outcome of the card game, they could tell ya who'd get a hit, who'd make an error."

The old clubhouse manager is already retreating down the hall when Kirby yells to him, "What was that guy's name?"

"Pete Sheehy."

As the stop and go traffic inches off the expressway toward the South Station exit, Charlie is resisting the urge to drive with both feet. He strategizes out loud. "Okay, I'll pull up just beyond the doors and put the flashers on, you run in and find him." Charlie guns the car forward a few yards. "Except you don't know what he looks like, and he doesn't know you either."

"Just pull up and leave the keys with me. If I have to move, I'll circle the block."

"But with the construction I don't think there's a block to circle."

"I know, I'll pull into the Post Office parking lot. But only if I have to move. Otherwise, I'll sit right there."

Charlie nods. Ruth's with him on this and that feels good. Charlie has been worrying whether she and C.J. will get along, not even allowing himself to wonder if *he* and C.J. will get along. What is it Jimmie's always saying from those motivational tapes he listens to in his truck? Seize the opportunity. Yes, it was kind of weird for Marisol to call up and after years of refusing to let the kid visit, to suddenly force him on Charlie for a week. But at the same time . . .

The minute he had hung up with Marisol, he phoned Jimmie, who had season tickets down the right field line, and pulled in a heavy duty favor (plus forked over a good amount of cash) for the seats to tonight's game. The plan had been pick the kid up at the train, head straight to the park, sit in the stands eating hot dogs and watching batting practice, joking and laughing and telling stories. Charlie knows this is a Hallmark card scenario, and so probably not realistic, but it's the only thing he's got to go on, so he's sticking with it. He follows the car in front of him as they both run the red light and sees the train station up ahead. The gap of a fire hydrant approaches and he pulls the car over. Charlie gives Ruth a quick peck on the cheek and then bolts out the door.

The station is busy, crammed with commuters. Charlie checks the big board overhead—C.J.'s train came in already, so where is he? He hopes the kid didn't give up and start wandering around the city. Charlie starts looking at the people sitting around the Au Bon Pain.

There he is. Charlie sees him, head bent over a magazine on the table, bobbing to some kind of music in his headphones. The music's so loud Charlie can hear it even over the din of a thousand commuters. He walks right up to him but C.J. hasn't noticed Charlie standing there.

"Hey. Hey C.J."

But C.J. can't hear him. It's just as well because Charlie's voice sounds weak and unsteady, and he'd rather the kid know how happy he is to see him. Better try again.

Charlie drums his fingers on the table, and C.J.'s head pops up. He whips the headphones down in almost the same moment. "Oh, hey Dad," he says, leaning back in his chair. "How you doin'?"

"I'm good," Charlie answers automatically. Okay, so, no rushing into each others arms or nothing. It's obvious C.J. is too old for that little kid stuff. "How was the ride?"

C.J. shrugs.

"C'mon, Ruth's illegally parked out there." He picks up the duffel bag, C.J. shoulders his back pack, and the two of them walk side by side toward the doors. "I have a little surprise for you," Charlie says.

"Oh yeah? What kind of . . . shit." C.J. forgot to zip the backpack shut and two CDs clatter to the floor. He whips around to pick them up, and that's when Charlie sees something that gives him a shot of ice water veins.

There on the back of C.J.'s head is the dreaded interlocking N-Y. Charlie can barely get the words out of his mouth. "Does you mother let you use language like that?"

"Sorry." C.J. shrinks back a little, remembering his plan to try to be invisible this week. "So, what's the surprise?"

No, this reunion's definitely not going the way Charlie wanted, but a plan is a plan and he sticks with it. "Want to go to a baseball game?" Charlie gets a little dab of gratification when he sees C.J.'s eyes light up for a second before dimming back to their usual guarded level.

"What game?"

"I've got tickets for tonight. I figured we'd go straight to the park."

C.J. isn't a dumb kid and he remembers when he was five years old and Charlie took him to games a couple of times. But he doesn't really recall Fenway, and he doesn't really remember any details from those games other than sitting in the sun and getting to throw peanut shells on the floor. He doesn't know what Charlie expects, and he's a little afraid to find out. But Sox/Yankees! The guys are going to be green when he gets back. How could he say no? His head is still killing him from the train ride, but he slaps his old man on the back of the shoulder. "Sounds great," C.J. says.

Jimmy's tickets are box seats down the right-field line. It's noisy here, very noisy, as Yankees fans and Red Sox fans try to shout each other down, men attempt to hawk soda and ice cream on top of that, and the scoreboard erupts from time to time with bursts of organ music and snippets of pre-recorded songs. Depending on your point of view, Fenway's size is either its greatest charm or its worst shortcoming. It isn't just that the park has the fewest seats of any in the major leagues, it's that the seats themselves are smaller, and closer together, than any others. In the grandstand at field level, you become very intimate with your neighbors. And the "bleachers" at Fenway aren't true bleachers in the sense of benches, they just happen to be the furthest seats from home plate. As actual seats to put your keister in, though, they're some of the nicest ones in the park, much better than the wooden slatted antiques you'll get twenty rows behind home plate.

Charlie, Ruth, and C.J. are fortunate to be sitting in molded plastic seats, just a few rows back from the field, though these seats are angled to face the outfield instead of home plate. Above the wall to their left, they can see the back of the head of the ball attendant who works the right-field line, a college softball player by the look of her. And a little further up they see the retired numbers painted into the facing of the roof deck.

Originally the numbers up there were painted in the order they were retired. 9 for Ted Williams. 4 for Joe Cronin, 1 for Bobby Doerr, and 8 for Carl Yazstrzemski. But placed that way, these numbers spelled out the date of the end of the franchise's final world championship season: 9/4/18, September 4, 1918. The next day, the World Series began, and the Sox defeated the Cubs in six games. Back then the Red Sox were the cream of the crop, on top of the world, aces. But they hadn't won the World Series since. So that date hung like the sword of Damocles over every game at Fenway. But simply re-arranging the numbers didn't solve the problem. For example, they could spell out 1948, a painful year when the Red Sox found themselves tantalizingly close to victory, only to lose in the playoffs. Or they could stand for .984 with 1 error, which was Bill Buckner's fielding average in the 1986 World Series. The numbers were minefields that had to be handled with care. So when Fenway was renovated for the umpteenth time in 1998, they were placed in numerical order: 1, 4, 8, 9. No bad memories with that arrangement, but the Sox still hadn't won the World Series.

As the game enters the sixth, Ruth wonders if now would be a good time to visit the ladies room. C.J. and Charlie haven't spoken to each other since the fourth inning ended on a close call, and she's running out of polite ways to restart the conversation. It had been difficult enough the whole first hour: she'd ask C.J. about school or something and he'd answer, she'd try to draw Charlie in with a comment, and then something would happen in the game that would put the two of them at odds again. The final straw was a close play at the plate. From where they are sitting, pretty close to the field but up the right-field line, neither of them could see whether the runner was safe or out, but that didn't matter. To Yankees fans, he was clearly out; to Sox fans, it was a bad call. Even though she's rooting for the Sox, Ruth thinks the runner actually was out, but she isn't about to tell Charlie that. Meanwhile, people are climbing past them in the cramped aisles, trying to get to the beer stands and the restrooms. Maybe I'll wait until next inning, Ruth thinks.

The batter stands in to start the top of the sixth, and she is relieved to see the two of them start to talk to each other. C.J. leans over to Charlie and shows him something on the scorecard. Charlie points at something across the field. Ruth hopes that this constitutes male bonding and, eager not to disturb its mysterious workings, says nothing. But then there is a called third strike. Charlie shouts that the ump is blind, while C.J. records something in his score book a little too gleefully, and they fall silent again.

Ruth slips out of her seat and goes down the dark runway into the bowels of Fenway. It's crowded back here, with people lined up for refreshments and pouring out of the restrooms, walking around, searching for a better food stand or the right ramp to their seat section. Ruth stands about five-foot-three and has to weave her way through to the ladies room door. There's a beat-up bullhorn in a concrete corner above the doorway that's broadcasting the game, but it's so noisy she can't hear what the announcers are saying. The crowd erupts though—something good must have just happened for the Sox. She can ask C.J. when she gets back to the seats since he's writing it all down. That'll give her an excuse to talk more with him.

From what she can tell, C.J. seems like a good kid. She doesn't have to be a psychic to see it's going to be a struggle for C.J. and Charlie to find a comfort level. Charlie has had his cap in his hands all night and has been wringing it so much she thinks he might need a new one before the game's over.

Ruth spends a good minute ducking her head in and out of stalls in the ladies room looking for one that has paper. Her uncle once took her to a game back in the seventies, when she was only eight years old, and back then it seemed like there was only one ladies room in the whole stadium. Times have changed a bit—Ruth doesn't really remember what the crowd was like back then, but she's surprised at how many women are here tonight. In fact, it seems to her almost 50-50. When she comes out of the stall, she sees she was lucky—now there's a line out the door.

Ruth doesn't escape the lines completely, though, as she gets absorbed into the hot dog line forming just outside the ladies room door. It's less of a line and more of a mob, and Ruth's really not sure how she should maneuver through it. Somehow it seems as if more and more people keep appearing in front of her, and after a few minutes she hasn't moved forward an inch.

She looks around her, for a security guard, another hot dog vendor, something. But all she sees is a tall man leaning against a concrete pillar, watching the scene. He's young and clean-shaven, with penetrating blue eyes and a smile when he sees Ruth looking at him. Ruth turns away, hiding a little blush—after all, it's not everyday that a handsome stranger smiles at her. A minute or so later she turns around, and he's still looking at her, his lips pulled in like he's trying to keep from saying something.

Ruth turns toward the concession stand again. She hasn't moved—in the strange convection of the crowd, people keep slipping in the sides. After they get their order, they are forced to back their way out through the middle of the crowd. Ruth can't even see what's going on up there. She crosses her arms, hoping to shoulder her way in, but all that happens is more people pile up in the scrum behind her, trapping Ruth in place.

She feels a tap on her shoulder. "Can I give you a hand with something?"

It's the guy from the pillar. He's got a slight drawl in his voice—she's not sure if it's Midwestern or Southern. He crowbars his lanky body in between people to reach her.

"Just trying to get a dog and a Coke," she tells him. She sees his hat's got no affiliation on it, and that gives her an idea. "Do you want one, too?"

"No, thank you," he says, just like his momma taught him to.

"Then make it three dogs, three Cokes. Do you think you could help me carry them up to the seats?"

"I sure could." He takes the wad of bills she's handing him.

"I'll be right back," he says, and wades into the crowd. Ruth backs out and takes his place by the pillar.

He emerges from the crowd a few minutes later, hot dogs, napkins, and ketchup packets heaped together on a flimsy cardboard tray, two Cokes jammed down into the corners, and another one held in his long fingers. He hands her the loose one, a few damp dollar bills plastered to it. "Your change."

She notices he did get a dog for himself after all. "Thanks. So," she says, as they move toward the concourse, "do you know anything about baseball?"

"Excuse me?" This wasn't a question he had been expecting. "Do I know . . . ?" He'd smile if he wasn't so surprised. He's not sure how to tell her he's a player, or he was, or maybe he still is, since right now he doesn't know what will happen next season. And he doesn't want to sound like a big shot. "You could say that I do." How to put it? "I used to play in Pawtucket." When she looks blankly back at him, he adds, "In the Red Sox system."

"Even better!" Ruth says, more to herself than to him. "Would you mind sitting down with my boys for a little while? I think they could use another opinion." Yankees 5, Red Sox 4, Ruth 1, she thinks.

Kirby nods and holds up the dogs. "No problem."

They pick their way back to the seats; if the look on Charlie's face is any indication, not much has changed since Ruth left. "Hey guys," she says, sliding into a vacated seat behind them. "Brought you some food. And this is . . . " She blushes, realizing that she doesn't know his name.

Kirby sits in what had been her seat, next to C.J., and hands the tray to Charlie. "Kirby," he says.

"He's a ballplayer," Ruth puts in and then sits back to see if the male bonding thing will happen.

Charlie's mouth hangs open, and C.J. takes over doling out the hotdogs and condiments.

"Kirby, not Kirby Wilcox?"

"Uh, yes sir, that's me."

Kirby is surprised to find his hand being shaken. "Amazing! Great to meet you! I remember when you were drafted, what, fifth round?"

Kirby and Ruth are both staring at Charlie now. C.J. is too, though his is less a look of astonishment than disbelief that his dad is being such a dork. There's a little admiration mixed in there, too, though. After all, how many people remember the names of fifth-round draft picks? Only those who live and die by their teams. And Charlie is the type of man who remembers not only the draft picks, but also where Carl Yastrzemski was married (Raleigh, North Carolina) and what Broadway musical Harry Frazee financed with the profits from selling Babe Ruth to the Yankees (*No, No, Nanette*).

"Sixth, actually," Kirby says, blushing all the way to his ears." That's, uh, that's not what most people remember me for."

"Oh, uh . . . " Charlie remembers and then he blushes, too.

"What?" C.J. asks him. "Dad, what?" He turns to the ballplayer. "What do most people remember you for?"

Charlie hushes him. "Eat your hot dog before it gets cold. So where have you been playing? I lost track of you after . . . after you left the Sox."

"Tacoma." Kirby shrugs. He catches Ruth's eye then, and she's looking at C.J., who has folded his arms in a youthful sulk. "So hey," he says to the kid. "What's been going on in the game?" He leans over C.J.'s scorecard, and C.J. begins to point out the crucial plays.

It's been a dogfight, this game, a seesaw, a run scratched here or there, a man cut down at the plate, an RBI bloop double that just landed on the chalk. That cheer Ruth heard was the tying run, and now it's five all.

Kirby wolfs down his hotdog while C.J. is talking. He hasn't eaten since the end-of-season postgame spread yesterday, or was it two days ago? There were those peanuts on the plane. The front office secretary in Tacoma didn't know why he wanted to go to Boston instead of Florida, but she booked the ticket for him just the same.

After the ride on the T, Kirby's got about 17 dollars to his name. He points at the scorecard. "This fielder's choice, did he beat out a double-play ball?"

"Yes," Charlie says.

"No," C.J. replies. "Hit too slowly," he adds.

"Looks like I've been missing a great game." Kirby's sitting the furthest to the right of the three of them, and he has to fold his long legs up to fit in the seat. Kirby angles himself toward the plate, diagonal in the chair.

Charlie asks the question before he thinks about whether it's polite or not. "So what are you doing here, anyway?" At least he stops himself before adding something like: I thought you'd never want to see this place again.

"I'm looking for something," Kirby says. "I'm on a kind of mission, I guess."

C.J. is all ears. "What kind of a mission? Like a scouting thing?"

"Not exactly." Kirby's not sure how to say it, it sounds so stupid, so desperate. But then he sees a woman coming up the aisle, couldn't be more than 22, with shoulder-length blonde hair, and cute. She's wearing a white t-shirt emblazoned with a blue and red lettered slogan: Reverse the Curse. She sees Kirby looking and smiles. He smiles, too, but he's transfixed by the lettering on her chest. As she goes by, the woman huffs, disgusted, and Kirby has no way to apologize, to explain it isn't what it looks like, since he has no way to explain what it is, either. He hangs his head and Charlie catches Ruth's eye behind them. She's looking at Kirby with the same facial expression she had when a black and white kitten appeared at the back door, lost.

Kirby leans down and the other three follow him by instinct, cocking their ears. "I'm looking for something that'll help me . . . but it's not here. I think I have to go to New York."

"That's where I'm from," C.J. says, his mind leaping ahead. "Are you going to take the train?"

"I, uh, I don't know how I'm getting there, yet. I think I'll have to . . . "

Kirby hears the crack of the bat, sees the blur out of the corner of his eye. He ducks, pulling C.J. down with him. Kirby doesn't even think about it, he just responds to the danger-whizz only ballplayers can hear and gets the hell out of the way.

The ball is a line drive slicing foul, and poor Charlie has no chance. The line shot ricochets off the arm of the seat in front of C.J. and hits Charlie square in the forehead. The ball's energy is dissipated by the two hard bounces, one off metal and one off skull, and so it falls quietly into C.J.'s lap.

Charlie is out cold, his hands still wrapped around his cap.

Kirby leaps to his feet, motioning for an usher. People are standing all around them now, staring at the man slumped forward in his seat. C.J. is still clutching the ball, guiltily wondering if they're on TV, and Ruth is staring with her mouth wide open, shaking Charlie lightly on the shoulder. Meanwhile, Kirby frantically tries to get the medics over, completely certain that this is all his fault.

Finally the medical personnel arrive and get Charlie onto a stretcher, the other three following behind. C.J. is the only one who looks back as they head down the ramp, just in time to see a ball sail deep into the dark sky above the Green Monster. 6-5 Yanks, he thinks, that's not bad—and then C.J. follows the others inside.

The strange procession weaves through the crowded, dingy concourse to a door in a cinder block wall. They all go in, and the door shuts on the cramped room. Kirby explains what happened to the EMT there, who flashes light into Charlie's eyes and waves some smelling salts under his nose. Charlie is alive, obviously, but still out.

"What do we do now?" Ruth asks Kirby.

"Just wait, I guess."

The EMT is an overweight guy with a friendly face. "You're lucky it hit the rail first," he says, "otherwise we might be looking at a cracked skull."

"You don't think he has one?" Ruth asks.

"Well, you probably want to go over to the Brigham for some x-rays," he suggests, "just to be sure." Then the EMT opens a small refrigerator and takes out a blue cold-pack wrapped in a paper towel. He hands it to C.J. "And you definitely want to stick that on there."

The swelling in the center of Charlie's forehead is visible now, quite a red lump coming up. C.J. thinks he can see the ball's stitches like a zipper mark on Charlie's skin. He puts the cold-pack down on top of the lump and holds it there.

Kirby is shifting from foot to foot like he wants to get out of there. "I'm so sorry," he says to Ruth. "I'm so sorry."

"Oh forget about it," she says automatically, then tries a joke. "Nothing you could do without a glove, right?"

"No, really." He eyes the EMT who is fiddling with a portable radio on his desk, trying to get the game to tune in. "It's my fault. I'm . . . I'm sort of a magnet for this kind of trouble."

Ruth knows better than to laugh. After all, she hears people's weird superstitions every day. But C.J. doesn't. He's still holding the ball in one hand, the other pressing the cold-pack on Charlie's head. "Are you a jinx?"

"Kind of."

"It's about what happened to you. The thing Dad didn't want you to say."

"Yeah."

"And that has to do with your mission, too."

"Yes."

At that moment Charlie opens his eyes and moans.

Everyone talks at once. Ruth is asking him if he knows where he is, C.J. is telling him about the ball, Kirby is apologizing. Kirby's voice finally wins out. "I'm so sorry, sir. You see, it's all my fault." The others are staring at him now. "Ever since that call-up, I've been cursed." He looks into Charlie's live-by-the-Sox, die-by-the-Sox eyes, and suddenly it doesn't sound as stupid. "That's why I'm on a quest now, to reverse the Curse of the Bambino."

Maybe it's because Charlie's just been hit in the head, but everything Kirby says makes a strange sort of sense to him. Charlie sits up and the cold-pack falls into his lap. The mark on his forehead is lurid now, the bruise purpling everywhere but the distinct stripe of the ball's seam. Ruth gasps when she sees it. Charlie feels it with his fingers. "Reverse the Curse?" he asks.

"Yessir."

Charlie stares around the room, suddenly realizing where he is. "What happened?" He touches his forehead experimentally with the tips of his fingers.

"Honey, maybe you should lie back down."

"No, I'm okay," Charlie says, swinging his legs around.

The EMT puts a hand on his shoulder. "Are you sure you're all right?"

"I'm fine."

"Are you sure?" the EMT repeats, but not forcefully.

Charlie nods and stands up. "I'm okay," he says again, but his attention seems far away.

"He's okay," Ruth repeats to the EMT. C.J. hands him the ice pack, and Charlie puts it automatically to his forehead. C.J. takes a last look at the ball, noticing the colorful gash where it hit the railing, the smudge of the trademark where the bat made contact, and then stows it in his backpack.

When they emerge from the first aid station, Charlie is surprised to find how crowded it is. There is a crack of thunder, though, and he suddenly understands. People are pouring into the concourse from the grandstand, programs held over their heads, coats up over their shoulders.

"Honey," Ruth says, pointing to the ladies room doorway. Charlie nods and she goes around the cinder block barrier that blocks his view into the room. The men are now left trying to find a place to stand in the increasingly chaotic underbelly of Fenway Park. They are just edging up a concrete ramp slightly, their backs to a brick wall, when a flash of lightning blinds Charlie for a moment and an almost simultaneous thunderclap deafens C.J.

Charlie has never been in a war zone, but he has witnessed a hurricane, and he figures this is something like both. There's thunder, there's lightning, and there are crowds of people—Red Sox fans, Yankees fans, stadium employees—rushing every which way. Charlie doesn't even realize it, but he has C.J.'s wrist in a death grip. The crowd jostles them and Charlie pulls the kid toward what he thinks will be a more sheltered spot. Eventually they hunker up against the ladies room wall.

Charlie's thinking ten things at once, at least two of which are, what the hell happened to Kirby? and, if the game is called off for weather, the Yankees will get the win. For that matter, where's Ruth? Did she come out already? Each thought seems to throb through the bruise on his forehead.

Small rivers of rain are pouring down the ramps and pooling around their feet. Charlie sees a woman with red hair—but it's not Ruth. Charlie's afraid she's been swept outside by the human tide. Some folks are fleeing the storm, running now toward parking lots or side streets where they've parked illegally. Others are huddling inside the park, waiting for the downpour to slow.

C.J. has finally built up enough sweat and rain on his arm that he slithers it out of Charlie's hand. "Do you think she went to the car?"

For half a second Charlie can't remember where the car is, then he recalls finding a spot on a side street after refusing to pay 20 bucks for gas station parking. "What was the name of the street?" he asks C.J.

The very New York seeming tuft of blond hair sticking out of C.J.'s cap waves like a damp feather as he shakes his head and sighs. "Queensberry Street."

"Are you sure?" He has to yell to be heard over the din of the rain and crowd.

"How could you forget a name like that?" C.J. has given up looking for Ruth and instead stares straight up at Fenway's dingy innards. Even on a sunny day, the walls in here are damp with condensed hot dog steam and a near-century of beer belches. C.J.'s nose wrinkles as a drop of something falls and hits him.

"I'm just checking." Charlie tries to get up on tip toes, as if that extra inch or two might make a difference, and then he sees her. Somehow, she has come out of the restroom and is walking in the wrong direction.

Preemptively, C.J. grabs the sleeve of Charlie's jacket, and the two of them start cutting across the crowds toward the ramp she is now climbing. They are really getting jostled, and people in the crowd are shouting like the game is still going on.

For some of them, maybe it is. Charlie hears someone close behind him yell "Hey Yankee Fan!" and then there's a tug on his sleeve. Out of the corner of his eye, he sees the jock knock C.J.'s cap off his head. He turns and catches the cap, but C.J. isn't next to him anymore. Instead there's a sudden scrum of guys in red and gray jerseys clobbering each other. C.J. is on top of a guy who must outweigh him by a hundred pounds. Charlie's not sure whether to feel a swell of parental pride as C.J., backpack and all, downs the jock and then disappears in the tangle of bodies.

Before Charlie can pick him out again, he feels someone grab *him* by the wrist. Bouncers and police are arriving at the edges of the fight. It's C.J. now on the other side of Charlie, pulling him away from the melee. The two of them run up the ramp into the rain, and then C.J. slows instantly to a nonchalant walk.

Charlie wants to ask if the kid's okay, but doesn't want to mother hen him. "Hey," he says, "I got your cap."

C.J. whirls around, the rain matting his hair. "You did?"

Charlie holds up the equally soggy cap, and C.J. clutches at it. For a second Charlie thinks the kid's going to hug him, but then he just says "All right, Dad! Thanks."

Then they go down another ramp and find Kirby and Ruth standing there, protected from the crowd by a large garbage container. Reunited, the four of them move off into the crowd as if they planned the rendezvous. No one says anything.

When they come out onto Yawkey Way, the rain seems to be letting up a bit. There are pieces of tree branches strewn about, leaves plastered to the streets, and the wind is still whipping hard, but the raindrops seem fewer and farther between.

They don't stop until C.J. leads them across an intersection and down a tree-lined street to where the car is parked in front of an apartment building. Charlie's heart skips a beat as he sees something colorful on his windshield—but it's just a leaf flattened against the glass. "Man, no ticket, that has to be some kind of a sign," he says.

A good-luck sign? Kirby thinks to himself. That would be a change. Maybe he had better stick with these folks for a while and see what happens. "So, uh, can I get a ride?" Kirby asks.

"Sure thing, kid," Ruth says. Then she looks at Charlie, cold-pack in his hand. "I better drive."

Fischer at Fenway

Mitch Evich

Fischer was a college student at the time, a history major, and although he tried to bear the burden of the past stoically upon his slender shoulders, he regretted enrolling in courses on Czarist Russia and Nazi Germany in the same semester. It was spring, the merry month of May, and Fischer was learning more than he had ever intended about pogroms and blood libels and the vast managerial chore of exterminating millions. After a while it got to him, and so one morning of dazzling sunlight, Fischer, who almost never missed classes, walked right past the building where the lecture would be taking place, down Commonwealth Avenue and into Kenmore Square, and then over the bridge across the Turnpike and down the street to where the ticket office was. It was a rare weekday afternoon game, and Fischer was able to get a seat within 20 rows of the Red Sox dugout. He put his knapsack in the empty seat next to him, signaled to a vendor that he wanted a beer, and settled in to watch the game.

The innings passed swiftly, thanks to good pitching and some crisp fielding plays, and Fischer ordered a hot dog and then a second beer, letting the alcohol and the springtime heat and the murmur of the crowd lull him into a state of languid contemplation. He would be a senior in the fall, he wasn't sure what he would do when he graduated, he was tired of people asking, he was tired of thinking about his student loans. He was tired, period. He yawned and rubbed his eyes, and then heard the crack of the bat, the whiz of the ball as it passed. It struck an empty seat about 20 yards to the right. A woman crouched over, hurriedly retrieving whatever it was that had fallen out of her lap, while other fans scrambled for the ball. An overweight man in a short-sleeved shirt emerged with it held proudly above his head, to scattered applause.

Fischer was not a Red Sox fan, the outcome of the game couldn't have mattered to him in the least, and yet when right fielder Dwight Evans drove a pitch into the center-field bleachers to give his team a 2-0 lead, Fischer was on his feet with the rest of the crowd, shouting his appreciation. When Evans crossed home plate he pressed hands with the runner who had scored in front of him, then walked toward the dugout like a presidential candidate, acknowledging the crowd with a brisk wave before disappearing down the dugout steps. Fischer was grateful to be included in the gesture; Evans wasn't a famous player, like Carl Yastrzemski; yet Fischer remembered as a child watching on TV as Evans made an incredible catch, right here in this stadium, in what everyone said was the greatest World Series game ever played.

A young relief pitcher entered the game in the top of the eighth inning and surrendered a run on three straight singles. While the crowd booed (Fischer himself did not boo) the young pitcher stood quietly and waited for the manager to remove him from the game. The next pitcher struck out the first batter but then gave up a three-run homer into the netting above the left-field wall, and the Red Sox trailed 4-2. The crowd grew silent; the sun was oppressive, not pleasant; the second beer had given Fischer a headache. In the previous lecture the Nazi Germany professor had talked about the failed plot to assassinate Hitler, and then Hitler's suicide as the Russians and Americans closed in. It was a good thing, Fischer knew, to be on the winning side. If Fischer's great-grandfather hadn't emigrated to St. Louis, would Fischer's dad have been a storm trooper instead of a sailor on board an aircraft carrier in the South Pacific? It was a silly question, since if Fischer's great-grandfather hadn't emigrated, Fischer himself—this Fischer, with the first name of Marty and an occasional craving for Hostess Ding Dongs and a habit of drawing flying machines on the margins of his lecture notes—wouldn't exist. He wouldn't be sitting here in a small green metal chair, his long legs constrained by the next row of seats, wondering how those two relief pitchers, two men barely older than he was, had managed to ruin such a splendid afternoon.

But he didn't particularly like the Red Sox, Fischer reminded himself. He didn't particularly like the idea of "liking" a particular team. He hated seeing people "praying" for such and such a millionaire to deliver a key base hit. Was their religion so threadbare that they let themselves believe that a divine being actually gave a damn who won a baseball game? For Chrissake, he couldn't even find time in his busy schedule to attend to the fate of *six million* Jews!

Fischer wondered if other people's minds worked like his, practically shouting at itself, probably ratcheting up his blood pressure a notch or two. People could be so maddening, the way they accepted the conventional wisdom, the way they did as they were told, sitting in traffic for God knows how long so they could get to jobs that consisted of shuffling papers all day or convincing people to buy more things they didn't need. The world had too many things already, and too many people.

He wished he could order another beer; it might calm him down. But the rule was no beer after the seventh inning—people couldn't handle it, they couldn't handle any of the freedoms they were supposed to enjoy as Americans—so instead he ordered a Coke. It lasted throughout the bottom of the eighth inning, during which the Red Sox loaded the bases with one out but did not score. "Damn it!" Fischer said when the final batter swung and missed.

It was unfair, he told himself. It was unfair that he should be here to see Dwight Evans hit a majestic two-run homer on this picture-perfect spring afternoon, the ball rattling around in some empty bleacher seats, two boys racing over to claim it as their prize, and yet the home run had been rendered meaningless because the bullpen couldn't hold the lead.

Dwight Evans had a thick black moustache and slashes of oil paint beneath his eyes. He wasn't exceptionally tall like a basketball player or huge like a football player; he looked like someone who might have been playing baseball at the start of the century, when the players wore those itchy-looking uniforms and stubby gloves. His number, 24, was divisible by 2, 3, 4, 6, 8 and 12. He was a decent, dignified man, not at all brash or obnoxious. Fischer wanted the Red Sox to win this game for Dwight Evans. Would he get one more chance to bat?

A man sitting close to Fischer said that for Evans to get to the plate again, the Red Sox would have to get two men on base. The first guy walked, the next guy popped up to the shortstop, the third guy hit a weak grounder and barely stayed out of a double play. Fischer watched as Dwight Evans moved leisurely into the on-deck circle. The batter at the plate took two called strikes, and the crowd booed the umpire. Then everyone was quiet. Fischer tried to relax. He wished he had something to hold in his hands: a beer, a hot dog, the handle of a baseball bat. He clutched the nylon carrying loop at the top of his knapsack, and tugged on the strap until the weight of the knapsack offered some resistance. The batter swung and just barely got a piece of the ball, deflecting it so it smashed against the catcher's mask. Then there was a pitch in the dirt, and a pitch that just missed being strike three. The crowd was clapping rhythmically for the batter, some had their hands clasped together. Fischer said to himself: Please let him get on base.

He slapped the next pitch between the first baseman and the second baseman into right field. The crowd roared. The runner on first base went all the way to third. Dwight Evans walked slowly toward the plate. Everyone was standing now, chanting Evans's nickname: "DEW-ey! DEW-ey!" The count went to 2-2, and then . . .

Dewey lined the pitch down the first-base line, past the diving first baseman, and the crowd roared.

The runner that was on first circled second base, determined to go all the way around and tie the game.

Heading for the right-field corner, the ball bounced just in front of where the box seats jutted out along the field of play.

A man wearing a dark blue t-shirt and a Red Sox cap reached out over the waist-high wall and backhanded the ball with his fielder's glove. He held the glove above his head, the ball still inside. The crowd stopped roaring. The umpire was pointing to second base. The ball was dead. The runner who had been on first base stopped just before he reached home, heeding the order of another umpire who sent him back to third.

"That prick!" someone yelled, and although it wasn't Fischer, he had been thinking the same thing. The moment had been despoiled. Evans, standing with his hands on his hips at second base, had been deprived of his majesty.

But the crowd was still on its feet. The Red Sox still had a chance to win. Evans was now the winning run. A single might bring him home, sliding heroically across the plate. But the next batter, a left-handed hitting catcher, flailed at the first pitch and popped it into the air. The third baseman caught it just a few steps from his team's dugout.

The players on the field congratulated the relief pitcher. Fischer turned his attention to the fan who prevented the Red Sox from tying the game. He couldn't find him. Was he already down on the beer-stained concrete, being spat on, kicked in the groin? No; Fischer caught sight of the blue t-shirt, the fan standing patiently with all the other fans, waiting to move up the stairs and into the short tunnel that led beneath the grandstand.

Fischer wanted the blue-shirted man to pay for his transgression. Fischer didn't want him kicked in the groin. But the fan shouldn't have been allowed to get away with that. He shouldn't have been allowed to keep the ball. He should have given it to a young boy, someone who was untainted.

Fischer grabbed his knapsack and hoisted it on to his right shoulder, then took his place in the line of people moving cattle-like toward the upper exit. For a moment he thought about going after the blue-shirted man himself, but the weight of Fischer's books reminded him that he had a lot to do that night. He had a paper to write on the abolition of serfdom. He had a half-pot of coffee to drink. He had much to think about, much to plan. He would conclude the night with an ambiguous fantasy involving a long-legged Jewish girl from his Nazi Germany class. He wanted to wait until the final moment before deciding how it would end.

The Prophecy
A Red Sox Alternate History

SAM AND CHRISTINA POLYAK

In late October of 2004, the world came perilously close to a disaster of unprecedented proportions. Until recently, the full story had remained a mystery. But recently declassified documents enable us to piece together the events of that fateful Halloween. Now, for the first time, the truth can be told.

Early on the morning of October 31, 2004, a group of heavily armed, bearded men broke into a guarded compound on the outskirts of Bushehr, Iran. In an efficient manner they disposed of six ill-prepared security guards at the front gate. A few moments later, an explosion broke the silence, and the men raced through a giant hole in a thick metal door. Two more armed guards were quickly dispatched. The alarms inside were deafening, but the men remained silent, focused on the task at hand. One of them reached into the crushed ice of the red cooler he had been hauling and took out the amputated hand of an Iranian General. The General had fallen victim to an 18-inch sickle just hours earlier as he lay asleep with his wife. Now, his bloodstained hand was quickly cleaned off and placed on the facility's state-of-the-art identification device.

Three more thick metal doors swung open. Two more guards and four engineers in white coats were shot dead. As the intruders entered the control room, they closed all the doors and shot out the electronic lock activation systems. These men knew that this room would be their death chamber, but no one wavered. Strict silence was maintained as the code was entered and the missile's warhead enabled. The countdown had begun. 5 . . . 4 . . . 3 . . . 2 . . . 1. "*Ravane Kardan* (Fire)!" the men shouted. "God is great . . . death to non-believers!"

It took the Boston Red Sox only five games to dispose of the New York Yankees in the American League Championship Series (ALCS). After losing Game Seven of the 2003 ALCS to the Yankees in such heart-breaking fashion, the Sox made sure their 2004 rematch wasn't even close. Curt Schilling and a rejuvenated Red Sox pitching staff shut down the potent Yankee lineup, as Gary Sheffield, Jorge Posada, Alex Rodriguez, and Derek Jeter batted a combined .173. The St. Louis Cardinals put up more of a fight, but as Game Seven of the 2004 World Series wound down, the Red Sox appeared to be on their way to ending 85 years of frustration and finally snapping the infamous Curse of the Bambino.

George W. Bush turned the baseball game off in the seventh inning; he needed to get some rest ahead of the next day's breakfast speech before the Shaker Heights chapter of the AARP. Bush had been busy campaigning in Ohio and Florida in the final days before the election, and the way things were going, he would need every vote. A slowing economy, instability in Iraq, and failures in public debates had caused the incumbent to fall 5% behind Senator Kerry in the latest polls, a fact that Bush's chief strategist Karl Rove never failed to mention during their daily breakfast meetings.

And in the last few weeks, his daughter Jenna had been keeping the president on his toes as well. In mid-October Jenna had been picked up by the Secret Service at a nightclub outside Gainesville, Texas. She had been drinking too much and was doing a striptease act on the bar. Unfortunately, someone there had a video camera. The Secret Service had spent the majority of their time since the incident attempting to find the tape before it surfaced on the Internet.

The phone rang and shook the president out of his stupor. Bush was sure that the call would have something to do with Jenna. But it did not.

In the sixteenth century, a French mystic named Nostradamus predicted the end of the world. According to Nostradamus, a crazed madman from the Middle East would fire a great destructive weapon on the metropolis of the West (assumed to mean New York City). But the timing of this event had never been clear.

In March 2004, a Swiss historian by the name of Jean-Claude Lavesque discovered that there was more to the prediction and a date was available after all. It turned out that Nostradamus wrote his predictions in a series of 942 four-line poems called quatrains. For the last five centuries, everyone had assumed that each quatrain was an independent thought. But by loading all the quatrains onto a supercomputer, Dr. Lavesque discovered that a code connected a number of quatrains that would otherwise have appeared to be unrelated. The scientific community dismissed Dr. Lavesque's research as a form of data mining, but he pressed on and by August had arrived at a perplexing observation. It appeared that the prediction involving the destruction of the world was linked to another quatrain that mentioned "an end to an 85 year curse."

After completing his research, Dr. Lavesque mentioned it in passing to an American colleague in an email. The response was eye opening. Dr. Clarkson Brown held a Ph.D. from the University of South Carolina and was also an avid baseball fan. He immediately made a connection between the Nostradamus prediction and the

Red Sox ending 85 years of frustration. But who would ever believe that story? Dr. Brown and Dr. Lavesque made a number of attempts to warn the Department of Homeland Security, but with the upcoming election, little attention was paid to their calls.

The World Series with the Cardinals had the best ratings in the history of televised sports. The Red Sox suddenly became America's team, a symbol of every working class hero who came close to getting a big promotion, believed his marriage would last forever, and hoped his child would not make the same mistakes that he did growing up. And the Red Sox responded, going toe-to-toe with the powerhouse Cards for six games and then taking a 4-3 lead late in Game Seven. Unlike the previous occasions when these two teams had met in the World Series, this time the Sox star hitter was up to the task. Ted Williams never really lived down batting only .200 in his sole World Series appearance in 1946. Manny Ramirez, on the other hand, was ready to roll.

After hitting 45 home runs during the regular season, Manny took the team on his broad shoulders during the playoffs by hitting .380 and driving in almost one run per game. He hit the winning home run in the clinching game of the Oakland series. He then had four hits and threw out A-Rod at the plate of a crucial Game Five in the Bronx with the Sox up in games 3-1. In the World Series, Manny had already exploded for three home runs and was batting .340. With a 2-4 night at the plate behind him, Manny just needed to concentrate on his defense to bring a title to a city that had waited for so long.

Finally, the bottom of the ninth arrived. As Keith Foulke sprinted in from the bullpen, the fans were bursting out of their shells. Not a seat was being used and the concession stands had tumbleweeds blowing through them. Thanks to a sacrifice fly from David Ortiz in the top of the inning that gave the Sox a 4-3 lead, only three outs stood between the Red Sox and the end of the Curse.

Bush: Get me Dick Cheney, Donald Rumsfeld, and Karl Rove on the phone, now!

Assistant: They are holding on Line 2 along with Condoleeza Rice, Paul Wolfowitz, and Colin Powell, Mr. President.

Bush: Dick, is this for real, or are you guys playing a joke on me again?

Cheney: I'm afraid that this time is the real deal. We still aren't sure who's responsible, but Khatami claims it's a militant group not affiliated with the government.

Rumsfeld: Iran's not responsible! Are you kidding me?

Powell: Mr. President, our local sources along with British intelligence confirm that there was a break-in at their nuclear facilities, and it looks like those perpetrators began the launch sequence.

Wolfowitz: Can you really count on British intelligence after the WMD fiasco?

Powell: That is not the point, Paul!

Rove: Let's get back to the matter at hand . . . did we even know that Iran had long-range capabilities on their nukes?

Powell: We don't have time to argue about 'ifs' and 'hows,' Karl. We need to make a decision. Judging by the missile's trajectory, the Pentagon thinks it's headed somewhere in the Northeast—probably New York City. But we can't go to the press just yet—panic would ensue.

Rove: Hey, if we shoot this thing down, that would be an election check-mate.

Powell: Will you stop it with the election, Karl. This is serious!

Bush: Colin, let him finish.

Rove: Thanks. As I was saying, a successful intercept would be enough to swing the independents on Tuesday.

Cheney: Are the F-16's in the air already?

Rumsfeld: Yes.

As he took his warmup pitches, Foulke could feel the electricity in the air. There was a sense of destiny in the Fens. The Cardinals had the bottom of their order due up, and Foulke had been perfect in six playoff save chances.

Mike Matheny, the Cardinals catcher, swung at the first pitch and hit a soft grounder to second base. 4-3 putout. One away! The roar of the crowd was deafening. Tom Werner and John Henry, the Red Sox owners, got ready to jump over the short wall in front of their seats next to the Red Sox dugout.

Next, second baseman and number nine hitter Tony Womack took a fastball on the inside corner for a strike. A leadoff hitter for Cardinals during the regular season, Womack had struggled mightily in September. Cardinals manager Tony LaRussa had decided to move him to the bottom of the order for the playoffs, but Womack still couldn't break out of his slump.

Foulke could feel the excitement of being only two outs away from history. As he looked in for a sign from Jason Varitek, he noticed a lady in her late 70s or early 80s praying with her rosary a few rows behind the plate. Wow, Foulke thought, some people think this is an event of biblical proportions. He began to consider what he should do to celebrate after the last out. Should he point to the sky? Should he throw his glove, or just pump his fist? SportsCenter watchers would want something special.

Distracted by these thoughts, Foulke fired ball one and then ball two. "Stop thinking about the celebration and make your pitches," he muttered. "Wake was awesome today and I have to save this for him."

Womack fouled off the next pitch, and the count ran even. Cheers began to pick up again. Another foul ball, and then three more followed. Foulke was trying to pitch inside, but Womack wasn't giving in. "Time to go outside with this one. Let's see if he swings!" Foulke thought. Ball three. "That's it! No more pitches to waste . . . . Let's see if he can hit my change." Strike three! Expecting the fastball, Womack had been way out in front of that one. Now there were two outs. Could 85 years of futility be about to come to an end?

Bush: Have we heard from the pilots?

Rice: Still no word, Mr. President.

Rumsfeld: What is the ETA for this thing?

Cheney: Fifteen minutes.

Rove: We have to contact the press.

Bush: Yes, do it, Karl.

Rumsfeld: Wait! I'm getting a Blackberry from the Pentagon: 'Code Red! The intercept failed!' What should we do now?

Wolfowitz: Donald, if we had only spent the 1990s finishing 'Star Wars,' this wouldn't be an issue!

Powell: Now is not the time, Paul.

Rove: Get the camera crew in there, now! George, do you want to review what will be on the TelePrompTer?

Bush: No, I can read good.

Now Foulke faced the top of the Cardinals' order, Edgar Renteria. While 2004 was not his best season, Renteria finished strong in September by batting .360 and scoring 18 runs in a limited role.

The roar of the crowd was deafening; Fenway Park was awash in red. Young boys were wearing Pedro shirts, while old ladies held up signs saying "I love Jason Varitek." The bars from Lansdowne Street to Dorchester to North Conway to Fall River were overflowing with anxious fans, all packed in together. They were sweaty, intoxicated, and unlikely to show up for work the next day.

Of course, the boundaries of Red Sox Nation extended well beyond the state line. In Arlington, Virginia, a young father watched the game anticipating that his three-month-old daughter would be up in a couple of hours. He knew his spouse would have little sympathy when he asked to sleep in the next morning.

Meanwhile, a family of four in Southern Florida was glued to the television set. The parents had decided to let their nine- and twelve-year-old boys stay up to watch the game even though it was a school night. Although the nine-year-old had been asleep for two hours now, his parents decided to wake him just so he could forever say he saw the Sox win it all.

In a nursing home just outside Barre, Massachusetts, a 75-year-old widow was quietly sewing a sweater for her granddaughter in front of the television set. She had almost finished with her eighth cup of coffee that day, and as she watched Foulke peer in for the sign from Varitek, she thought of her husband, who had passed away two years ago. Going to games together in the '50s and '60s, she had always wondered what his reaction would be if his beloved Red Sox ever won "the whole thing."

Now Foulke's first pitch was on its way . . .

"<<Beep>> <<Beep>> This is the Emergency Broadcast System. This is *not* a test!"

Bush: My fellow Americans, the country of Iran has launched a nuclear weapon that is presently headed for the Northeastern United States. Our intelligence indicates that the destination is likely to be in the corridor between Boston and New York City. The military command has made a number of attempts to intercept the missile, but have yet to find success. We will continue trying. In the meantime, we have armed our nuclear facilities so as to permit a swift boat, I mean, swift response to this clear act of aggression from a rogue state. If you reside along the eastern seaboard between Boston and New York City, please listen to the emergency instructions on the radio and television. If you have a loved one in the affected area, please join me in praying for their well-being. I will update you with further developments as I retrieviate them. Thank you, and God Bless America.

A silence fell across Fenway after Bush's message was seen on the Jumbotron. The umpires huddled at home plate. After several minutes, they decided to continue playing until further notice. A few people headed for the exits, but the majority of the crowd remained to support the hometown team. Foulke threw a strike, then bounced a ball in front of the plate. Renteria stepped out to check the sign. Foulke got the ball back and began his wind-up. Renteria fought off the inside fastball by wristing it into the net behind the plate. Now the Sox were just one strike away from putting the Curse to rest.

Meanwhile, Iranian President Ali Mohammad Khatami was on the phone with George Bush.

Khatami: Mr. Bush, you have to understand this is not an act of aggression by my government; this is terrorism! What if the hijackers of September 11 had flown those planes into the British Parliament; would this be considered an act of aggression by the United States against Great Britain?

Bush: The analogy is pointless. I really don't see the connection. To put it bluntly, your country has been a thorn in our side since the hostage crisis of 1979. It's time to remove that thorn.

Khatami: I feel like I'm talking to a man whose mind has already been made up. So I will leave you with just one thought. If we had one missile that could reach your shore, what makes you think that we do not have more?

George Bush slammed the phone down and immediately called Dick Cheney, who was just hanging up the other line.

Bush: Do you think he's bluffing?

Cheney: We'll soon find out . . .

Bill Mueller sprinted to the pitcher's mound from third base to give Foulke one last word of encouragement. With a glove over his mouth, Mueller whispered, "This is it, Keith . . . he's not going to want to end this thing with a bat in his hands, right?" Foulke smiled and nodded.

The Sox closer reared back and threw. The pitch was low, but Renteria took a big hack at it anyway, not even close to making contact. Was that it? The Boston cops moved into position, ready to keep the Fenway faithful from rushing onto the field.

But wait . . . the ball had bounced on the front right corner of the plate and skidded by the catcher. An alert Renteria hustled to first base as the ball squibbed all the way to the backstop. By the time

Varitek reached it, he had no play. A chill blew through the ballpark. Were they going to do it to us again? To come so close and not be able to pull it off . . . this couldn't be happening!

In the bleachers, a flustered 33-year-old lifetime Red Sox fan began shouting expletives as he crushed the half-empty bag of peanuts in his coat pocket. His face looked pale. This fan was only 15 when Bill Buckner let the famous Mookie Wilson bleeder seep through the five-hole. He was hoping never to have to experience that kind of agony again. His fiancée started pulling at his shirt.

"Why is that guy on first base?" she said. "I thought he swung and missed. Isn't that an out?"

"He can go to first base if the catcher can't hold on to strike three, unless the catcher can throw the guy out."

"Well, that doesn't seem fair!"

Meanwhile, the crowd began to get excited again as Jim Edmonds stepped up to the plate. This was the heart of the Cardinals order, but all the Sox needed was one more out. Even the best hitters make an out two out of every three times. Right?

But Edmonds swung at the first pitch and lined a double down the first base line. Only the hustle of Gabe Kapler, a late-inning defensive replacement, kept the speedy Renteria from scoring. Fenway went quiet.

Cheney: What's the ETA?

Rumsfeld: Five minutes!

Wolfowitz: Can we launch our missiles before the damn thing lands?

Rice: No, Paul, that would be preemption and we don't want to go down that road again.

Cheney: You are right, Condi. We'll have plenty of time to take out Iran.

Powell: Donald, my sources tell me that two doctors working on the Nostradamus code contacted the Department of Homeland Security a few months ago and predicted just this sort of thing would happen.

Rove: Good point, Colin. What if they go to the press and make us look like idiots? Let's get a few aides to start digging up dirt so we'll be ready to discredit them.

Cheney: Good idea!

Powell: That wasn't my point. My point was that—

Cheney: We know what your point was, Colin. Unfortunately, we don't have time for this right now. Karl, what else should we be thinking about?

Rove: Do we know how many more long-range nukes they have?

Powell: The CIA thinks three or four.

Cheney: Should I get in the bunker again?

Rove: You'll have plenty of time for that later, Dick. The missile is nowhere near you.

There were now men on second and third, with still two outs. Sox manager Terry Francona jogged to the mound. "Don't worry about the guys on base," he said. "Just make your pitch to Pujols and you'll be a star in this town for decades." Foulke nodded.

As the likely winner of the National League Most Valuable Player Award, Albert Pujols didn't let pressure faze him. Batting .391 for the Series, he was now in position to make or break the Curse.

Strike one. Foulke fired an 89-mph fastball on the outside half of the plate that Pujols just missed. The fans were on their feet again. Some were hugging, some were holding hands, some had their fingers crossed, and some had turned away because they couldn't bear to look, but everyone seemed to have forgotten the potential catastrophe that was about to befall the world outside Fenway Park.

Varitek called for another fastball on the outside part of the plate, but Foulke shook him off. No one would remember Varitek making a bad call with a pitch, but everyone in Red Sox Nation would recall Foulke blowing yet another Sox chance at the brass ring. "I have to go with what got me here," Foulke whispered.

Varitek signaled for a change up, and Foulke nodded stoically. The pitch was away and well over the plate. Pujols swung and made contact—

At that precise moment, Dr. Brown was yelling to Dr. Lavesque on the phone. "Are you seeing this, Jean-Claude?"

"Seeing what?" Dr. Lavesque responded in a sleepy voice. The Swiss rarely stayed up to watch American baseball.

"It's happening exactly as Nostradamus predicted. World War III is about to begin, just as the Red Sox win the World Series."

"That can't be! I meant to call you a few weeks ago, Clarkson. I re-ran my program to check some of the other linked predictions, and I discovered that I'd made a terrible mistake. There actually are no statistically significant connections between the quatrains."

"Turn on the news, Jean-Claude!" an exasperated Dr. Brown replied.

With just 25 miles left to New York City, puffs of red smoke started pouring from the missile and it began to lose altitude. Could this North Korean manufactured killing machine reach its destination? The news was relayed to the president's makeshift War Room.

Pujols hit a towering fly ball to left field. Manny Ramirez moved a few steps back but remained well in front of the Green Monster. Edmonds and Renteria were running full steam, but Ramirez appeared to have this one lined up.

Bush: Is the missile going to make it to Manhattan?
Rumsfeld: We don't know yet; it might just crash in the water.
Bush: Let's keep our fingers crossed!

The ball hit the tip of Ramirez's glove and fell behind him. Johnny Damon had been running over to hug his teammate, wanting only to celebrate the end of the game, the Series, the season, and the Curse. But now he was forced to retrieve the ball to try and keep Edmonds from scoring. Unfortunately, Damon wasn't known for his arm, and the winning run crossed the plate.

Almost simultaneously, the 500 lb missile crashed harmlessly into the ocean off Long Island. George W. Bush immediately alerted the country and gave full credit to his team for engineering a successful outcome. Then he returned to his private residence and popped open a can of Pepsi Edge from his personal fridge. The disaster had passed. And really, Bush thought as he sipped from his soda, things could have been a whole lot worse.

The call could have been about Jenna.

Life, Death, Love, and Baseball

Skye Alexander

Here in Boston, time begins on Opening Day—not on January 1, but in the early part of April, when the sun is in Aries. The field at Fenway Park gleams bright as Easter basket grass and the sweet-sour smell of hot dogs grilling wafts seductively through the stands. The Green Monster beckons like the Sirens of old and we rouse ourselves from our long winter's nap, dig out from under the snow banks, and begin to hope. Hope, after all, is what spring is about. And nowhere does hope cling with such tenacity by so fine a thread as in the heart of a Red Sox fan.

Just because Opening Day is the official rite of spring doesn't mean it will be warm at the ballpark. My husband Mark and I have sat through many a game in our long underwear and down parkas, coffee cups clenched between frozen fingers. But not today. Opening Day 1981—which also happens to be my birthday—is as glorious as it is rare. Baseball weather at its best. In the bleachers the yowling yahoos have stripped off their shirts and wave them in the air like lassos as the team takes the field: Evans, Rice, Miller, Perez, Stapleton, Hoffman, Lansford, Allenson, and Eckersley. Seeing

Carlton Fisk in a Chicago uniform, though, is like a pair of pruning shears in the gut. It's a wound that will fester by the end of the day and never heal.

Eckersley has a three-hitter going for the first four-and-a-half innings. Then in the bottom of the fifth, Destiny, disguised as my bladder, forces me out of my seat and down to the stinking catacombs under the bleachers. How different my life might have been if only I'd waited a few minutes more, until after Dewey hit his homer. But of course, we can't know what the future holds—home runs or heartbreak—and even if we did, it's doubtful that we could change it. Free Will is just something cooked up by the Early Christian equivalent of ad men to keep us in there for the full nine innings, instead of heading for the showers before we even get up to bat.

There are 7,420 seats in the Fenway Park bleachers; today every one of them is filled. By now, a fair number of the occupants are drunk, and the aisle is an obstacle course of bodies. When someone jostles me from behind, I stumble and smack domino-fashion into the guy in front of me. It's really not my fault that his cup of beer empties itself on his Official Red Sox Team T-shirt, but I feel responsible anyway.

"Oh, Jesus, I'm sorry," I apologize quickly. Without thinking, I dab ineffectually at his stomach with my handkerchief until I realize I'm rubbing the rounded belly of a total stranger with the familiarity of a mother spit-cleaning her toddler's dirty cheek.

"It's okay," the man assures me. "I've probably had enough anyway."

He is about 50, I guess, with droopy blue eyes that flash like Vegas neon when he smiles, transforming his face from plain to fascinating. His pale, soft skin is already turning a blotchy magenta and will cause him nearly as much pain tonight as Fisk's eighth-inning, game-winning homer.

"Please let me buy you another beer," I offer.

He waves me away. "No need, really."

"It would ease my guilt."

"Ah-ha. So in fact, the beer is for you." He glowers, eyes now as cold as deep space, and leans toward me until the brim of his baseball cap nearly touches my forehead. "A gift with strings attached is a noose."

Then he turns away, merging into the roiling crowd, and is gone.

The Red Sox go on to lose the game 5-3. Hope's hold on the thin thread begins to slip. It is an omen, I suspect, though of what I'm not sure yet.

When I walk into the Flower Child Garden Shop Saturday morning, my boss Charlie Mercer glances up from his newspaper. "Read your horoscope today, Jess?"

He never tires of teasing me about astrology, which he thinks is complete hokum even though, like most skeptics, he's never bothered to investigate it.

"That's not real astrology," I tell him. "It's just for fun, like fortune cookies."

"Well, it's right on today: An unwise gamble could be costly," he says, holding out his hand. "Five bucks."

I give it to him. For three years now, Charlie and I have been betting on Red Sox games. I always take the Sox. Charlie, who likes to be contrary, takes the opposing team.

"If they'd sent Fisk his contract a few days earlier, it would've been a different ballgame," he says, pocketing my five.

"You won the bet, don't rub it in."

I pour myself a cup of coffee from the pot Charlie makes first thing in the morning and keeps warming all day long, so that by mid-afternoon it looks like the La Brea Tar Pits.

"There's a shipment of grass seed in the back that came in yesterday. Unpack it and put it out front, by the fertilizer. Then deliver these two FTDs, and when you get back you can start pricing those cement tchotchkes." He means a shipment of lawn ornaments that arrived yesterday—concrete and polymer statues of swans, turtles, bunnies, cherubs, St. Francises, and Madonnas posed demurely in front of mini-amphitheaters that Charlie calls "Marys-on-the-half-shell."

"Slow down, chief, I haven't even had my coffee yet. As we were saying only a moment ago, look what happened when management didn't appreciate Carlton Fisk."

"Is that a threat?"

I smile sweetly. "I'll let you off with a warning this time."

Although our bantering might sound hostile to an outsider, in truth Charlie and I get along quite well considering that we have to work together every day and that, like most Ariens, I have about as much respect for authority as a skunk has for a pesky dog.

I am halfway through my coffee when the door of the shop opens in a tinkle of Indonesian bells and a vaguely familiar-looking middle-aged man walks in. Like most people, he looks different without a hat and it takes me a moment to place him. He recognizes me immediately, though.

"You!" he says. It's the guy from the bleachers.

"What a coincidence," I quip.

"There are no coincidences," he answers, spearing me with his stare. Then he shakes his head slowly and tosses me a rueful smile. "It had to be Carlton Fisk."

I take this as a truce. Baseball is the common ground on which we can build.

"I wish it gave me satisfaction to say I told you so."

"Once again . . . " His voice trails off, then he suddenly hops back on his train of thought and asks, "You do landscaping, right?"

"That's what it says on the sign."

"So it does. Well. I need some. Landscaping, that is."

"What did you have in mind?"

"Nothing major." He seems to be trying to determine how much hoeing and digging a medium-sized 29-year-old woman can reasonably be expected to do. "Just some flower beds. They need replanting."

"Where do you live?"

He gives me an address in one of the classier suburbs and I check my appointment book. "How about Tuesday, 11 o'clock?"

"Fine."

"We charge $30.00 an hour, two-hour minimum, plus the cost of the plants and other materials."

He nods. "Tuesday, then."

I write down his name, Patrick O'Neal, and phone number in my book. Before he leaves, he dazzles me with a baby-blue smile and I take it we're friends, or at least on the same team.

"So, you going to get that TV antenna put up this weekend, or what?"

Tony is our landlord, a fat, bug-eyed, irritating little man who chain-smokes unfiltered Pall Malls even though he has emphysema and sometimes gets coughing spells that make me think he might turn inside out. A bachelor, he lives on the first floor of our triple-decker Victorian where he spends his time doing crossword puzzles, playing solitaire, and reading Louis L'Amour novels. Tony's great regret in life is that he was born six days after the Sox won the World Series in 1918; he's been waiting ever since.

Mark mumbles something noncommittal. He doesn't want to admit it, but my rugged, athletic husband is afraid of heights and is trying to find a way to get out of erecting the antenna on the roof of the three-story building without revealing what he considers to be an unmanly weakness.

"Lord knows why I bother to watch 'em, the bums," Tony grumbles.

The bums are the Red Sox, of course.

"Why do you then?" I ask.

He looks at me as if I've uttered the unthinkable. "What else can I do?"

When you're in the landscaping business, time really does begin on Opening Day. We have so many customers in the Flower Child Garden Shop this morning that I'm almost half an hour late getting to Patrick O'Neal's place.

"I thought you weren't coming." He sounds worried.

"I would've called," I say, climbing out of the van. "Sorry I'm late. It's been incredibly busy at the store lately."

I hand him a pot of Portofino tulips. "Since you wouldn't let me buy you a beer, I brought you these instead. No strings attached."

He takes them from me and says, "Thanks. Much better than a beer, especially that watered-down ballpark stuff."

O'Neal's lawn is a multi-cultural affair with at least two dozen varieties of weeds. I follow him around to the south side of the house where the flower beds are. By now I've pretty much seen it all—the plant world's equivalent of a big-city police officer. Even so, the wreckage is startling. Hundreds of tulips and daffodils have been ripped from the ground, the bulbs still attached to the stems. Their lifeless carcasses are scattered about the yard like tornado victims. Many of them haven't even had a chance to bloom. The ground is full of holes, but it's obvious they weren't dug for planting; they've been hacked and gouged with a sharp instrument in a wildly haphazard manner.

"My wife's parting gesture," O'Neal explains. "She was jealous of the flowers."

I can't help wondering why he has just left the debris lying around. And how can a person be jealous of flowers? But I'm a gardener, not a psychiatrist, so I keep my mouth shut and bend down to examine the remains.

"We can save most of the bulbs and replant them. Of course, they're not going to bloom this year." I start collecting the bulbs that haven't been crushed beyond recognition. "Did you have anything in mind for these beds?"

"I want to see flowers all the time," he says, more to himself than to me.

"We'll have to make do with annuals this spring, but I can plant perennials and bulbs that will bloom during the summer and fall."

He's making me nervous the way he keeps standing there staring at the ruined flower beds and clutching the pot of Portofinos like a lonely kid with a teddy bear.

"I'm just going to clean up this mess, take some soil samples, and measure the area so I can do some sketches," I explain. "It'll take me an hour at the most."

When he doesn't budge, I resign myself to his awkward company and collect my tools from the van. He hangs around until I've gathered up the last of the ravaged foliage and raked the soil smooth, then he turns abruptly and goes into the house. I feel strangely like an undertaker who's just laid a loved one to rest.

I spend another half hour collecting soil samples from several spots and roughing out a plot plan. When I've finished, I knock on the door to tell O'Neal I'm leaving and to schedule another visit. I prefer to plant flowers during the waxing moon, which encourages growth, and if possible when it's in either Libra or Taurus, the signs that rule flowers. According to the ephemeris, this coming Friday is perfect.

"Want some lemonade?" he asks.

"Sure, thanks."

He holds the door for me and I step into an over-decorated kitchen. If I'd known about Martha Stewart back in '81, I'd have said he was her biggest fan.

"You can wash your hands in there," he says, pointing to a lavatory at the end of a long hall.

All up and down the hall hang framed black-and-white photographs of flowers. Shamelessly sensual photos. Roses with dewdrops glistening on their fleshy petals. Daylilies with darkly inviting centers. Hibiscus with pistils lewdly erect.

When O'Neal comes up to me with a glass of lemonade, I feel myself blush.

"What do you think?" he asks.

"If you're the photographer, I can see why your wife was jealous."

There are dozens of photos in the living room. Strange, haunting images with women in them as well as flowers. A pretty woman lying corpse-like on a bench beside an old-fashioned stone swimming pool, roses tumbling from her hand into the empty pool. Female feet and calves fleeing a vase of flowers smashed on the floor beside an overturned glass of wine; the dark wine flows between the flowers like blood. When I come to one of a little girl smiling from the back of a convertible like a Homecoming Queen, an enormous bouquet in her hands, I start to cry.

"What is it?" O'Neal asks.

I just shake my head and keep crying. I am embarrassed to be weeping in front of a stranger—and because the pictures have stirred up such unexpected feelings—but I can't seem to stop myself. Through O'Neal's lens I see how men view women: as fascinating objects. And I see us women struggling to maintain the fantasy, adapting our lives to their images and expectations at the expense of what we truly long for: equality, friendship, and understanding, but most of all to be loved with the same passion O'Neal bestows on his photography.

O'Neal leads me to a chair. For a long time he holds my callused, dirt-and-grass-stained hands in his soft, white ones.

Finally he says, "You've never been cherished."

What woman has? I want to ask. I think about my jock husband's obsession with sports, my father's devotion to his job. I think about O'Neal's flowers.

"Why did your wife leave you?"

"I drink too much, I don't know the right people." He runs his hand through his thinning, sandy hair. "She had reasons."

But I know it was because he loves his art more than he could ever love his wife.

When I tell Charlie that O'Neal's job will easily run into four figures, he nods indifferently and passes me the joint. Charlie and I are in the tool shed, smoking pot as we sometimes do to unwind at the end of the day. Of course he grows his own. It's interspersed between the Japanese red maples and the Lombardy poplars on the lot behind the store. He believes the best way to conceal something is to hide it in plain sight. Once I suggested he sell it—pot is more profitable than flowers.

"I don't sell weeds," he said flatly.

An aging hippie who got his start pedaling flowers on the Haight in 1965, Charlie is an anachronism in an age when cocaine is king and greed is good.

"Who's your favorite player?" I ask, thinking I should know this already.

"Pete Rose."

"Because he's a such good hitter?"

Charlie shakes his head.

"Because he's such a fierce competitor?"

"Nope."

"Okay, I give up. Why?"

"His name."

"Charlie Hustle?"

"Rose."

O'Neal, it turns out, is an Opening Day fan. He knows the starting roster and the Sox's standing in the League—who doesn't? In Boston, baseball is the great equalizer. "So, how 'bout those Sox?" is a guaranteed conversation starter in any bar or coffee shop. But he's useless in a debate about whether Dwight Evans's arm or Mickey Rivers's speed is the greater asset in the outfield, or whether it's more important for a team to have a catcher who can hit for power than one who calls a good game.

His knowledge of flowers is equally limited. Although he behaves almost reverently toward them, he doesn't have the slightest interest in knowing about their genus, soil and sun requirements, or peculiarities. His is the blind idealization we reserve for all our deities. Mark is the same way about athletes—he hates to hear them being interviewed because it makes them too real.

Nevertheless, I talk to O'Neal about the new plants as I tuck them into the soil. His omnipresence makes me uncomfortable and I talk to fill the silence. Maybe some of it will sink in. But after spending a few days working in his garden, I realize he is probably incapable of remembering to water, feed, and weed according to the schedule I've so meticulously outlined for him.

"If you don't take care of these plants, they'll die," I warn him. "Not only will your investment will be wasted, but you'll have their deaths on your conscience forever."

He smiles ingenuously and holds out his hands, palms up in a gesture of helplessness. He reminds me of the Jesus statues we sell at the shop.

"Maybe you'd better arrange some sort of on-going garden care for me," he says.

I have a feeling this was his idea all along.

O'Neal's shade garden has fared better than the sunny ones. Lily of the valley border the flower bed, perfuming the air with their delicate fragrance. Behind them are a pair of bleeding hearts, several handsome hostas, and a variety of ferns. Columbine show off their purple trumpet-shaped blooms in back, interspersed between yellow Siberian iris, foxglove, and wolfsbane. All I'll have to do is fill in the front section with white impatiens to brighten the area.

I make a mental note to warn O'Neal that the wolfsbane is deadly poisonous and the foxglove can do a job on you, too. Not that he's likely to eat it, but I don't want to be sued if he gets wolfsbane juice in an open cut and goes into convulsions.

Meanwhile, Tony is planting a border of tacky red geraniums all along the front of our house and down the edges of the sidewalk. Every year I offer to put in something more interesting, volunteering my professional services free of charge and providing all the plants at wholesale, but he won't hear of it. He actually likes supermarket geraniums the way some people prefer Wonder bread to homemade pumpernickel.

As I pull into the driveway, he scowls at me and yells, "Bernie got my squirrel."

He means my cat who is named after Bernie Carbo. Most people don't remember that without Carbo's three-run homer in the sixth game of the 1975 World Series, Carlton Fisk wouldn't have had a chance to hit his famous game-winning blast.

"You can't change nature," I shrug.

"That squirrel ate peanuts right out of my hand. Came up on the kitchen windowsill every morning, you know that?"

"A squirrel's a wild rodent. Why don't you get a real pet?"

"I didn't want you kids to have that cat in the apartment, remember? But I let you, against my better judgment, 'cause I don't like to say no. I never knew he was a killer."

"Look, Tony. I'm really sorry, but Bernie can't tell the difference between your pet squirrel and any other squirrel. You can make a pet out of another one."

Tony grumbles a bit, then changes the subject. "When's that husband of yours going to put my TV antenna up anyway?"

"I'll remind him."

Mark tosses the sports section of the paper on the floor and goes into the kitchen for another cup of coffee. "That broad still hasn't learned that baseball is a man's game."

I grab the paper, indignation bubbling up from my belly like hot lava, and find the piece he's referring to, an article blaming the Red Sox's inability to win the World Series on the peculiar physical characteristics of Fenway Park. The author is Penny Baker. Accompanying it is a picture of a pretty woman about my age who looks oddly familiar. It takes me a moment to remember where I've seen her before: in O'Neal's photograph, the woman lying beside the empty stone swimming pool.

"You know this woman?" I ask. During his years in the minors, Mark got to know a lot of people connected with the game, including the press.

"Yeah. She's one of those pushy types who think women reporters ought to have the same access to ballplayers as the men."

What he means is, Penny Baker feels the practice of interviewing athletes in the locker room after games is exclusionary, designed to keep women out of this old boys' club. I happen to agree with her. Mark's a Capricorn, traditional as they come, who believes in doing things the same way they've always been done. I think the status quo could use a good kick in the butt. It's one of many ways we disagree. If I'd known astrology before I married Mark, I might have thought twice about hooking up with someone so different. All the books say Aries and Capricorn are incompatible signs. But of course Ariens thrive on conflict, and I'd probably be bored silly if we got along.

What really intrigues me, though, is why this female sportswriter posed for O'Neal. "What else do you know about her?"

"She's smart, headstrong, knows her baseball—kind of like you, Jessie," he says. "Used to be married to some rich older dude. Last thing I heard, she ran off with a guy in the Dodgers' farm system."

"Maybe she got tired of Boston winters," I suggest, quickly putting two and two together to see if they make four. I wonder how Penny Baker feels about flowers.

By June, talk of a strike is everywhere. Worried fans keep hoping the owners and players will reach a last-minute agreement—there has never been a mid-season strike in baseball's long and colorful history.

"A summer without baseball is like a summer without sunshine," Mark moans. "They can't do this to me."

Like every Boston fan, he takes the whole thing personally.

"Look at it this way," I say, trying to be optimistic. "The Sox are in fifth place. Maybe a break will give them a chance to regroup and come back stronger."

Oddly enough, the fans blame the ballplayers for demanding a bigger piece of the pie instead of the owners who still think like plantation bosses. It is a poignant sign of how the times they are a-changin'. Before the '80s are out, we will be blaming homeless Vietnam vets for their heroin habits and children on welfare for being born.

We all knew it could happen, still it's a bit like the death of someone close. You try to prepare yourself, yet when the time comes it's a shock and you don't know how to fill the emptiness.

On June 12 the strike begins. There are no more games to bet on so Charlie and I bet on when the strike will end, but when it drags out far beyond our expectations we don't have the heart to bet again.

"Greed is what this strike is all about," Charlie grumbles. "Millionaire athletes who don't appreciate their good fortune and fat cat owners who want every crumb."

Things between Mark and me aren't good these days. We have reached that dispirited, restless stage in our marriage when we realize we're not going to be able to change each other into our romantic ideals, but haven't yet learned to accept the way we are.

The strike only makes things worse. Without baseball, we don't have much to talk about. When we do talk, we end up arguing. I don't understand where these arguments come from or how they explode—they seem to have a life of their own.

One night I forget to call Mark to tell him I'm working late. When I finally get home, he is standing at the stove, stirring a pot of spaghetti sauce with the intensity of MacBeth's witches at their cauldron. From the look on his face, "double, double, toil, and trouble" is sure to be my fate.

"Where have you been?"

His voice is suspicious and accusing, and even though I know I'm wrong, I bristle like a fighting cock.

"Trying to earn a living," I snap back, my feisty Aries temper flaring.

"Something wrong with the phone?"

"Okay, I should've called. It was really busy, I just forgot the time. Give me a break, will you?"

"I've been holding dinner for an hour."

"What do you mean? That's spaghetti sauce from a jar."

I see the pot coming just in time to duck out of the way. Spaghetti sauce splatters like blood on the kitchen wall. If Mark had really wanted to hit me with it, he would have. He used to be a minor league pitcher, after all, and can still hit a spot the size of a dessert plate from 60 feet.

I slam the front door behind me and eat at the diner down the street. Then I go to a movie. When I get home, Mark is in bed pretending to sleep and I spend the night on the sofa.

Aries people have a low tolerance for boredom and one slow afternoon I phone the sports desk at the newspaper to inquire about Penny Baker. A man with a gravelly voice answers, then coughs twice without covering the receiver.

"I used to enjoy reading her articles, but I haven't seen any in the paper lately," I tell him. "Is she on vacation?"

"Haven't heard from her in a while. She missed her last deadline."

I thank him and hang up, then call information for the number of the Los Angeles Times. Maybe she's covering the Dodgers now. Before I can dial the West Coast, the door of the Flower Child Garden Shop swings open, Indonesian bells tinkling, and my boss walks in.

"Hey, Jess," Charlie says, waving the newspaper he's carrying. "Read your horoscope today?"

"I told you, I never read that drivel."

"I know, I know. But listen to this: 'Keep digging and your efforts will pay off.' I couldn't have said it better myself."

"What's that supposed to mean?"

"Remember those roses you were supposed to dig up and take over to that customer in Newton?" Charlie glances at his watch. "If you get finished by the end of the day, you can keep your job."

I often wonder how things might have been different if I'd made that call to L.A. Not for Penny Baker, but maybe for me.

This afternoon I plant daylilies in O'Neal's garden. Six varieties, three of each. Showy hybrids I drove all the way to Cape Ann to buy from a grower who has over 400 different types.

As I'm setting them in, the back of my neck starts to prickle and I look up to see O'Neal taking my picture. Caught in the act, he gives me one of his charming, innocent grins to show he means no offense, but I still feel a little violated. He should have at least asked permission. But I guess I ought to be flattered too—he's a damn good photographer, after all. Maybe I'll go down in history like the raggedy woman in Walker Evans's famous image or the naked Vietnamese girl with napalm on her skin. If I ever write a book on gardening, I can use his photo on the cover.

That evening Mark meets me at the door, his face the color of putty.

"What's wrong?" I ask. "You look sick."

"Tony's dead."

"What happened?"

"I just found him downstairs in his apartment, when I went to pay the rent," Mark continues. "On the toilet."

"You mean he died taking a dump?"

"Apparently. Probably had a heart attack. He wasn't exactly a picture of health, you know."

I flop down in an overstuffed chair and try to imagine it, but the thought makes me feel as nauseated as Mark looks. When my time comes, I sure hope I can arrange a more dignified exit.

"I called the cops. They'll be here any minute." He opens the front door and leans against the doorjamb, watching for the black-and-white. "He died without ever seeing the Sox win the Series."

"We probably will too," I point out. "Now you won't have to put up that TV antenna."

After 49 desolate days, the strike ends. Ironically, the "second season" as it's called, begins rather like the first one, with the Red Sox playing Chicago. Once again Eckersley pitches, and once again Boston loses. It's an ugly game. In the first inning Eck hits Carlton Fisk with a pitch. The White Sox steal five bases. The Red Sox get 10 hits yet only manage to rack up a solitary run, leaving 11 runners stranded on base.

That night, I go to bed with O'Neal. It's my idea. Although he's been fantasizing about it since Opening Day, he would never have made the first move. We leave the radio on the nightstand tuned to the ballgame, not so we can follow the action, but so I'll know when to expect Mark home.

Why did I do it? It certainly wasn't passion. I could say it's because my marriage is like a vase that's been broken and badly glued, so that now when I look all I see are the cracks. But it's really just a case of Saturn Return I'm going through, that painful stage when Saturn has completed its first cycle through the birth chart and come back to the position it occupied at my birth. At 29, I fear I'm getting old. Recently I noticed the first gray hairs, the first wrinkles. I need to feel that men still find me attractive.

I'm used to Mark's lean, hard body; O'Neal's soft, paunchy one is a surprise. So is the tentative, adoring way he touches me, as if I were a gardenia whose flesh will bruise simply from the heat of his fingertips.

It is strangely soothing not to experience desire. When O'Neal embraces me I feel warm and comforted, like I'm sinking into an eiderdown quilt. His desire, though, is self-evident. What turns him on is paying me homage. He kneels before me and kisses my feet. He brushes my hair 100 patient strokes and anoints my body with oil.

Most of all he likes to photograph me. I pretend I am a famous artist's muse, playing Venus to his Boticelli, striking poses that make me blush to recall. I'm not the type for black lace and silk stockings—I have to don filmy lingerie his departed wife left behind in a closet filled with a whole lot of expensive designer clothing, because all I own are cotton Jockey briefs—but O'Neal's photos transform me into a sultry vixen. Except for my small breasts, I could pass for a Victoria's Secret model.

I love the way he becomes aroused while ogling me through the camera lens. Sometimes I won't let him touch me at all; he's only allowed to look. Like the Fenway Park Wall, I giveth and I taketh away.

Our affair spills over into chrysanthemum season. There are pictures of me all over O'Neal's walls now. Exotic, lustrous, lewd, and disturbingly provocative. The photos of Penny Baker disappeared long ago.

One day when I come to prune the roses, he carries me into the bedroom and scatters their red petals on the sheets. He is trying to be romantic, but they make me think of virgin blood and I push him away, savoring the dejected look on his face and my power to inflict pain. Power, it's been said, is the headiest of aphrodisiacs—especially when you haven't had it for 3000 years.

I am no longer a nubile nymph, a charming and helpless plaything. I have ceased being one of Maxfield Parrish's dewy-eyed maidens and become Manet's haughty harlot Olympia.

I could say the planets conspired against me and it wouldn't be far from the truth. Even a novice astrologer could look at my birth chart and predict stormy weather. With Pluto, the destroyer, square to Venus, the planet of relationships, my love life was sure to take a few hits—I just didn't realize how hard those blows would be.

On September 26, I make the mistake no cheating wife can afford. I forget to tell my friend Karen that she is my alibi.

When I come home that night, the apartment is dark and I

assume Mark must be out. These days he doesn't tell me where he's going or when he'll be home. Then I hear something rustle in the living room.

"Jessie?" His voice is as soft as a fly buzzing against a screen.

"Hi, I didn't know you were home. Why are you sitting in the dark?"

I start to turn on a lamp, but he stops me.

"Don't. Where have you been?"

There's something forlorn about the way he asks. He's not the cocky, jeering antagonist I've grown accustomed to, spoiling for a fight, but someone who's frightened and in pain.

"I called Karen's place to tell you Nolan Ryan was pitching a no-hitter, in case you wanted to watch. She didn't know where you were."

There's no good way to break this kind of news, so I just give it to him straight. "I'm having an affair."

He waits a moment, as if trying to decide whether he wants to hear the rest, before asking, "Is it serious?"

That's a good question, one I haven't dared ask myself. "I don't love him, if that's what you mean."

"Are you going to keep seeing him?"

I've never considered what I'd do if it got to this point. Now I realize I can't continue with O'Neal. I'm not sure I even want to.

"No."

"What's going to happen to us, Jessie?"

"I don't know," I answer truthfully. I really don't.

Astrologers say the full moon brings hidden matters to light. On this mid-October afternoon, I can already see the full moon in Aries hanging ghostly pale in the eastern sky as the sun begins its slow descent. Maybe that's why I feel an impulse to dig deeper in O'Neal's garden than is necessary to plant the flowers his wife ripped out six months ago—and keep digging until my shovel hits something that shouldn't be there.

The scene on the 11 o'clock news reminds me of the first time I saw O'Neal's garden. Flowers, ripped from their beds, are strewn about on the lawn. Police carry away a stretcher bearing a form that, although covered with a tarp, is too easily recognizable.

Mark takes my hand and holds it with what seems like genuine concern. "That could've been you," he says.

I can't stop thinking the same thing.

When I see the stack of photographs on the fat cop's desk, I know I'm in shit deep enough to fertilize half the world's gardens. You wouldn't have to be the sharpest knife in the drawer to size up my relationship with O'Neal and figure me for his accomplice.

"But I'm the one who turned him in," I remind the cop.

"Guilty conscience. Happens all the time."

He flips slowly through the lewd pictures, apparently enjoying himself. He selects one and holds it up, comparing the wanton temptress in the black-and-white image to the tomboy seated before him.

"So you're a gardener," he says.

I nod, too embarrassed to speak.

"Then I guess you'd know that wolfsbane can cause heart failure."

"You mean he poisoned her?" I ask, incredulous. Evidently O'Neal wasn't as ignorant about flora and fauna as he pretended.

The fat cop raises his left eyebrow. "He says *you* did it."

In this year and decade of greed, it seems only fitting that the two richest teams with the largest audiences and the biggest attitudes—New York and Los Angeles—should play each other in this misbegotten World Series. The Red Sox finish second in the "second season." Like all Boston fans, I never truly believed they could win, but I still hoped.

Just like I hope the jury will find me innocent of Penny Baker's murder. My attorney thinks my chances are pretty good now that police have exhumed the body of O'Neal's first wife—the rich one who died 12 years ago, leaving him a great deal of money. Her history of high blood pressure and coronary trouble kept everyone from asking questions when her heart stopped beating one evening, not long after she'd eaten a Caesar salad sprinkled with diced wolfsbane.

Mark has been unexpectedly supportive during this whole ordeal. Capricorns are noted for being steadfast and dependable; I know I wouldn't be so valiant if he were in this situation instead of me. Charlie, however, fired me the instant the story hit the news. I can't say I blame him. Even if I'm found innocent, I'll probably have to find another vocation. Maybe I could be an astrologer. I can't see the stars at night anymore, but I've read plenty of books over the past few months and I'm getting pretty good at doing readings for my fellow inmates—most of whom wouldn't be here if they'd made better choices about the men they let into their lives.

The indicators for the day my trial begins look promising: Jupiter in my ninth house suggests good luck in legal matters, plus favorable influences from the sun and Venus should help me present a positive image to the twelve people who will decide my fate. Who knows—after knocking me around with a fungo bat for a while, perhaps the cosmos will start being kind again and I'll spend next Opening Day inside Fenway Park instead of this cell.

Ice Age
A One-Act Play
David Kruh

A man and a woman, both wearing white lab coats, stand beside a tank, which is bathed in a green glow. A cable extends from the tank to an outlet, and there are gauges and switches prominently displayed. Phillip Harkin, a thirty-something man, walks around the tank, his eyes full of amazement. Following him with her gaze is Dr. Helen Martin, an older, dignified, and patient woman.

PHILLIP

(Touches the outside of the "tank.")

So, he's in there?

HELEN

(As she efficiently checks the readings on a display)

That's right.

PHILLIP

I thought it would feel cold, you know.

HELEN

It's extremely well insulated. Remember, the whole idea is to keep the body that's inside cold.

PHILLIP

This is so fantastic. So how many of these have you done?

HELEN

Me? Personally? I've attempted ten.

PHILLIP

And did you thaw them all out okay?

HELEN

We prefer to say resuscitate.

PHILLIP

So did you?

HELEN

We learn more with each revival, of course, so the chances for success keep going up. Of the last five I've done, all are living.

PHILLIP

Fantastic. You know I didn't even know I had a relative in here until your people called me.

HELEN

Most families don't. It's been hundreds of years since these patients were alive and in most families this usually ends up becoming hearsay and legend.

(indicating the tank)

PHILLIP

There had been rumors, you know? I remember my great-grandmother telling me a story when I was nine or so, but you know how it is when you're nine and someone a hundred years old starts talking about the past. But I do remember her saying something about a relative and freezing, but it never sank in. But when I looked him up in the family databank after your people called, sure enough, there he was. My great, great . . . times eleven, I think, grandfather. Turns out he was quite a guy.

HELEN

(Still checking the machinery)

What did he do?

PHILLIP

He played baseball.

HELEN

(Stops what she is doing)

Played what?

PHILLIP

That's all right. I didn't know either. I had to look it up myself. Baseball was a sport that was big during the late industrial and early computer ages.

HELEN

Never heard of it.

PHILLIP

No reason you should. No one's played it professionally for almost 250 years. Sometime around the fourth year of the Middle East War people stopped going to the games. With no oil and no gas and the economy in pieces there were just too many other things on their minds, I guess. Anyway before anyone knew it teams were going bankrupt and around 2012 the league just folded up.

HELEN

Your ancestor would seem to be in line for a shock.

PHILLIP

I don't understand.

HELEN

The sport from which he made his living no longer exists.

PHILLIP

But it does. You see there are people . . . recreationists . . . hobbyists, I guess you'd call them, who still play it. They've formed teams and schedule games and pretty much everything the old ballplayers had. Except fans to watch them. And get paid, of course.

HELEN

So it's exactly like it used to be.

PHILLIP

I don't follow.

HELEN

No fans or money.

PHILLIP

Oh. Yeah. Funny. But you'd be surprised how much the latter isn't true.

HELEN

What do you mean?

PHILLIP

(Evasive)

Never mind.

HELEN

(Suspicious)

So . . . was he any good?

PHILLIP

Are you kidding? This guy here was one of the best there ever was. He was the last man to bat over .400.

HELEN

Excuse me?

PHILLIP

I had to look that up, too. It was a highly regarded record in the sport. There was a player, see, called a pitcher who stood about 60 feet away from another player on the other team who was called the batter, and this batter had to hit a ball thrown by the pitcher. Which wasn't easy. These pitchers could throw over 90 miles an hour, which meant the batter had less than a second to swing his bats. Which makes it all the more remarkable that one season this man—

(bangs on the tank)

HELEN

Please don't do that.

PHILLIP

Sorry. One season this man hit the ball more than four times out of every ten tries at bat.

HELEN

And that was good?

PHILLIP

You were considered great if you got three out of ten hit. And most players got less than that.

HELEN

So you can be very proud of him.

PHILLIP

So . . . how long will it take? You know, to wake him up.

HELEN

Well first of all, let's make sure we're clear on some things. Your ancestor is not asleep. He's dead. Has been for over 300 years. The process by which we restore cognitive functions and mobility are complicated and even though, as I mentioned before, we're getting better at revival, there are still dangers.

PHILLIP

But the prognosis is good.

HELEN

Again, prognosis is a word I would use for a living patient.

PHILLIP

Sounds like a lot of double talk to me. Are you a doctor or a lawyer?

HELEN

I am a professional who has obligations to the living, the dead, and to this institution.

PHILLIP

(Nervously disingenuous)

I'm sorry. I did not mean any offense. I was just curious when you can begin.

HELEN

You seem to be in an awful hurry to see your ancestor revived, Mr. Harkin.

PHILLIP

If you had found a long-lost relative, wouldn't you?

HELEN

I think I would want to be sure of that person's health and well-being.

PHILLIP

He'll be well taken care of.

HELEN

I am not talking just about his physical well-being, Mr. Harkin. These are human beings who, from their perspective, are suddenly thrust 300 years in the future. Imagine the implications. Everyone they have known and loved has been gone for three centuries. And in his case the sport he clearly loved is gone as well, for all practical purposes.

PHILLIP

Doctor, this man was a fighter pilot in two wars. He was even shot down once. He's strong. He'll adjust.

HELEN

I am sure that Mr. Williams was very brave, but what we're talking about here is way out of the realm of normal human experience. Trust me, I've witnessed enough of these cases to know.

PHILLIP

Look, doctor, all I want to know is how long it will be until he's normal.

HELEN

Normal? This man is being revived after being dead for 300 years. That's not normal and never will be.

PHILLIP

Fine. I guess what I mean is how long will it be until he's be able to function.

HELEN

I'm not sure I follow.

PHILLIP

How can I put this delicately? When will he be able to work?

HELEN

Work? Mr. Harkin, your ancestor is being revived from the dead. It's not like we've removed his appendix or tonsils. It will take time for his body to gain enough strength for him to be even able to feed himself.

PHILLIP

I'm not talking about a construction job, here. All I need to know is when will he be strong enough to write.

HELEN

I beg your pardon? Write?

PHILLIP

His autograph. How long until he can sign his name?

HELEN

I don't understand . . .

PHILLIP

(Showing her what is on the hand-held device)

These family databases are amazing. Turns out this guy was making money—a lot of it—even after he was old and in a wheelchair.

HELEN

Lots of people are productive members of society well into their advanced years.

PHILLIP

But this guy did it with his pen. When I did my research I discovered that his son—I guess that's my great times ten grandfather—anyway, he built a whole business around his father signing baseball-related items—baseballs, bats, uniforms, things like that—items that he sold to baseball fans all over the world.

HELEN

His son sold his father's autograph? You'll forgive me but that sounds a bit grotesque.

PHILLIP

Lots of players used to sell their autographs. Back then it was a huge business. And it still can be.

HELEN

(Disgusted)

Do you mean to tell me that you intend to make money off your ancestor that same way?

PHILLIP

You make it sound as if I don't care about him and that's not true. Think about how great this will all be for him. Out there are thousands of passionate baseball fanatics whose hero—one of the greatest men who ever played the game—is suddenly going to re-appear after three hundred years. Imagine the adulation he'll experience when I announce that Ted Williams is back among the living.

(Gets an idea)

Say, maybe after he's recuperated we could offer hitting lessons? Imagine what that would be worth?

HELEN

(Horrified)

I can't even begin to speculate.

PHILLIP

So you can see why I'm anxious to get things started.

HELEN

Yes, well, just as I am sure you can understand there are few matters that must be attended to first. And, as I mentioned, it's a very delicate process that—

Phillip rolls his eyes impatiently. Now Helen is getting angry.

HELEN

Mister Harkin, please understand that as a doctor I have a responsibility to my patients.

PHILLIP

You said before that they were all dead. So how can they be your patients?

HELEN

Whatever word you wish to employ they are human beings who deserve some measure of dignity.

(Struck by a thought. Pauses. Then, to herself, as she touches the tank)

Dignity . . .

PHILLIP

What was that?

HELEN

Nothing. Never mind. Tell you what, Mr. Harkin, this may take a while. Could I ask that you wait in our guest lounge? Or you can go back to work or your home and we'll call you when we have any news.

PHILLIP

No, I think I'll hang out here.

(Caresses the tank with gleeful greed)

I can get some work done on the press release and the brochure while I'm waiting.

HELEN

It really could be while.

PHILLIP

That's all right.

Helen rolls her eyes with disgust as Phillip crosses to the door.

PHILLIP

(With a smarmy smile)

Doctor.

Helen watches Phillip exit. She pauses, then reaches behind the tank and pulls a plug out of the wall. The green light turns red and an alarm bell rings. She stares sadly at the tank as the alarm stops.

HELEN

Rest in Peace, Ted Williams. And this time we mean it.

Blackout

(END)

Green Monster

Adam Emerson Pachter

Around the time El Guapo started loosening, I decided to write a will. Sometimes being a Sox fan will do that to you. I didn't know if I'd finish it in the bleachers that night, but thinking about the bullpen was a good start. "El Guapo" meant the handsome one, but this season nothing looked good about Number 34. His ERA had nearly doubled since last year, his innings were way down, and hitters looked forward to his arrival like they would the substitution of a softball. As Guap waddled towards the mound, I began to search through my jacket for a blank piece of paper.

Don't get me wrong; life isn't really like the Red Sox bullpen. For one thing, life doesn't usually come with your own pitching coach and set of tomato plants. And besides, you may never know when you're going to meet that One Great Scorer in the Sky, but you can be pretty sure when the Old Towne bullpen's gonna kick the can.

El Guapo, or Richard Alan Garces Mendoza, if you wanted to use the name in the Red Sox media guide, started sending his warm-ups towards the catcher while the runner on second tapped his spikes and gave Nomar a few words. With only one out, ordinarily you would think that the Devil Rays would need another hit in order to score, but since Wake had started this particular catastrophe, Mirabelli was squatting behind the plate, and that, combined with Garces's natural indifference towards men on base, meant that the runner would definitely try to steal third. I'm sure Nomar knew all this, but, like swinging at every first pitch, it seemed to be something he couldn't really control. He took his usual spot well off the base and kicked at some dirt. Maybe El Guapo would just serve it up and at least he could make a play in the field.

We had just begun the seventh inning, so you knew it was too early for Uggie to be called in to close this particular disaster. I say disaster even though we were still up by a run. But in a way I was relieved they'd summoned Guap rather than trying to stretch Uggie into a three-inning stint. Unlike Urbina, Garces usually kept it in the park.

I thought about putting my headphones on and getting Joe and Jerry's take on things, but I figured their talk might distract me. If the Red Sox ended up pulling this one out, Joe would probably give his trademark "had 'em all the way" speech, and if not he'd say something about "another frustrating outing" for the guy that took the loss. Even though it was still late July, and there was a lot of baseball left to be played, I had a feeling this would be one year we wouldn't catch the Yanks.

As it turned out, I was glad I didn't try to get the radio play-by-play, because with the headphones on I probably would have missed the sound of the bag of peanuts whizzing through the air next to my head. Behind me some drunk bleacher bum made a swipe at the bag and missed, sending half his Bud onto the woman next to him. I knew why they couldn't sell glass bottles at Fenway, even if we were only playing the D-Rays, but sometimes a little glass would sure help keep the beer in the cup.

"Hey, watch where you're throwing that," another fan yelled. "You hit me, I'll sue you for negligence."

"If I'd hit you," the Peanut Man replied with a sharp look, "you couldn't get me for negligence; it would have been an intentional tort."

The fan didn't know enough law to talk back. But it gave me an idea.

"Hey, Peanut Man," I said as he gathered the change from the row behind me. "Can you help me write a will?"

The Peanut Man turned his yellow shirt towards me as he sized up my proposal. "All right," he said. "That'll be four bucks."

It wasn't a bad offer—same as for a bag of peanuts. And since prices for everything jumped as soon as you entered Fenway, I probably wouldn't find anything for less. Not that there weren't plenty of doctors, lawyers, and businessmen at tonight's game—I could see them reach their field box seats around the third inning, baseball caps still the original dark blue with the bright red "B" standing out nice and clear. Obviously their caps got kept on a shelf until game time, unlike my own faded number. But that wasn't the only difference between me and them—they bought 60-buck field boxes when they couldn't get their companies to spring for the 200 dollar seats that the new Sox owners had installed right by the dugouts. The pure fans had complained that these seats would cut down on the amount of foul ground and might result in a crucial out landing in the seats—and the way they described it, that would happen with Jeter at the plate in the deciding game of the ALCS. I guess I wasn't a purist, but only because I didn't spend a lot of time thinking about seats I could never afford.

Right on schedule, El Guapo served up a meatball to the first batter, and that batter did what you always do with a meatball—he sent it banging up against the Green Monster, about ten feet above the mechanical scoreboard. It made a nice ping—well, nice if Nomar or Manny had launched it, not so good when it meant the D-Rays had just plated the tying run. Manny grabbed the ball on a hop and fired it in somewhere around second base, but the batter just took a wide turn around first and then retreated to the bag. Nomar thought about hurling it in there, but Tony Clark waved him off. And since the only help Tony gave us was with his glove, Nomar listened to him and held on to the ball. Everybody just stayed cautious, which helped the D-Rays out more than us. After all, there was no need for them to try and stretch a single into an out, on the off chance that Manny's throw to the infield might be accurate. Not when the next batter would see a pitch just as good.

You see, Guap didn't exactly have the finer points of control down, not this year. And he was never a nibbler—he'd just fire in the next pitch and dare the batter to take a hack at it. The batter would, and I had an ugly feeling he'd connect. But, I reminded myself, at least they hadn't put Uggie in the game. With our luck, the first pitch he'd throw would be sent right out.

Mirabelli took a stroll to the mound, and I squinted over at the Green Monster, trying to see if I could make out where the ball had hit. That was the great thing about baseball; there were always plenty of pauses where you could grab a peanut, take a sip, or try and steal a look. And I had decent seats, Section 35 near the Triangle. I had a better view of the Monster than any of the folks higher up. But tonight I couldn't make out any dent, not from my angle. Still, I liked the breaks in the action. If football was a movie, all big bangs and quick cuts, baseball was more like a book—whenever you needed, you could just take a break and pick things back up later when you were ready. Especially with a Stephen King novel or something like that. Sure, I'd read John Updike's farewell to Ted—every Sox fan had to. But King loved our team just as much; he even wrote a book about Tom Gordon. And King's stuff was a lot more exciting to me.

I handed the Peanut Man my money and he promised he'd be back in the seventh-inning stretch. El Guapo shook off whatever it was Mirabelli had tried to tell him, and his next pitch was a mile high. Even a Devil Ray knew not to chase that junk, and the batter just settled down to wait for something better. Watching it happening while knowing what was gonna happen, I started to get that ugly feeling in my stomach. It almost didn't matter what the sign was or who the D-

Rays had at bat. I knew—no, thousands of people knew—that Guap was going to serve it up.

I used to come to more games before my dad got sick—I collected tolls at the Cambridge/Allston stop on the Mass Pike, and I set up my schedule so I usually got off by game time. I liked sitting there by myself in the toll booth, and I had plenty of time to read when it wasn't rush hour. Only problem was I picked up all the smells of the cars coming through, and so I always sat in the bleachers because everyone smelled a little funny out there, and the stink from a thousand tailpipes just mixed in with the stink from spilled beer and summer sweat and crushed peanuts until none of them really smelled that bad—it was all just a part of the game.

Before Dad got sick I used to make at least 20 games after May 1, which was when they pushed the night starts back to 7:05 and made it more likely I could get to them. I didn't want to show up late, to miss the first pitch and "The Star-Spangled Banner" and all the excitement from a game that could go either way, the point where it was all in front of you and you just didn't know how this one was going to turn out, where you could hope Pedro's shoulder held up or Lowe continued his dominance or Wake could somehow float that knuckler just a little longer, or that Nomar and Trot and 'Tek had one of their nights where they put the game out of reach by the end of the third.

Those were the games you prayed for, and before the first pitch you never knew whether tonight would be one of the ones they'd talk about—in a good way, I mean. I said that I would never miss a first pitch or a last out, and for 15 years I kept that promise. With Dad sick I still did, but it meant I had to cut back on the number of games.

My dad grew up a dime's hop from Yawkey Way, back in those days when the Yawkeys actually lived and ran the place. He grew up rooting for Teddy Ballgame and the other DiMaggio, courted my mom during the Impossible Dream season ("There were two impossible dreams that summer," he always said, "but only one of them came true."), and even told his drinking buddies that a well-placed foul ball helped bring me into the world. You see, my mom was pregnant all that summer and fall of 1975, and the World Series opened about two days after I was due. My folks watched the games inside with their jackets on—ready to leave in a Boston minute if it came to that, and my dad plotted out four different ways to get to Mass General just in case the traffic was bad.

When Fisk hit that ball in Game Six, everybody knew it would be foul, had to be foul, there was no way any Red Sox player was gonna get lucky on an extra inning drive like that. But my mom and dad both leaped up, waving their hands, pushing that ball fair just like Fisk was doing, and when it hit the pole and the Sox won the game, my mother gave the kind of shriek that you don't normally hear from women during sports, and when my dad looked over there was a puddle under her. Luckily all three of us made it into the car and off to the hospital before most of the fans had reached the streets—they were still celebrating inside the park when we drove by. But the stadium lights never looked that bright on any other night, my dad always said, in one of the few times he ever talked so deep.

Of course, being my dad and a true Sox fan, he soon found the cloud in that silver lining. "It's always Game Six for us," he often told his beer. "Never Game Seven. Every Red Sox World Series appearance since 1918 has gone the distance, but we never win the final one." Then he'd turn to me. "I only wished for two things that year: the Sox would take it all, and I'd have a son. I got one of the two, same as always."

"So you're batting .500," I said. "That's not bad."

"But life ain't baseball, Mike; just be sure you remember that. Life ain't baseball, not by a long shot."

I still don't know whether he was passing judgment on the world or the Red Sox, but I tried to keep them separate after that. It didn't work, of course. I was born on the Fourth of July for Red Sox Nation, maybe the best night we ever had. There wasn't any chance I'd be able to have a life away from my team with a start like that.

It's funny how your thoughts fit into the time you have for them, especially at the ballpark. I figured I'd snuck off into a massive daydream, and I wouldn't have been surprised to find the game was over when I came around. But the truth is, El Guapo hadn't even made his next pitch. And when he did he surprised everyone except the batter—the pitch was high and away, but the batter never even flinched, much less took a swing at it. Guap just shrugged in some kind of defeatist way, and then I knew, he knew, everybody knew that even though our tight stomachs were praying for something different, the next one would be a fastball right in the batter's wheelhouse, and once again our necks would snap back on contact.

Sure enough, the D-Ray drove it as hard as he could, right out towards the Triangle, and Damon had been playing in, maybe hoping to hold the runner to one base, and so even though Johnny was fast and had a great glove, when I saw him running back I knew he wasn't going to get to it, and just as Damon moved out of my line of sight, down and to the left, I figured it for a triple at least. Maybe the batter could have gone inside the park, but why get thrown out at the plate? The Triangle was the deepest part of Fenway, more than 400 feet near straight-away center, and I guess I should have been grateful because that location kept it in the park. Johnny played the carom nicely, same as he always does, and he hit the relay man dead on. Sanchez fired it in to home plate, but the batter had stopped at third. There was no need to stretch things, not at this point. They had the lead, and Guap looked like he was going to have a heart attack.

Grady had been talking about his new quick hook, at the same press conference where he said that catching the Yankees was just like dieting—you could only do it one pound, or one game, at a time. But the Bronx Bombers had one of their mid-week day games against the O's, and the Rocket had already put them down in a three-hit, eight-strikeout performance. So if the new Devil Ray lead held up—and did anyone in the park doubt that it would?—we'd be going backwards, at least tonight. Tomorrow was another day, another possibility, and since I was born in October 1975 and will always be a Red Sox fan, I had already turned to tomorrow and the hope that Burkett might be scratched and somebody else would be pitching.

Anyway, Grady was true to part of his promise (another example of getting half of what you wish for, I could almost hear my dad say), and so he yanked Guap and signaled for someone else to join us from the pen. Garces walked with his head down towards the home dugout, and when he got near those new seats he just flicked his glove off into the stands. Sayonara, just like that. Watching him leave, I had a feeling that more than a game had ended that night. El Guapo, Mr. Handsome himself, might not be back.

"So, who gets your stuff?"

I turned around and saw that Peanut Man had returned at the seventh-inning stretch, just like he said he would. Garces's replacement had made quick work of the D-Rays, but a deep fly to Nixon in right let the runner on third tag and score, so we entered the stretch with a two-run deficit.

"What do you mean?" I said.

"That's what a will is all about—your stuff. You don't have kids, right?"

"No, I'm not hitched."

"Well, then you don't have that problem to deal with, so it's mostly about stuff. You must have something valuable, right? Something that someone else might want after you're gone? Everybody has something."

I thought about that. I had grown up during the late 80s, and posters of the Rocket, Gator, and Dewey had covered the walls of my room.

"I do have a signed Don Baylor bat," I said. "He gave it to me one day when I came to the park early to watch them warm up."

"Don Baylor, huh? Nobody took it on the shoulder like him. He didn't even make an effort to get out of the way of those baseballs. Bet he set some kind of record for that. I even saw him snap a bat across his knee once after he had struck out."

"My bat's not broken, though. It doesn't even have a crack. And he signed it, too, with his number and everything."

The Peanut Man nodded. "That's cool, even if Don Baylor never had what I'd call national appeal. Still, it might fetch something, so you'd better make sure it goes somewhere you want. You die without a will, the state takes most everything you got."

"How do you know so much legal stuff?"

He smiled at me. "Think I've always been a Peanut Man? I once tried for a real career, even went to law school. Now I'm givin' out legal advice for four lousy bucks."

"Cheap for wills, but pricey for peanuts," I said.

"Don't I know it. Anyway, what else you got?"

I thought back to all the games my dad had taken me to, all the batting practice balls I'd scooped up and held out to be signed. We'd even saved up enough to go down to Spring Training one time, and I'd come back with a whole bag of gear. Players were more relaxed down there, and they would sign just about anything.

"I've got a Mike Greenwell jersey from one time when we went down to Florida. He liked it down there a lot, he told me it made him sad each time the regular season started."

"That's why they called him Gator," the Peanut Man said. "Yeah, that'd be worth something."

I nodded, back in the dreams of my childhood. "And then there's a Bruce Hurst baseball. He was going to be the Series MVP, you know."

The Peanut Man nodded solemnly. "Yep, they had the champagne all ready, and the scoreboard said 'Congratulations Boston Red Sox, 1986 World Champions.' Now why'd they have to go and do that? Why'd they have to put it down in writing like that?"

"You don't always get everything you want."

"No kidding. Well, look, we're up to bat. Now, who's your best buddy?"

"Rich," I said. We had gone to school together, and after my dad got sick and before he got married, Rich came to most of the games with me. "Yeah, Rich is my bud. But his wife isn't into the team so much these days—they're trying to have a baby. So maybe I should just give the stuff to you, Peanut Man."

He shook his head. "No, no, that's not allowed. I can't draft the will and also be named a beneficiary."

I just stared at him.

"Law school, remember? I got all the legalese. Now look here," and he took the piece of paper from my hand. "I, fill in your name, being of sound mind, do solemnly declare that I leave all my Red Sox paraphernalia to my good friend Rich, add his last name here. And just sign your name down there and get someone to witness it. In the law, they love words like 'paraphernalia.' If you've got any more stuff you wanna give to somebody, you just put it in the lines below. Look, I gotta run. Anything more, it's gonna cost ya another four bucks."

The Peanut Man took his bags and started to walk away.

"Hey Peanut Man," I said. "How were you in law school?"

"I did pretty well," he replied.

"Then why'd you quit?"

He smiled. "I spent the summer after my first year working for a law firm, and they wouldn't let me out in time for first pitch. Gotta make the first pitch—it's not worth going if you're gonna miss that. Enjoy the game, now, okay?"

"Thanks."

I first noticed that something had gone wrong with my dad's head in April of 1999. We were watching the game on NESN because he hadn't felt like heading to Fenway; ever since my mom died, my dad had begun to prefer the warm indoors to the cold of springtime at the park. He sat there with a blanket over his knees even though the day hadn't been so bad; when I'd gone to work earlier, I hadn't even worn a jacket. Pedro was on the mound and throwing fire as usual, although that night his pitches were sailing a bit and so opposing runners were still getting on base. Plus he'd plunk a few from time to time, just to make a point, and as a result the sacks were full of Blue Jays.

"I hope Clemens has a better time tomorrow," my dad said after Pedro tossed another wild pitch. "They really need that one-two punch."

"Why do you care about the Rocket?" I asked. Besides, Clemens had just pitched the day before and had gotten shelled by the Twins, something I was happy to see.

"Why do I care? I care because he's our workhorse. I care because Pedro's got a glass shoulder, and we need good things from Clemens if we're ever gonna catch the Yanks."

"But Clemens plays for the Yankees now. . . . " I started to say, but my dad didn't hear me. "I bet Bruce Hurst turns it right around," he continued. "Terrible what the Mets did in the Series. He was going to be the MVP."

A few days later I made an appointment with my dad's doc, and I told him to shelve the usual memory questions about day, year, and all that crap. "Ask him about baseball," I said, and the doc, who was also a Sox fan, promised he would. The results were sad and quick: Alzheimer's Disease, and it was already getting to a pretty serious stage. For my dad's memory, there would be no coming back, and the doctor warned me that pretty soon he'd start forgetting short-term stuff completely.

"When you see him, tell him your name. Always start with your name, and then keep on bringing it up," the doc said.

"You're telling me he's not going to remember my name?"

The doc looked at me. "I'm sorry, Mike, but eventually he won't. Keep bringing it up, though, and there's a better chance it'll stick."

"What about my mom? She's dead, and he still remembers her." I felt kinda hurt by this.

The doctor put his hand on my shoulder. "The thing is, Mike, that your dad knew your mom a long time before you came along. And long-term memories are the things that stay, even with Alzheimer's. You know how your dad keeps bringing up the '86 Series? Well, for him that memory's as clear as if it was just yesterday, while the real yesterday, whatever he said or did or ate for lunch, comes and goes like a glass of water. You can't remember the taste of a glass of water—once it's gone, it's gone. Short-term stuff is just water to your dad's brain, while long ago still sticks around like a mug of beer."

"Are you saying my dad's always gonna think that Roger Clemens is still pitching for the Sox?"

The doc just shrugged. "That wouldn't be so bad, would it? The way Clemens got himself back in shape, I'd love to see him and Petey go one-two in the rotation." Noticing the down look on my face, he said, "Look, my advice is don't push him too much on the current Sox—that'll just confuse him and frustrate you. Stick with the past when you talk—hey, you're a Sox fan, so you know all the old stuff. With any luck, maybe he'll slide his mind all the way back to Fisk's shot. That wouldn't be a bad place to stop."

"Sure," I said, trying to sound more cheerful than I felt. "Just so long as his last thought isn't of Bucky Bleeping Dent." Then I shook the doc's hand. It wasn't his fault he had such bad news. And, as it turned out, the doc was right. After that conversation my dad lived for about six months on his own, but by the time the Sox got booted in five by the Yanks, sent home for the winter in the last Fenway games of the twentieth century, he was already in a Southie nursing home.

Thinking of my dad and the way the game had gone south didn't exactly put me in a laughing mood, and they'd stopped selling beer in the seventh, so I decided to distract myself by focusing on the park, instead of the field, for a while. What I saw put the smile back on my face, at least for a little while. After all, Fenway on a nice July night is a beautiful thing. The ladies in the bleachers weren't wearing much more than their tan lines and baseball caps; the beachballs were floating around the stands, just one bounce ahead of security; the folks around me were munching their peanuts and Cracker Jack; and the scoreboard was putting up its usual silly list of fan birthdays and strange player facts. Now, I'm pretty die-hard for the Sox, but even I had no idea of all the info they could pull from Nomar's first year. Longest hitting streak by a rookie, huh? They must have dug deep to come up with that one.

The wave made it through my section while I looked, and I stood and put up my hands in the same silly way as everybody else. Then they played "Sweet Caroline," and everybody sang like it was their favorite song. From my seat I could see down into the bullpens, and chuckle at how the groundskeepers put wavy lines in the visitor's grass, just to throw 'em off a bit, while the marks in our pen were nice and straight. And the lights above the Green Monster were sharp and bright, and I thought about how new ownership was floating the idea of putting seats up there, and wouldn't that be something else. And then as I thought, I heard that nice thunk of ball on bat and jerked my head over in time to see Manny finish off one of his smooth power swings, left hand already falling off the handle as he watched his drive float over the Monster and the screen and onto the roof of the parking garage across the street. And I thought about how his first hit as a member of the Sox had been a three-run homer over the Monster, and I had been there to see that, and maybe acquiring him would turn out to be all right. And unfortunately that one tonight was just a solo shot, but now we had Shea Hillenbrand at the plate with only one man out in the ninth, and if he could just stop swinging at every ball a foot over his head then he could probably launch one too and then the game would be tied. And if the game got tied here in the bottom on the ninth, we would definitely pull this one out; for some reason I was sure of that.

I put all this together in the time it took Shea to work an even count, but he wouldn't let them put him on, and the pitcher for the Devil Rays had read the right scouting reports. He threw it a foot outside and Shea went flailing, hacking away at a clear ball three, and out in the bleachers folks started to think that maybe this wouldn't be our night after all. And next up was Brian Daubach, one of the team's best-loved "Dirt Dogs," but he'd had a terrible interleague trip out to the West Coast, and all he could manage tonight was a weak grounder to first, and you knew he wasn't going to win the footrace to that bag. So the game ended and the scoreboard thanked us for coming and told us that attendance was closing in on the two million mark and would probably end up setting some kind of record.

And I went home and listened to Joe and Jerry wrap things up on WEEI, and then for good measure I turned on NESN and got their post-game chat, and then it was time to go to bed because they didn't change my start time at the toll booth just because the

Sox had lost. I got up the next day and I went to work and then I had a beer and then I visited my dad, and he was looking old and small and a little bit afraid in the middle of all the nursing home crap. But I told him my name and I was wearing my cap, and it turned out sometimes he keeps the TV on after lights out because his roommate is a Sox fan too, and so my dad caught the game last night, and even though I wasn't sure how much he remembered, he still wanted to talk about it.

"Did you see Manny hit that shot over the Monster?" he said. "Did you see him swing that bat? A one and two count, but he still knew that he'd get his pitch. Must've traveled 500 feet. And I bet it would've hit the Pike if some poor guy's windshield hadn't gotten in the way." My dad glanced out the window and did a little kind of smile. "That was like Hendu's blast against the Angels. That was the kind of shot that wins games and sends us on to championships."

I looked at my dad and then I held his hand and felt the grip go tight. "You're right, Pop," I said. "It was just like that."

A Sox Fan's Wildest Dream

Bill Nowlin

Joe Castiglione shouts, " . . . and the Red Sox win the World Series!"*

The End

* *This shortest of short stories was written on October 3, 2004, the final day of the regular season. It came true on the evening of October 27, when Joe Castiglione made the following call: ". . . swing and a ground ball . . . stabbed by Foulke . . . he underhands to first. . . . and the Red Sox are World Champions . . . for the first time in 86 years, the Red Sox are the champions of baseball . . . CAN YOU BELIEVE IT!?"*

Contributors

Skye Alexander is the author of numerous works of nonfiction and fiction, including the mystery novel *Hidden Agenda*, which won the Kiss of Death award for best book of romantic suspense. A Red Sox fan since moving to Boston in 1974, she believes the 2004 World Series win is a sign that all of us can overcome seemingly insurmountable odds and make our dreams come true if we just believe.

Mitch Evich is the author of *The Clandestine Novelist*, a semi-autobiographical novel. He moved to Boston in time for the 1986 baseball season and suffered the consequences for the next 17 years.

Tracy Miller Geary's stories have appeared in numerous literary magazines, and she is currently the co-fiction editor of the *Harvard Review*. Unlike the character in her story, Tracy has never dated a Yankee fan, and actually met her husband while watching the Red Sox at Fenway.

Matt Hanlon is founder of the weekly *Sane Magazine* (http://sanemagazine.com) and has been living in New York City, London, and now California since leaving Worcester, Mass. All those life events that had been on hold pending a Sox Series victory came flooding through shortly after, with a marriage to his muse and a baby on the way. It won't be the name on the birth certificate, but Pedro Curt Papi Manny Johnny Bronson Tim Derek Trot Jason Hanlon is bound to be a Sox fan.

Mary Kocol is an art photographer and filmmaker in Somerville, MA. You can see more of her work on her website: http://www.KocoMotion.com. Gallery NAGA, run by "wicked huge" Sox fans, represents her photography in Boston. Mary is still partying after the 2004 Red Sox World Series victory.

David Kruh is a published author and playwright, whose writing has also appeared in the *Boston Globe*, *Boston Herald*, *Yankee Magazine*, and *Boston Magazine*. **Steven Bergman** is an award-winning, published playwright, who has also composed the scores for a number of other musicals and motion pictures.

Bill Nowlin is author of nearly a dozen books on the Red Sox and Sox-related matters. His contribution to *Fenway Fiction* is his most succinct work to date. Bill is a co-founder of Rounder Records of Cambridge, MA, and current vice president of the Society for American Baseball Research.

Jeff Parenti was a radio announcer for the Georgia Tech Baseball team while in graduate school and wants Don Orsillo's job, but for now is pro only as a civil engineer. He went deep into enemy territory to witness the '04 Game Seven Red Sox victory from the bleachers in the Bronx and fondly remembers Bob Zupcic's rookie season.

Elizabeth Pariseau has worked as a reporter for several Massachusetts newspapers and publishes a blog, Cursed and First, devoted to the Red Sox and Patriots. She will always regret not being old enough to have seen Carlton Fisk in action.

Sam and **Christina Polyak** reside in the Metro-West region of Massachusetts. Although they both grew up in families where sports were an afterthought, they have managed to make it to a good share of memorable Sox games in the last seven years, including the Pedro/Zimmer smackdown, Darren "Kung Fu" Lewis charging Jaret Wright spike-high, and the Offerman phantom tag.

Jennifer Rapaport's short fiction has appeared in *Quarterly West* and *Paragraph*. So far as she knows, her husband has no plans to begin a major league pitching career.

Andy Saks is the founder of Daydream Believers, an organization that helps people create their best careers. He's a lifelong Sox fan, and will be naming his first-born child "Papi."

Tom Snee lives with his wife and son in Iowa City, where he works for the University of Iowa. He has been published in *The Long Story*, *Exquisite Corpse*, and *The Wapsipinicon Almanac*. Tom once lived in Portsmouth, NH, just an hour's drive from Fenway Park.

Rachel Solar is the author of *Number Six Fumbles* and a widely published freelance writer whose work has appeared in the *Boston Globe*, *Boston Herald*, *In Style*, and the *Pennsylvania Gazette*, among others. She is still waiting patiently for Manny to call.

Cecilia Tan lives in Cambridge, Massachusetts, and for five years lived two blocks from Fenway Park. A writer and editor by trade, she writes fiction of many kinds (erotica, science fiction, etc.) and nonfiction about her many passions, of which baseball is the chief one. She is the author of *Fifty Greatest Yankee Games* and co-author with Bill Nowlin of *Fifty Greatest Red Sox Games*, and edited *The Fenway Project* with Bill. She considers the Yankees her childhood sweetheart and the Red Sox her troubled roommate. Find out more at http://www.ceciliatan.com.

Bob Weintraub lives in Newtonville, Massachusetts, with his wife, Sandra. His novel *Best Wishes, Harry Greenfield*, will soon be followed by a collection of baseball fiction.

Jonathan Winickoff is a pediatrician at Massachusetts General

Hospital and a lifelong Red Sox fan. He conceived of and adapted this piece of Soxspeare just prior to the 2004 ALCS Game Seven. (Thanks to David Winickoff and Adam Pachter for their editorial assistance.)

Call for Submissions

Have you written a piece of fiction inspired by the Boston Red Sox? If so, you are invited to submit your story for possible inclusion in a future anthology. Short stories in any genre, excerpts from plays or screenplays, and the like are all welcome. If you'd like more information, please contact the editor at adampachter@yahoo.com or send your completed story to:

Rounder Books
Attn: Fenway Fiction
One Camp Street
Cambridge, MA 02140

We look forward to hearing from you!

About the Editor

Adam Emerson Pachter is the author of the novel *Ash* (ISBN 0-89754-192-8) and numerous short stories. He edited an edition of *Let's Go: Europe,* the world's best-selling travel guide, and won the Improper Bostonian magazine's inaugural fiction contest for his story, "Lotion." Pachter lives in Arlington, MA with his wife and daughter.